the Book of
Three Pages

By

Jim Lindberg

Breezeway Books

This book is entirely a product of the author's imagination. All incidents, locations and characters or uses of names are intended as fiction. Any similarity to actual events concerning people, living or dead, is purely coincidental.

ISBN: 978-1-62550-591-0

Library of Congress Control Number: 2011905438

ACKNOWLEDGMENTS

Many thanks to Rex Douglass for encouraging me to write this kind of fiction, and to Rex Hammers, who enjoyed the manuscript enough to read it twice. Special thanks to Sue Rawers for catching a lot of subtle grammatical blunders and other errors, and to Claudia Macias and Jean Setne for proofreading my manuscript, and for constructive criticism.

DEDICATION

In memory of Rex Hammers, one of the strongest characters I have ever known, and as good a friend as a guy could ever ask for.

It is a rare thing in anyone's lifetime to meet such an individual as Rex. I believe that since the dawn of time two of the finest things a man can do in this world are to raise a solid family to enrich future generations, and, when times require it, to stand up and defend home and country with all he has to give. Rex has done both remarkably well, and all of us will forever be in his debt. I spent many hundreds of hours around the coffee pot with Rex, discovering what a well-read and knowledgeable man he was. Memory of those hours is one of the great treasures of my life.

TABLE OF CONTENTS

Author's Introductlon   *i*

The Book of Three Pages   *1*

The Waterhole   *89*

Timetangle In Talavera Canyon   *115*

A Tale of Two Friends   *153*

AUTHOR'S INTRODUCTION

One of the real pleasures of writing entertaining short stories is that once in awhile the characters take hold of the tale and pull the author along. That's usually a good sign; it means the story has real depth and a natural feel, with a nice mix of things like adventure, romance, action, or maybe even a touch of the supernatural.

The story "The Book of Three Pages," from which this book takes its title, was originally intended as a short story, but came alive as a novelette. Set in both old Mexico and the modern day Mexican border country, it's a captivating tale that will grab you and not let go.

The three stories that follow it were also influenced by the characters themselves. One, set in nineteenth century Southwest, is about two young men from vastly different cultures who fate has thrown together in dangerous circumstances. Another tells of a university professor and a soldier, each highly suspicious of the other, who must cooperate to survive in a wilderness beyond either's understanding. The last tale tells of two orphaned, teenage boys who grew up as best of friends, only to see their lives take a surprising twist.

I consider reading fiction of any kind to be one of the finest ways there is to relax. Whether by the fireplace in the evening, in the back yard with a morning cup of coffee, or when waiting for an airline flight, it's always nice to have truly entertaining fiction handy. The fiction I write is intended to be just that and I sincerely hope you enjoy reading this book as much as I have enjoyed writing it.

THE BOOK OF THREE PAGES

Rancho Soledad

Silence. The sudden, frightening kind that few pilots ever hear and all dread, deep down inside. At more than a mile above the desert of Northern Mexico, the engine of Frank's single engine Cessna 180 stopped. Without warning or complaint of any kind, it just stopped.

Dr. Francisco Jensen was a well-trained pilot and immediately performed all the appropriate emergency procedures. Nothing helped. He was thankful that he had just finished crossing the rugged mountains of the Sierra Madre Occidental and that he could see the gleaming white surface of a dry lake bed within gliding distance off to his right. He knew that one way or another he would be on the ground in just a few minutes. On the ground in the vast desert of the Mexican State of Chihuahua.

Like several American doctors who lived near the border, Frank occasionally traveled to Mexico to donate a few days of his time and skills to help rural Mexico develop better medical facilities. Having just spent two days at a hospital in La Paz, he was flying home, a trip he had made several times before.

***

Half an hour later, standing on the salt flat where he had landed, Frank added more sun block lotion to protect the fair complexion that, along with his blue eyes and blond hair, came with the European part of his ancestry. Everything he could check about his engine said it was in good shape. But the engine would not start.

Even with his aviator's sunglasses, the downed pilot found himself squinting his eyes against the brilliant sunshine reflected from the dry lake bed. The white, salt-covered sand stretched in all directions, like a field of new fallen snow. From his navigational chart Frank determined his location reasonably well and knew that he was a long way from anywhere.

Even in the vastness of Northern Mexico there are occasional roads, ranch houses, or small, communal settlements called *ejidos,*

1

scattered here and there. But during the several minutes of his glide to a landing, Frank had searched for a place to go for help and had seen nothing. Not a mark on the land anywhere to indicate human activity.

Frank walked a little distance away from the stricken airplane and, shading his eyes with his hands, looked around. The dry lake was miles across and he had chosen a landing site about half way between the center and the western edge. He found that he could only see for a few hundred feet in any direction because of mirage generated by the heat of the summertime sun. All around the view was the same, an almost painfully white, flat surface surrounded by a wall of shimmering heat waves, like a circular prison that blocked any view of nearby hills or mountains. Frank walked back to the shade provided by the wing of his airplane and sat down on the dry, salt and gypsum surface.

As he sat in the shade, Frank noticed just for a moment the faint sensation of something pleasant and vaguely familiar, something that was gone before he could identify it.

Frank could find north from his aircraft's magnetic compass and he considered removing it from its bracket on top of his instrument panel so he could carry it with him as he began his walk for help. He had the emergency water supply he always carried and some food, but only enough for a day or two in the summer heat. And yet how could he choose a direction? What would he try to walk to?

As he stared helplessly at his chart lying on the glistening sand, Frank thought of the airport in Ciudad Obregon where he had stopped for fuel little more than an hour earlier. He thought of the offer of an orange soft drink he had declined while his plane was being refueled. He would not refuse it now.

Frank climbed back into the cockpit and tried radio calls again. No response. He remembered the mandatory flight plan he had filed in Ciudad Obregon and knew that it offered little help. In Mexico such things don't get as much attention as they would north of the border.

The cockpit had become unbearably hot in the sunshine. So, with a heavy heart, Frank climbed out and sat again under his airplane's wing on the crusty-dry lake bed. He let his head drop to his arms across his knees as he realized how much alone he really was.

Then Frank noticed the odd sensation again. Stronger this time, pleasant and flowery for a few moments and then gone like it had been carried on a fickle evening breeze.

Was he imagining things? Frank knew he had to get hold of himself and make some attempt at a survival plan. He stood up and stepped to the baggage compartment to inventory his resources. As he did so he looked across the fuselage at the mirage in the distance.

Was there something out there? The mirage wall seemed a little different in just that one spot. Or was it just his imagination overworked by the one hundred degrees plus heat?

Frank laid one bare arm on the aircraft fuselage and then pulled it back from the hot aluminum surface. He stood for a few seconds with his eyes closed then looked up at the clean, blue sky to let his eyes rest on something more than the world of white he felt trapped in. Then he looked back at the mirage, and yes, something was definitely taking shape in the dance of heat waves in that one particular direction.

Again using his hands to shield his eyes, Frank squinted at the spot that was fighting the atmosphere's thermal turbulence to take shape in his vision. How far away; how big is it? Again he closed his eyes and turned aside. Whatever it was was not moving fast, but it was coming straight at him.

After a time Frank decided that it was a vehicle. At least it seemed to have wheels of some kind. A blob with large, narrow wheels, and some sort of bobbing up and down going on in the middle of it.

Minutes later the nearly new two-wheeled chaise came to a stop about twenty yards from the airplane. Flicking of its ears and quick head motions showed that the well-groomed black mare pulling the vehicle was not pleased with Frank's airplane and its odd smells of gasoline and engine oil.

The vehicle's single occupant stepped down and stood quietly beside the black chaise and horse. The small-framed old man's dark, leathery face and hands looked almost black against his white, pajama-like clothing. Two white eyes peered out from under a straw hat. A *campesino*, a farm worker, one who had spent more than half a century in Mexico's desert sunshine.

For a moment Frank looked up again just to see the clear blue sky, to shake the feeling that everything he was seeing was either black or white.

"Hello," said Frank as he stepped toward the man. "I'm sure glad to see someone out here. I've been forced down and need to find a mechan—"

The old man raised his hand to stop Frank, as awed by the big machine he saw in front of him as was his horse. Moments later he lowered his hand and nodded for Frank to continue.

"My name is Jensen, ah, Frank, call me Frank."

"Yes Señor, I am Paco. I have seen you fall from the sky."

Paco's voice had a gentle softness befitting his small, frail frame. With a wave of his hand he indicated to Frank that he was welcome to join him on the chaise's single, bright red, leather upholstered seat.

Happy to have been rescued, Frank stepped forward and then turned back to the airplane. He collected his water bottles, a suitcase, and the small medical bag he always carried when traveling. He carried them to the chaise, placed them on board, and took his seat next to Paco.

With just a touch of reins from Paco the black mare turned the two-wheeled vehicle around and headed back the way she had come.

"Do we have far to go?" asked Frank, remembering that he had not properly attended his airplane. "I can't leave my plane without tying it down."

"Only a few minutes Señor," said the soft voice.

"Wait, I can't leave it—"

As Frank spoke he looked over his shoulder to find that his aircraft was nowhere to be seen. There was nothing in sight but the flat, white, dry lake bed with its fence of shimmering heat waves in all directions.

Paco said nothing more, and Frank sat quietly watching the horse as the little chaise, moving only slightly faster than a man's walk, rolled toward the wall of dancing heat waves that seemed always to stay the same distance just ahead.

Casually looking off to one side Frank was surprised to see another shimmering object hanging in the air above a mirror-like mirage. As it moved nearer he saw that it was a rider on horseback traveling in the same direction as they. The horse seemed to be walking on the lake that was the false water of the mirage.

Again the faint scent, the same as before. Pleasant, either sweet or flowery, Frank could not be sure.

Thinking that he might be suffering from too much sun, he remembered his water bottles. He offered one first to Paco, who, glancing skeptically at the two liter plastic bottle, declined. Frank drank a generous amount himself, then looked back at the rider who had drifted nearer to the vehicle.

A rider dressed all in black. Very nicely dressed Frank noticed. Even the rider's round, flat brimmed hat had decorative tassels, each with a small black ball at the end. Not a good choice of color for the summertime heat.

But one thing was clear to Frank. He was seeing a rare example of horsemanship, the smooth blend of motions that come when a practiced equestrian and a well-trained animal have gotten to know each other well. Clearly, the lady was a superb rider.

Now that she was nearer Frank noticed the white blouse at the neck of the lady's dark riding jacket, and a bit of white handkerchief showing from a breast pocket. She smiled politely at Frank and waved a white-gloved hand. Then, changing to a faster gait with no apparent signal to her mount, she moved into the distance ahead without splashing any of the shimmering mirage into which she disappeared.

As the one horse-chaise reached the edge of the dry lake, Paco began following a faint track that wound its way into the nearby hills. At least now they were off the monotonous, white surface and the mirage was gone.

"Paco, did you see that rider? Who was she?"

"Si Señor; she is La Señorita."

"Señorita?, Señorita who?"

"La Señorita Victoria, de la casa Hidalgo."

"She's beautiful," said Frank. His comment was not well received by Paco whose shrug indicated that the conversation was over.

The little track they were following finally wound its way to a greasewood covered ridge-top from which Frank could see a broad valley spread out below him. There were small fields, trees, and several buildings. Two fences built from carefully fitted rocks stretched with geometric precision out of sight over the next ridge. "A cattle ranch," thought Frank, "and apparently a prosperous one."

Minutes later Paco brought the chaise to a stop just inside an iron gateway in a high adobe wall. Through the gate Frank could see several adobe buildings. One, clearly the main house, had carved double doors fitted with decorative, and undoubtedly effective, wrought iron reinforcing plates in the early 19th century Mexican style. Surrounded by well-tended gardens, stone patios, and fountains, the home was clearly that of a successful *hacendado,* a man of property.

Wondering how he could have failed to see all this from his plane as he landed just a few miles away, Frank gazed in wonder at the building, its grounds, and at the open gate with a single letter "H" prominent on its wrought-iron, overhead cross piece.

"You are expected, Señor," said Paco as he looked away from Frank, seemingly dismissing him.

Frank knew that in the Mexico he was familiar with no one would have a home as lavish as this in such a remote area without ready access to the outside world. And yet he had seen no sign of an airstrip, or even trucks or cars. Such opulence suggested the presence of an influential politician or highly successful businessman, and the nature of the man's business might make him disinclined to have uninvited visitors.

Gathering his things, Frank stepped down and, with some apprehension, walked to the huge double door. It opened before he could knock, and a young girl, dressed as a housemaid, motioned for Frank to enter and, with a polite curtsey, said "Good day Señor. I am Maria. Please come in."

"Thank you Maria," said Frank as he stepped through the door into a large, relatively dark room where he heard another feminine voice.

"Good afternoon kind Sir! Welcome to Rancho Soledad. I am Victoria."

Frank looked toward the far end of the room where the words had come from. He was in the presence of a young lady seated in a carved mahogany and woven palm wingback chair. Instantly he was struck by her voice, as soft as the whisper of a breeze so that Frank might have just imagined her words, and yet as clear as mountain spring water, leaving no doubt that it was real. All concern about what sort of reception he might receive in this odd place evaporated, not so much because of the pleasant message the woman's words conveyed, but because her presence gave Frank an inexplicable sense of well-being.

Standing there in his well-worn cowboy boots, faded jeans and sweaty, blue, chambray shirt, Frank could only mumble polite thanks and mention his name. A country bumpkin in the presence of elegance.

Clearly this was the girl Frank had seen earlier on horseback. But no riding costume now. Her long black hair was a length that came well below her shoulders, and was arranged down the right side of her face to the front where it ended just below the bust of her dress. The skirt of the pale-violet colored dress was full and flowing over countless petticoats, bringing to Frank's mind the elegant styles of American Civil War movies. In her lap she held a small, red, leather-bound book. Presumably a prayer book of some kind.

The young lady stood up but did not take even one step. Still holding the little volume in one hand, she extended both in a welcome and smiled at Frank with genuine happiness. Her expression, coupled with her flawlessly smooth, copper-brown complexion seemed so radiant to Frank as to be unreal. *Piel canela*, or cinnamon skin, indicating some Indian ancestry, noted the confused flyer. Victoria was naturally endowed with an appearance that would be the envy of any California beach bunny and with a charisma that could melt a man's heart.

Then, with her almost breathless voice that made Frank's knees weak, Victoria said, "Please make your self comfortable, Señor. My father will be with you shortly." With just the slightest hand gesture she indicated that Frank should enter the adjoining room. He did so, wondering whether her voice was more like music or the rustling of tree leaves in a soft, evening breeze. Immediately Maria closed the heavy door behind Frank, who found himself alone, but with a faint feeling that he had known Victoria all his life.

Frank was impressed by the intricately carved wood furniture and bookcases that surrounded him in what was obviously a library and sitting room. Two things caught his attention. One was that the room was illuminated only by daylight coming from the large windows on one side. The other was the books. Some appeared new and some showed the normal wear of age and use. But all were leather bound, and two that Frank could see lying on a table showed colored, decorative scrollwork on the page edges. The illuminated binding style often used by 19th century printers.

Could this be a movie set? A large stone fireplace, though not in use, was clearly real. Frank walked to a bookcase to examine the contents more closely.

Among various old books Frank's attention fell upon one particular volume. A simple, black volume immediately recognizable as a copy of Andrew Motte's translation of "The Principia," by Isaac Newton. Not able to resist, the fascinated visitor pulled it off the shelf, knowing that it was a work originally written in 1687 and was one of the most important books in the history of both science and mathematics. The leather bound volume also had the colorful illuminated page edges, and bore a printer's date in the late eighteenth century.

Holding the volume in his hands Frank glanced at other titles and quickly realized that the library was not just for show, but the property of a well-educated man who took reading seriously. And then he felt another presence in the room.

"You are perhaps a man who likes books?"

The resonant voice and quiet appearance of a frail, slightly built man who was obviously his host, startled Frank. At least he hoped he would be considered a guest in this strange place.

"Ah, well, yes, actually."

"Good, good. Perhaps we will have time to talk of such things during your visit with us. For my home is yours as well, as we Mexicans are fond of saying." The elderly man extended his hand to Frank.

"I am Señor Rubén Hidalgo Cantenera de Silva, and you are now my guest."

Though the man's demeanor was quite friendly, his use of the word "guest" conveyed a slight tone of "whether I like it or not."

"A charismatic fellow, this elderly country gentleman. Gotta be a politician," thought Frank.

"I am Frank Jensen," said Frank, accepting his host's hand and noticing that his own name seemed anticlimactic compared to the formal, Spanish rendition of Señor Hidalgo's name.

"I suggest that we sit and share some tea, or coffee if you prefer, while you tell me what brings you to my small part of Mexico."

"Coffee would be nice," said Frank.

Rubén nodded and Maria, who had been watching unobtrusively, left the room's doorway, presumably heading toward a kitchen.

"Well, Señor Jensen, you have an accent that I cannot place and are certainly not Mexican, yet you speak the Spanish language. How does that come to be?"

"Yes Señor Hidalgo. My mother's parents were from Chihuahua and my father was European, from Sweden. In fact my first name is actually Francisco. My mother insisted on it."

"Ah, Francisco, a good Mexican name," replied the distinguished gentleman. "So, perhaps here at Rancho Soledad I may call you by its familiar form, Pancho."

"So, what brings you to my ranch and my home, places that do not get visitors that do not have business here?" There was a distinct note of sternness in Rubén's question.

"Well Sir, I've had some difficulty with my plane and I need some help if I am to get home any time soon."

"Your plane? I do not understand."

"Yes, you see, I spent the weekend in Cabo San Lucas, near La Paz, and was flying home when my engine quit. If you have a radio telephone I'd like to let my office know that I'm going to be late."

Rubén said nothing. He sat quietly watching his guest until Frank spoke again.

"Señor? Have I said something I shouldn't have?"

Like many Americans of Mexican descent in Southern New Mexico, Frank spoke a reasonably good, but highly colloquial version of Spanish that is different from that of the Mexican interior. His host's language was precise and fast, in the style of Mexico City, and many words were different from Frank's experience.

Before Frank spoke again, Rubén broke the silence.

"You say you were traveling from near La Paz to your home. Where, may I ask, is your home?"

"Oh, ah, Las Cruces, New Mexico. I left Cabo this morning and stopped in Ciudad Obregon to refuel. I should have been home a couple of hours ago."

"La Paz and the Sea of Cortez I know well. I know too of Ciudad Obregon. But where, Señor, is Las Cruces?"

"Oh, it's in New Mexico, about seventy kilometers north of Juarez, north of El Paso."

"Then perhaps you are an American? Please do not take offense, but that would explain your speech."

Frank nodded affirmatively and his host continued.

"Señor Jensen, I know of the name Juarez. It is an important one, but there is no Mexican locality that bears it. Of what place are you speaking?"

Uncomfortable with his host's strange statement, Frank tried to explain. "The large city on the Rio Grande, a few hundred kilometers north of Chihuahua City. You know, Ciudad Juarez." Frank hoped he didn't sound condescending.

"I see. You are speaking of El Paso del Norte, just across the river from the American city of El Paso."

"Si Señor," said Frank, and made a mental note not to use the modern name of the old Mexican city again.

Again, Rubén sat for some time looking at Frank, and finally rose to his feet.

"Perhaps it is better if we move out into the courtyard. It is quite pleasant there later in the day and the light is better."

9

The two men walked to a patio near a carved stone fountain under an arbor rich with the scent of its ripened Concord grapes. Just as they sat down at a small table, a servant arrived with coffee. Rubén nodded thanks and, after taking a small sip, continued his scrutiny of Frank, who busied himself with his own cup.

After another long pause, Rubén spoke again.

"Señor Jensen, you have me confused, and I suspect you have not been frank with me. I offer you, a stranger, the hospitality of my home and you respond to my proper inquiries about your background with statements that are incomprehensible. My daughter tells me that you 'fell from the sky' and Paco, one of my workers, says that he saw you do so. You say that you are a traveler, one who left the vicinity of La Paz one morning with the intent of arriving near El Paso del Norte on the same day. That is a journey of many days under the best of times, one that is nearly impossible under the current circumstances. I feel that a guest owes his host a more reasonable explanation than I have thus far been given."

"What have I gotten into", thought Frank.

"With all due respect, Señor Hidalgo, I was flying my own airplane. It's only about six hours from La Paz to El Paso or Juar—ah, El Paso del Norte, by air."

"Señor Jensen, I am an old man who does not know of all modern things. Your language and mine may have their differences, but I know that words like 'airplane' and 'radio telephone' have no meaning in anyone's Spanish."

While listening to his host, Frank thought about what he had heard. A "many day" trip? One that is "impossible under the current circumstances?" The knot in Frank's stomach got tighter.

"Señor Hidalgo, may I respectfully ask you a question?"

Rubén nodded in response.

"You said a trip like mine is impossible under the current circumstances. May I ask what circumstances?"

Rubén looked hard into Frank's eyes as he answered.

"The revolution, of course. Maximiliano's Federales."

"Jesus, this guy's talking about what happened over a hundred years ago!" thought Frank, as he slumped back in his chair, certain that he was in the hands of a demented old man. Rubén sat quietly watching him. As he sat, Frank thought of all he had seen. No motor vehicles on the ranch. No roads beyond mere horse or wagon trails, and no electric lights. A ranch as prosperous as this would surely have an engine-driven power plant. Frank again felt a wave of despair.

"Perhaps we should continue this subject tomorrow," said Rubén. "A pleasant meal, without such strange thoughts on the table, and a good night's rest will bring a new day. Perhaps one that is more amenable to difficult conversation. We here at Rancho Soledad always find the evening meal to be a pleasant and light-hearted time. I trust that you and I shall keep it so."

"Si Señor, of course. But, ah, just one more question, Señor Hidalgo. What time is it, that is, what is today's date?"

"That is an odd question to come from an apparently educated man. Nevertheless, I will answer it. Today is the 28 day of the month of September, Year of our Lord 1865."

The Vaqueros

Clearly, Rubén had his own reservations about the mental state of his guest. A servant, dressed exactly as Paco had been, showed Frank to a guest room with no conversation beyond polite amenities. Confused and apprehensive about what was happening, Frank stood in the middle of the room taking in his surroundings. Though lighted only by waning daylight coming through the single large window in one wall, the room was clearly well-appointed, almost opulent. A carved mahogany dresser stood in the middle of the wall opposite the window. The walls were made of well-fitted adobe bricks. One wall held a large mirror, framed in mahogany. On the dresser were clean, white, folded towels, a large metal wash basin coated with mottled blue baked enamel, two crystal drinking glasses, and a large pitcher of water. A large bed, a small bedside table with a kerosene lamp, and a leather upholstered chair, all built of the same mahogany, made a pleasant room. The oil paintings of hunting scenes on the wall and other minor decorations showed that it was a room intended for a man's taste.

Walking to the window Frank found an excellent view of Rancho Soledad's outbuildings, and noticed several workers busy at chores of ranch life. A corral with two well-groomed horses and a stable, which likely contained more animals, reminded Frank of the rider who had waved to him as he rode in Paco's chaise.

As Frank watched, two other riders arrived. Both were well dressed in the older Mexican tradition, complete with wide, round-brimmed sombreros, but made of felt rather than straw as were those worn by the two *campesinos* who immediately took their horses. The two vaqueros stood together talking, probably about the business of running a prosperous ranch. At least that is what Frank assumed.

Resigning himself to the bizarre situation he found himself in, Frank walked to the huge dresser. He picked up a small bar of soap from on top of the towels, and noticed that though unused, it had no impressed factory trademark. Clearly it was the product of simpler manufacture, having been cast in a small, wooden frame.

After the refreshment of clean water and towels, Frank lay on his back on the comfortable bed mulling over the events of his confusing day. He had no doubt that the *hacendado* was a demented old man. But the entire ranch seemed to be operating quite in concert with him. They can't all be crazy. But how could the old guy keep everyone in line?

Frank rested comfortably with vague thoughts of stealing some form of transportation, even a horse, and trying to get away. But where could he go? The next ranch? Where would that be? And those two vaqueros he had seen from his window had been wearing sidearms, and one was carrying a rifle. From their dress and their manner when dealing with the *campesinos*, Frank knew they were more than just working cowboys.

As Frank lay there thinking about what he had seen, he heard raised voices from near the corral he had seen below. He stepped to the window and saw that the two newcomers were still there, and a household servant, somewhat agitated, was speaking to one of the men. As he did so he pointed directly to the window of Frank's room. One vaquero, rifle in hand, turned and looked directly at Frank, then strode purposefully toward the rear of the hacienda.

Travelers

Just a few kilometers away from Rancho Soledad a jackrabbit, ears back, sat on a low hill. The only motion was the busy nose and mouth as the little fellow nibbled carefully at the succulent green pad of a prickly pear cactus at the edge of a two-rut wagon road. Suddenly the ears, nearly as long as the rabbit himself, popped straight up and the foraging stopped. Seconds later he scampered over to the security of a mesquite clump about fifty yards away. He had learned long ago to get quickly out of the way of the creaking, squeaking sounds of traffic on the road.

12

About to reach the top of the hill, several heavily armed men on horseback escorted three others in a small wagon rigged with a white canvas awning for protection from the sun. At the front of the group, Tito Rodriguez Hernandez continuously scanned the horizon in all directions around the riders. His right hand was steady on the grip of the Henry rifle he had to hold in front of him since his saddle scabbard was occupied by a double-barreled shotgun.

Nearly a mile away Enrique Mendosa Martinez ducked himself and his horse behind the crest of a ridge in time to avoid being noticed by anyone in the group on the wagon road. For a short time he carefully watched the wagon and counted all the riders he could see. Then he took to his mount and, riding at a lope, went cross-country to report to Señor Hidalgo.

The wagon, with Tito still at its head, continued its slow pace. With a determined attitude, the men headed directly toward Rancho Soledad. Ten minutes after they had passed the crest of the ridge, the jackrabbit crept back, to continue grazing on the succulent green of the prickly pear he had been working on.

Jose

Not particularly surprised, but with some apprehension, Frank walked from the window where he had been standing over to the door of the room. The knock he was responding to was strong and demanding, not the polite rapping of a servant.

Frank opened the door and the visitor stepped purposefully into the room without invitation and closed the door behind him. He was a large man, particularly for a Mexican, being well over six feet tall. He stood for a few moments looking at Frank, then indicated that Frank should sit down in the room's only chair. Frank declined to do so.

"You are a Gringo, yes?" The man, speaking English, deliberately emphasized the disparaging word for a foreigner from north of the border.

"I am a *Norteamericano*, yes. And you are a Mexican, no?"

"Do not make smart remarks with me, Gringo. I am here to tell you two things. But first I want to know what brought you to Rancho Soledad."

The visitor no longer had a rifle in his hand, but still wore a Walker Colt revolver on his right hip.

"I flew here in my airplane. I have had engine trouble and was brought to this house by one of your workers."

"Yes, by Paco. He say's you 'fell from the sky.' Gringo, you and I know that is not so—that's ridiculous. So, I ask again, why are you here?" The middle aged, rather handsome vaquero stepped slightly closer, his face only inches from Frank's.

"I, ah, I don't know how I got here—I really don't. But all I am trying to do is go home, back where I belong."

"Where is that, Gringo?"

"I am from New Mexico—"

"*New* Mexico? Ay Gringo, I told you not to be smart with me. You are no Mexican of any kind, old or new."

"No, I mean, ah, I'm from near Mexico, near El Paso, Texas."

"Ah, a Texan. A Gringo of the worst kind!"

"No man. I'm telling you the truth and I mean no harm. And, I should point out that your boss, Señor Hidalgo, has accepted me as his guest, in this room, and I suggest that you watch your own manners. I am asking you to leave, and as *su jefe,* Señor Hidalgo, has said, we will leave discussions about my presence here until tomorrow." Frank had switched to the use of his modest command of the Spanish language, just to make it clear that he wasn't all "Gringo."

The intimidating vaquero stood quietly for a few moments, then relaxed just a bit. "OK, *extraño,* we will see what tomorrow brings. You will confine your visit to Señor Hidalgo, or to me, or my men. These are bad times here in Mexico, and if you are not what you say you are, things will not go well for you."

The visitor then turned toward the door, opened it and stepped through.

"You said you were here to tell me *two* things," said Frank.

Jose stopped, without turning. Over his shoulder, eyes stabbing deep into Frank's, and with an acidic whisper, he made one more remark. "You will stay away from La Señorita Victoria or you will not survive, no matter who you are."

***

As Jose left Frank's room, he returned to the hacienda's library where he found Victoria, seated in her wheelchair.

"Ah, Señorita, I would like to talk to you about our visitor."

"Yes Jose. You have met him already?"

"Yes, and I am concerned because I—we—don't know who he is. He is a Gringo—uh—he's not one of our people, Señorita, and we don't know why he is here."

"I do know Jose, and there is no need to be concerned."

"You know why he is here?"

"Not exactly, but I know that all is well with his visit—"

"He's just visiting? How long will he be here?"

"Not long; he is here to help us."

Victoria watched the handsome, highly competent, ranch foreman as he stood in front of her chair. He was plainly uncomfortable talking to her this way. He seemed almost shy, like a young boy in the presence of a schoolgirl he was infatuated with. She knew that he would like to have a far less formal relationship with her, and was hopeful about what the future might bring.

"Well, I will be glad to see him leave," said Jose. "We should not trust any stranger these days."

Victoria almost smiled at Jose's remark, realizing that it reflected something more than just concern for the people of Rancho Soledad.

"Jose, please do not worry. Although things may not be as you would like now, I can promise you that the future is better than you can possibly imagine, both for you and for me."

Some seconds of silence passed as Jose digested the remark. Then he bowed ever so little in his best gentlemanly fashion and stepped back slightly.

"Si Señorita, but I will be sure that this Gring—this visitor does not harm you or our people. You be sure to call for me if you should ever need me for any reason." Then he added, "Any reason at all."

Visitors

After sitting in the single chair by the window looking at the distant hills that looked so familiar, and occupied by thoughts of what was happening to him, Frank dozed off, and was awakened by another knock at his door. This time a gentle tapping accompanied by a polite feminine voice from the hallway. Frank opened his eyes and momentarily stared at the wooden *vigas*, the hewn timbers of which the ceiling was constructed. Disappointed that he was not awakening from a dream, he answered Maria's summons.

"Good afternoon, Señor. The patron wishes you to know that the evening meal will soon be served in the small courtyard." After waiting politely for Frank's "Thank you, Señorita," Maria scurried back to her own world.

Minutes later Frank found himself seated just to the left of his host, who presided over the meal at one end of the large dining table. Clearly Frank had been given a choice seat, for he had an excellent view of distant mountains across the courtyard. A layer of high, thin clouds, faintly bathed with orange, hinted at the spectacular sunset that would soon come.

"We at Rancho Soledad prefer to take our evening meal outdoors at this time of year to appreciate the pleasant climate our country provides us," said Rubén.

Though still not sure what was happening to him, Frank could not help being impressed by the elegant setting among flowering trees and grape arbors, and the gentle sounds, like those of a bubbling brook, that came from the carved stone fountain. "One classy place," thought Frank.

Frank had been introduced to the others seated at the table, most of whom were present as he entered the courtyard. To his delight he found Victoria, already seated directly across from him, wearing yet another evening dress, this time pure white in color. Lying just beside her left hand on the white tablecloth was the little red book Frank had seen earlier. Now he could see it much better and notice its elegantly tooled cover. No title of any kind, just an intricate image of flower blossoms.

Several other members of the family were present, men and women of varying ages. Of some concern to Frank were three men whose body language made it clear that they were not happy with Frank's presence at Rancho Soledad.

"Jose, Emilio, and Enrique, three of my best vaqueros," Rubén had said as he introduced the men.

From their manner of dress and their demeanor Frank knew that these men were more than just ranch hands. He had noticed that behind them and lying near the fountain were three gun belts and two rifles. Clearly the weapons had been removed as a courtesy at the supper table, but were being kept nearby. Being well acquainted with 19th century firearms as a hobby, Frank noticed that the two Henry rifles and the one cap and ball revolver he could see well were quite consistent with his host's contention that the date was 1865.

The meal began with roast pork and, no longer really surprised by anything anymore, Frank found that it was served with a nice white wine from grapes that had been grown at Rancho Soledad. Resigning himself to the mildly disturbing presence of the three vaqueros, he began to thoroughly enjoy the evening. He found his host to be a pleasant conversationalist, and, although Victoria hardly ever spoke, Frank was completely captivated by the young woman seated across from him.

In an attempt to engage Victoria in conversation, Frank complimented her on her ability on horseback. This brought two results for Frank, one to be expected, the other not.

Emilio and Enrique momentarily stopped what they were doing and glanced at Jose, then resumed their meal. But Jose caught Frank's attention with an intimidating glare, and he held eye contact long enough to make it clear to the stranger in their midst that he was to drop any interest in the patron's daughter.

But far more important to Frank was Victoria's response. As she politely thanked Frank for his compliment, he noticed again the scent of many flowers in wild profusion, but always dominated by that of lilacs, just as he had experienced near his airplane on the desert dry lake. And her voice. To Frank it was at once soft and soothing like that of a mother comforting a frightened child, and then again like tiny bells tinkling in response to a gentle breeze. The stranded flier was overwhelmed with a sense that all was well in this place as long as that lady spoke.

As the meal continued, Jose again focused his attention on Frank. Finally, he spoke. "What is a Gringo," he began, and then as a result of a disapproving glance from Rubén, "What is a *Norteamericano* such as you doing in times like these in our country?" Frank noticed that Jose had pointedly not addressed him as Señor, as he should have.

"Jose, my friend," interrupted Señor Hidalgo, "This evening we are all here, regardless of nationality, to celebrate the fact that the Lord has given each of us one more day of life, including the glorious sunset we see to the west." With a sweep of his hand, Rubén indicated the deep blues and green of the sky that blended into the brilliant oranges that were silhouetting the distant mountains.

"We will leave such questions for tomorrow," he added while smiling at Frank.

The meal continued with the men's conversation running to activities of the French soldiers and the government that was run by

17

Emperor Maximiliano. At one point Jose asked, somewhat sarcastically, what the *Norteamericanos* thought about Mexico's efforts to rid itself of the hated regime of Maximiliano.

Still disoriented by a discussion of current events that he felt had happened more than a hundred years earlier, Frank was at a loss for words. Even though he had a fair grasp of 19th century Mexican history, he was not at all sure what effect an answer might have. He was about to reply with some noncommittal statement, but never got the chance.

A young man, dressed as a *campesino* just as Paco had been, rushed up to the table and quickly spoke a few quiet words to Señor Hidalgo.

"It seems that we are about to have more visitors," said Rubén to his three vaqueros. Immediately all three politely excused themselves from the table, picked up their weapons, and Emilio and Enrique immediately left the courtyard.

"I must apologize for the interruption," Señor Jensen. "In the past news of visitors to Rancho Soledad would be welcomed and mean that there would be additional settings at our table, for whoever they might be." There was a hint of disappointment in Rubén 's demeanor as he spoke. "But in these modern times we find it necessary to identify strangers before they get too close."

As Rubén spoke, a servant appeared with a wheelchair, one that to Frank seemed to be of primitive design. Then Jose stood, picked up Victoria in his arms, and placed her in the well-padded contrivance. He then turned and pointed his finger at Frank for just a moment, making it clear that Victoria was off limits. The serious vaquero then gathered his weapons and left the courtyard on the heels of his two colleagues. Just as quickly as he had appeared, the servant wheeled the young woman out of the room. But just as she left his view Victoria gave Frank a slight nod of the head and a smile that made him feel as though he had always known her.

Surprised by the discovery of the woman's handicap, and thinking of the exceptional horsemanship he had seen her perform, Frank felt a powerful desire to help and protect her. He sat staring at the doorway through which Victoria had disappeared.

Easily guessing Frank's thoughts, Rubén smiled and said, "My daughter is one of the finest caballeras in all of Mexico, and her Arabian mare, Mariposa, has legs enough for both of them."

Seeing in his mind again the delicate beauty of Victoria and her mount as he had first seen them on the dry lake, Frank smiled at the appropriateness of the Spanish word for butterfly as a name for the elegant, white, saddle horse.

A few minutes later Emilio returned, obviously quite excited. "Patron, Benito is with us! Come quickly."

"Do not speak that name, Emilio," replied Rubén with a glance at Frank. "Señor Jensen, a pressing matter requires that you excuse me for a moment." Rubén and Emilio hurried out of the courtyard into the large open area in front of the ranch house.

Now alone at the table, Frank stood and walked to the front door of the hacienda where he could see Rubén 's vaqueros who were obviously concerned about the contents of a wagon that had just arrived. But many other men were present too, some on horseback and all armed with long guns or revolvers. Two wore across their chests the crossed ammunition bandoleers that Frank had seen in so many Hollywood films.

Rubén, noticing that Frank was watching, stepped quickly to where Frank stood and said, "A friend of mine is quite ill and is being taken to Ciudad Chihuahua for treatment," and hurried back to the wagon.

Frank, feeling that he might be able to help, followed Rubén. As he approached the wagon he immediately found his way blocked by a huge bay mare with a surly looking man in its saddle. Armed with two Walker Colt revolvers and holding a Greener shotgun in his hand, Tito Rodriguez Hernandez did not look friendly.

Noticing the sudden movement of the horseman, Rubén stepped toward Frank intending to send him away. But Frank spoke first.

"Señor Hidalgo, I may be able to help."

"You must get away from here, quickly," replied Frank's host. Much of his gracious manner was gone.

"Yes, of course I will if you want. But I am a doctor, and I have medical supplies; I might be able to help."

Rubén looked directly at Frank and asked, "You are a physician?"

"Yes, and a surgeon."

"Señor Jensen, please forgive my rudeness this evening, but you must return to your room. These are serious men living in uncertain circumstances."

Frank turned and walked back to the patio, followed by the man on horseback who kept the bay close enough to Frank's back to nearly overrun him. Because of the man's dark complexion and his black, wide brimmed Sombrero shading his face, the whites of Tito's eyes seemed to bore right into Frank, and the shotgun never wavered as Tito kept it pointed at Frank's head.

Frank's Patient

From the window in his room Frank could see the activity around the wagon, but in the near darkness he couldn't make out any detail. Plainly an animated discussion was taking place. Finally, several men carried the sick man from the wagon into the house.

Frank sat on the edge of the large, soft bed for a few minutes thinking about his situation. He was wondering about his own sanity when he thought about the events that appeared to be going on around him.

His introspection was interrupted by a knock on the door, somewhat louder than that of the housemaid, Maria, earlier.

"Yes, come in."

The door opened and Rubén walked in.

"Señor Jensen, it appears that you and I cannot wait until tomorrow to clarify your presence here at Rancho Soledad. Is it true that you are a physician? I find that question to be of great importance in the present circumstances. I wish also to know about your experience and skill, and since a great many people's lives—including yours—may depend on a decision that I must make, I pray that you will answer with all honesty and candor."

Frank could see the sense of vulnerability in his host's eyes.

"Señor, Hidalgo, I am indeed a qualified surgeon licensed by the State of New Mexico where I have been a practitioner of internal medicine for more than twenty years."

"*New* Mexico? I know of only one Mexico. Are you Mexican or a *Norteamericano?*"

Frank realized that to his host the region to the north was just a territory of the United States, and that the State of New Mexico did not yet exist.

"Señor, I work and live in the United States of America in what you would call the Territory of New Mexico, but my medical training was carried out at universities in Texas."

"Ah, you are a Texan," replied Rubén. "I might have guessed from your attire. In any case, please come with me."

Frank thought again of his scuffed-up cowboy boots and smiled. Apparently, his host had made his decision.

Frank picked up his medical bag, glad that he had not left it in his airplane, and the two men walked along the hallway to another guest room. Frank, thinking it strange that such a group of armed men would be required to take a man to town for medical attention, asked, "Who is your friend Benito, anyway?"

At once Rubén 's manner became hard again. "I would prefer that you give your attention to your patient's well-being and be less concerned with his identity."

Chastised, Frank mentally slipped into the role of a practicing physician about to make a diagnosis.

In the room Frank saw immediately that the middle-aged man lying in the bed was in considerable pain and had vomited recently. He also found Tito and two other armed men, each clearly distrustful of the stranger in their midst and intent on preventing any hostile action on Frank's part. Tito now had his black sombrero off, but held across the back of his shoulders by a leather thong. In his hands he held a short, slim knife.

It took Frank less than three minutes to complete his examination and reach a solid diagnosis.

"Señor Hidalgo, your friend has acute appendicitis, and from what these men have told me about when the pains began, I can tell you that the situation is quite serious."

"Are you sure, Dr. Jensen? You did not take much time—"

"It is a simple case to diagnose because it is so far advanced. I must also tell you that his appendix will rupture long before you can get him to Chihuahua."

"And if it does?"

"Your friend will surely die unless I remove his appendix immediately."

"Surgery?" responded Rubén.

"Yes, and it would best be done in a hospital. But it can be done here."

Immediately, the man fondling the knife said, "If he dies, *gringo,* he will not die alone!"

"Now Tito," said Rubén, "We are friends here. We will all give the doctor any help he requires."

Frank, already thinking of the rustic surgery he was about to perform without modern anesthesia, mentally reviewed the contents of his medical bag.

***

Two hours later Frank sat in a chair as his patient slept reasonably comfortably. As Frank had hoped, the operation went quickly and routinely. Still, as a physician he had to marvel at the sturdy constitution of a man who had undergone painful major surgery in a semi-conscious state with just a shot of morphine and a little wine as anesthetic. Barring some off-the-wall infection problem, Frank was confident that this swarthy-complected fellow would make a quick recovery.

Tito, who had put his knife away and was sitting quietly beside the bed, spoke to Frank. "Señor medico, I think my friend sleeps well now, better than he has in two days." Frank could see in the man's eyes that he no longer regarded Frank as a threat to the sick man.

***

Three days later Frank, Señor Hidalgo, Jose, Emilio, Enrique, and all the visitors stood by the wagon in front of the ranch house. Victoria was there too, seated in her wheelchair. Frank was making one final exam of his patient to be sure that all that could be done had been done to make the man's journey comfortable. The patient himself, in good spirits and impatient to be on his way, was ordering everyone nearby to make haste in completing preparations.

"Please be careful Señor—, uh, please be careful for the next week or two; we don't want your stitches to tear. And as soon as you can, please be sure to get more medical attention," said Frank.

"Yes Doctor, I shall keep your words in mind."

Then Frank's patient continued. "As I suspected, and as my niece has confirmed for me, my friends have neglected to tell you my name. I am eternally grateful Dr. Jensen, for you have saved my life. For that I owe you much more than a formal introduction."

With that the rapidly recuperating man reached out his hand to Frank and said, "permit me to introduce myself. I am Benito Juarez Garcia, *yo estaré eternamente ha su disposición*, my friend."

Frank was surprised by the eloquent expression "I will always be at your disposal" rather than the more common *a sus ordenes*, meaning "at your command" that was common in the Mexico Frank was more familiar with.

Before releasing Frank's hand, the man added, "If there is ever anything you need during the new days that are coming for Mexico, you need only inform my people."

As Frank looked into the man's face he saw the determination of a man of destiny, and wished he could tell his patient that in years to come one of the largest cities in Mexico would bear his name.

Frank bade his patient good-by and stepped away from the wagon. All through the conversation he was aware that Victoria was watching him intently with a hint of admiration in her eyes and a smile that made his knees weak. As the wagon rolled on its way, Frank almost forgot about the peculiar circumstances of his presence in Mexico.

Then Frank was jarred back into reality, or lack of it, when he saw Jose leave his place near the wagon and walk toward him.

"Ah Señor Doctor Jensen. I must speak with you."

Frank said nothing, not particularly anxious to deal with the big Mexican any more than necessary.

"Doctor Jensen, I am happy to find that my concerns about your visit to Rancho Soledad were not important. I wish to thank you myself for what you have done for Mexico. New or Old Mexico, whichever." Jose grinned a little at his own lighthearted remark. "Forgive me for being extra careful, for considering the times we Mexicans are living in." With that, Jose turned and walked back to join Enrique and Emilio.

As everyone turned toward the house Frank deliberately walked beside Victoria's wheelchair. He had spoken to her father two days earlier and leaned enough about the lady's condition to understand that her left foot was deformed and that the condition was a congenital defect about which nothing could be done. As he walked beside the chair Frank felt a deep frustration because, with all his medical training from a hundred years in the future, there was nothing he could do to help her.

Frank started to gently lay his hand on Victoria's wheelchair, but the elderly woman pushing the chair casually changed direction, preventing the gesture. The action was subtle but deliberate enough for Frank to know that he was not to come that near to Victoria.

Glancing to the side, Frank saw that Jose was watching him from a short distance away. As their eyes met the vaquero slowly shook his head from side to side.

As Frank followed the wheelchair back toward the house he became aware of a small presence beside him. At his side was a smiling little girl about five years old, with captivating, jet black eyes and a simple, white cotton dress. As his eyes met hers, she reached up and took his hand as any child might when walking with an adult she trusted. The young lady walked with Frank a short distance as Victoria and her efficient chaperon disappeared into the house. When they too reached the house, she took her hand from Frank's, curtsied like a storybook princess, and in a sparkling little voice informed Frank that her name was "Lupita." Then, with the shyness common to all ladies of that tender age, Lupita blushed and ran away, leaving Frank with a lasting impression of just how lovely a child can be.

A Pleasant Day for a Ride

During the past several days Frank had occasionally taken short walks alone near the ranch house to pass the time. He had found that when he got out of sight of the ranch buildings the countryside looked completely familiar, and he could almost believe that he could go home again. Or that perhaps just over the next few hills he would be able to see a modern gravel road or electrical power line. But wherever he ventured all he saw was the familiar looking mesquite, greasewood, and yuccas of the Chihuahuan desert.

After the departure of his patient, Frank again felt that he would like to be alone. He approached Rubén to tell him that he was going for a walk. This time his host, who understood Frank's need for solitude, made a suggestion.

"Doctor Jensen—ah—Pancho, I know that you said that where you live people do not use horses as we do here. I find this peculiar, for surely they are available, are they not?"

"Yes, of course they are, at least on our cattle ranches," said Frank.

"Well then, I presume you can ride satisfactorily, and mounted you could see more of Rancho Soledad." As he spoke, Rubén gestured with his hand to a well-groomed sorrel mare, all saddled and ready to go, that a *campesino* was holding for Frank.

Having done some riding in the past, Frank appreciated the offer. He accepted the horse and climbed into the saddle as gracefully as he could, trying to avoid looking too clumsy. Immediately he noticed the six-inch diameter saddle horn, and smiled a little realizing he was about to ride a saddle that was considered a valuable antique by modern day horsemen in either the United States or Mexico. He found that the stirrups had been adjusted nicely for the length of his legs.

"Have a nice ride, Pancho my friend," said Rubén. Then, with a wink of an eye, he added, do not worry about getting lost; the animal knows her way home."

***

An hour later Frank had found a pleasant valley that to his surprise had a trickle of a stream in it. At one point there was a grove of scrub oak and juniper trees near a shallow pond of water. After letting the sorrel drink his fill, he dismounted, tied the reins to a small juniper, and then squatted down on the green grass at the edge of the pond. "A spirited, but well trained horse," thought Frank.

As many horses do, the sorrel had evaluated her rider and knew that she was carrying a timid amateur. Fidgety about attention she was getting from a fly, she was clearly thinking of heading back to the barn.

Very much appreciating the solitude and tired from the events of the last few days, Frank lay back on the grass. Through the green leaves of an oak tree that was providing some shade, he could see the rich blue of Chihuahua's clean, desert sky and a few puffy, white clouds. Like a chorus of tiny voices the tree's leaves rustled in the afternoon breeze as an accompaniment to the melody of the trickling water nearby.

Frank let his eyes wander and took in the texture of oak branches, the smell of nearby grass, and the familiar scents of the desert pond. Even the raucous call of a canyon wren and the distant screech of a red tailed hawk soaring high above seemed so familiar. Frank tried to relax and enjoy his surroundings but he couldn't avoid the hollow, empty feeling caused by his peculiar circumstances.

Alone in the countryside, Frank could almost believe that his situation—the whole visit to Rancho Soledad—had to be some sort of trick. Here he could see, feel and touch things that were exactly like home. As he thought about his plight, he watched a low flying marsh hawk hunting for mice along a nearby ridge and noticed one difference from the desert of his home in New Mexico. Even near the horizon the sky was deep blue and much clearer than it would have been in New Mexico. On every day he had been at Rancho Soledad the air had seemed unusually pristine. Frank had to admit that he was seeing the unpolluted environment of the 19th century, and his host's contention that this was a day in 1865 had to be true.

Yet all around Frank were the prickly pear cacti, mesquite, and greasewood bushes that were a familiar part of his life in New Mexico.

With a heavy heart he sat with his back against a comfortable scrub oak tree and tried to relax.

The saddle horse, grazing nearby, flipped her head and snorted some, enough to wake Frank and remind him of his situation. He realized that in spite of the idyllic and completely familiar surroundings in which he found himself, he had never before been so hopelessly lost. He was far, far from home—maybe impossibly so.

Frank sat up, with his arms around his knees, and spoke soothingly to the horse, just to break his own chain of thought. It didn't help much and counting back he realized that he had been at Rancho Soledad, or wherever he was, for nearly two weeks. Thinking of people and places at home in New Mexico made things worse. For short moments he would feel like his earlier life was just a memory, or hallucination, and Rancho Soledad was the only reality left for him. He stood up and walked a few paces, knowing that he had to get control of himself to avoid the depression he was sliding into.

Feeling a wave of despair, the stranded flier kicked some of the loose dirt at his feet and picked up several pebbles. He tried with moderate success to skip a flat one for a distance across the pond. Then he threw the handful all at once, disrupting most of the pond's surface as he turned back toward the waiting horse. He hardly noticed the animal's ear flip in response to one of the annoying flies that was bothering it. With tears beginning to cloud his vision and feeling unimaginably tired, Frank feared that he was losing control, or what little control he had, of the mess he was in.

But the physician in him and his natural strength of character made him stand up straighter for a few moments, and try to empty his mind of depressing thoughts. As he did so, he again heard a distant sound, like high-pitched notes of a flute but faint and without melody, and he felt the sound was coming from the pond behind him. And there was just the slightest suggestion of spices, and richly fragrant blossoms, both sounds and scents so subtle that Frank thought he must have been imagining them.

As he turned to look back at the little pond, he noticed that the water was calm again, no longer disturbed by the handful of stones he had disgustedly thrown in moments earlier. He could clearly see, reflected in the surface of the pristine pond, the inverted image of a ridge not far away. In the reflection, silhouetted against the blue Chihuahuan sky, he saw a rider dressed in black on a white horse standing on the ridge crest. Quickly Frank looked up, directly at the ridge, only to see the brilliant, blue sky where the rider should have been.

"Jesus, I'm losing my mind," thought Frank as he shook his head in a subconscious effort to clear his thoughts.

But as the scent of lilacs grew stronger, deep inside Frank knew that Victoria was with him, sharing his solitude. Feeling suddenly content, he sat down again with his back against the oak tree where he had a view of the image in the pond's surface. Soon he relaxed completely with a sense of companionship like none he had ever known. The faint, near musical, tinkling sounds Frank thought he could hear grew clearer as did the pleasant scent of lilacs. As the delightful sensations danced about his head he realized that they were almost words, or phrases, and yet faint enough to be nothing more than imagination. As he sat there his gaze never left Victoria's reflected image on the surface of the pond.

As the phrase-like sensations swirled through Frank's mind he realized that Victoria was telling him something. "You need not worry" he heard, or thought he heard. "All is just as it should be; there is no beginning; there is no end."

And then he clearly heard the sounds gather into the most important message of all. Frank felt Victoria's soft voice tell him, "We need only wait patiently, and then—"

A few more snorts and a little pawing of the ground by the impatient saddle horse broke Frank's concentration, and at that moment the delicate reflection in the pond became just an empty, inverted skyline again. The sorrel mare had just jerked her head some, again in response to the attention of a fly.

Frank was disappointed because of the interruption, he wanted to know what more was being said, and at the same time knew that he wouldn't. Was it all his imagination? Perhaps, but the lost traveler chose to believe that it was Victoria, and thanked the lady for giving him strength to carry on. Again he lay on the grass taking in the coolness of the gentle breeze, and letting his vision, slightly blurred by tears, walk among the cotton-puff clouds in the clean, blue sky above him.

***

Perhaps an hour later Frank woke up with a start. Without intending to, he had fallen asleep. Feeling much better from his little nap he sat up and looked toward the little juniper tree where he had tied his horse.

"Oh damn it! Now I'm screwed," said Frank. The sorrel was nowhere to be seen. Immediately Frank remembered how carelessly he had tied up the animal. Just looping the reins around the branch would have been OK for the docile farm horses he had ridden long ago when he was just a young boy, but he should have been more careful with the far more spirited, working cow-horse he had been given. He knew he was now afoot, faced with a walk of several miles back to the ranch house. An hour or two, that is if he could remember where the place was.

Rubén Plans Ahead

Just after breakfast Rubén called Jose aside in the open courtyard.

"Jose, I have an important matter to talk about with you."

"Si Jefe, I think I know what you have in mind."

"Yes, my friend, I know that you have as much love and concern for Rancho Soledad as I do. You have been my foreman and most trusted friend for more years than I can remember. I think you too have heard the bad news about our country's troubles."

"Si Jefe," troubles caused by the vile Maximiliano and his *Franchutes*, no?"

"Yes. Twice in recent days neighbors have sent me word that Maximiliano is sending soldiers to hunt down Benito, and anyone associated with him. I am concerned because they are sure to know of my respect for El Presidente, and will probably know that Benito was here."

"They will not like that," said Jose.

"No, most certainly not. I think we both know that there will be trouble, perhaps more than we are prepared to deal with, and it will come sometime soon."

"Señor, I have always been ready to help any way I can. You know that Rancho Soledad and its people are more to me than a job as foreman. This rancho, this land and its people are my home, my life. I will be here as long as is required to help you in any way I can and—"

"Thank you my friend. I have always known that."

"And, mi Jefe, I can promise you that Emiliano and Enrique both feel the same as I do. Like me, they are both more than just vaqueros if trouble starts."

"Yes Jose, life is better here at Rancho Soledad because of you three men and your vigilance. Now, I think it is time for us to make some preparations for the bad times that are surely coming."

"What can we do to help?"

"I think, Jose, that the time has come for us to move most of the livestock to a better location. I would like you to have your men take all but what we need for a fast departure to the Hernandez ranch. It is good country in the foothills of the Sierra Madre. They have been expecting me to make this move. They have more than enough grass and water to handle our stock, and have offered to provide shelter for our workers if needed."

"I will get this done immediately. Is there—"

"Yes, I want you to have Paco prepare a wagon with his family, his little Lupita, and for us as well. And Jose, be sure that all this is done quietly. It matters to me that our visitor should not know about this, or our coming troubles. That is important."

"Si Jefe," I would like the Gring—ah, the Tejano, to be gone from here, and away from our Victoria. But he is here, and I understand what you want, what we all need. And I want to tell you one more thing that is more important to me than my own life."

"You are thinking of my daughter, Victoria."

"Si Jefe. I want you to know that as long as there is breath in my body my—your—Victoria will be safe, anywhere."

Jose's Search

"Señor Patron, Señor Patron," called Gregorio, the *campesino* who had saddled the horse for Frank.

Rubén and Jose, who had been standing in the courtyard talking, turned to see what the excited young man wanted.

"Señor, the horse, she has come home. She has come back without the Señor Pancho! She—"

"I thought he told you he could ride," muttered Jose. "Now the *Norteamericano* must be rescued."

"Send two or three of your riders to look for him, Jose," said Rubén, "and—"

"I will find him myself, Señor. It will be easy to follow his trail."

Then turning to young Gregorio, Jose issued polite, but stern orders. "You will see that the sorrel the Gringo was riding gets some

29

water. Then saddle my black for me, and put the saddle the Grin—eh, the *Norteamericano* was using on a fresh animal. Choose one docile enough for a Texan to ride." Jose had again noticed his boss' displeasure with his use of the slang word Gringo.

***

Less than an hour later Jose, having easily backtracked the sorrel in the loose soil, sat easy in his saddle as he watched Frank in the distance plodding his way toward the hacienda in the afternoon sun. Smiling just a little at Frank's plight, the vaquero put his mount into a lope, leading the fresh horse Gregorio had saddled, and soon reached Frank. There he deliberately brought his big Morgan stallion to a stop right in front of the man on foot, almost running him down. Frank could feel the horse's breath mere inches from his own head.

"Aye Gringo, did you lose your mount? Or would you would rather walk than ride like a man?"

Frank, backing away from the big, black stallion, noticed that the rider was Jose, who had been none too friendly toward him earlier.

With a sarcastic tone Frank replied. "Sorry to have inconvenienced you; I was a little careless in tying her down."

"Why are you so far from the hacienda, Gringo? Have you found what you are looking for?"

"Eh, I'm not looking for anything. Just taking some time to be alone."

"Here is a fresh mount; try not to lose this one." Jose threw the reins of the horse he had been leading to Frank, then moved his own black Morgan in a tight circle around Frank and his new horse, forcing Frank to turn around awkwardly to keep facing Jose. Frank could not help noticing that Jose was heavily armed, as usual. The Walker Colt on a belt and a Henry rifle in his saddle scabbard.

Then the vaquero, who was clearly as much a soldier as a cowboy, stopped and stared directly into Frank's eyes. "Gringo, I want to know why you are here. You are not Mexican, not an *Indio*, and certainly not a *Franchute*. El Patron says you are a Tejano, but I do not think even a Gringo from Texas would be foolish enough to lose his horse!" Jose's manner was getting to be disturbing to Frank.

"I don't know, damn it, and if I did I doubt that it would be any of your business anyway!"

Again Jose moved the big black right up to Frank's chest, clearly demonstrating that he was a competent rider on a well-trained mount.

"Everything that happens on Rancho Soledad is my business. Especially anything concerning La Señorita Hidalgo. You would do well to remember that and stay away from her!"

"La Señorita—Victoria? I, uh, I have—"

"Gringo, I think you have been on Rancho Soledad long enough. You are not Mexican and not a vaquero; you are useless on any rancho."

Frank stepped forward and with his left hand grabbed the Morgan's bridle, to push the animal away from himself. With a jerk of his head to free himself, the horse caused a dollop of spittle to fall on Frank's arm.

"Careful, Gringo, you could get hurt. This animal is not a child's mount as is the gelding I have brought for you. He doesn't like useless Gringos any more than I do."

Getting pissed off at the belligerent man looming over him, Frank stepped toward the man in the saddle. "Look, damn you. You ignorant bastard! You have no idea what I could tell you about your future—" Frank stopped speaking, realizing what a bizarre situation he was really in and how out of his control things really were. Then he calmly said, "Let me remind you, damn it. Your recent visitor didn't find me useless!"

With that comment Jose sat up straighter in his saddle, dismounted, and stepped toward Frank, and stood quietly for a few seconds.

"Señor Medico, I must apologize for part—only part—of my remarks. You have indeed been of great use to not only this rancho, but to all of Mexico, and I will always be grateful for that. I would be ashamed for anyone to know of my foolish words." Then the vaquero remounted the black Morgan, and turned the animal in the direction of the ranch house.

"Have a pleasant ride back, Señor Medico, but do not forget that I have warned you to stay away from La Señorita. You could still get hurt!"

As Frank watched Jose ride away he again noticed the fine example of horsemanship demonstrated by both man and animal.

***

About an hour later Frank arrived back at the hacienda where he saw Gregorio waiting. "I will put the horse away, Señor. Did you enjoy your ride?"

"Yes, Indeed I did, and I thank you for choosing such a pleasant, ah, two pleasant animals for me," said Frank with a grin.

Frank then accompanied the man to the stable and unsaddled the little gelding himself, gave it a good rub down, and saw that the animal got water and feed. "He who rides 'em takes care of 'em," Frank had always been taught.

A Surprise for Frank

On his way to the house Frank saw Rubén sitting in the shady courtyard, clearly waiting for Frank's return.

"I trust you had a pleasant ride," said the elderly gentleman.

"Sure did. I found a pleasant little spring. Such a nice a place that I showed how careless I can be about horses."

"Yes, yes," said Rubén. "Your equestrian skills did not impress my vaquero, Jose. He has suggested that the horses know more about riding than you do," laughed Rubén.

"Well, I thank you for the use of such fine animals. I have noticed that everything here on your ranch seems to be top quality."

"It is our tradition here at Rancho Soledad to raise the best beef cattle in Mexico, along with purebred bulls that are sold for breeding stock, and others that are bred especially for the bull rings in the cities. To do all this requires that we raise good horses as well. You should visit Rancho Soledad during one of our *charreadas*, what I think you would call a rodeo. You would see Mexican vaqueros at their very best."

After his comments Rubén was silent as both men thought about the peculiar events surrounding Frank's current "visit" to the ranch.

"Dr. Jensen, when we first spoke you told me some strange things about your reason for being here, and we agreed to speak again on the subject more frankly. We have not done so. During the past few days I have concluded that you are not mentally deranged and are a man to be respected. But that still leaves me in a difficult position as far as your story about your home, and your tales of traveling from La Paz to El Paso del Norte in a matter of hours."

"Yes Señor Hidalgo. I know what I have said makes no sense. I too am completely confused about it, and to tell the truth, I have wondered if all this is a hallucination."

"I assure you, Pancho my friend, Rancho Soledad is not a hallucination."

"No, of course not," Señor. "I only meant—"

"I know what you meant," said Rubén with a smile.

Again the two men sat in silence for a few moments.

Frank wrestled with the idea that he was speaking with a man who clearly had been born near the end of the eighteenth century. Should he tell his host that the revolution currently in progress would be successful for the people of Mexico and that yet another revolution was coming only a few decades after this one? Should he speak more of airplanes, automobiles, the great wars, of telephones and radios?

No, Frank decided he should not do that. Such talk could do nothing but mark him as a screwball after all.

Finally Rubén broke the uncomfortable silence.

"Dr. Jensen, anyone who lives long enough in this world comes to realize that there are things that do not bear discussing in too much detail. They may be of great interest, but talking of them is only entertainment."

"Yes, Señor Hidalgo—"

"Please, let me finish," said Rubén with a slight raise of a hand.

"In rural Mexico, away from the cities, we know that life itself is much more complicated than just being born, working and then dying. Here we know that some people are different from others in ways that do not meet the eye. Sometimes these people understand things that the rest of us do not. With us at Rancho Soledad there is such a person. She is my daughter, Victoria." Rubén paused, and poured a glass of water from a pitcher that was sitting nearby.

"You have met my daughter, of course. But you have never talked with her, other than to make the formal courtesies of day-to-day life, not so?"

"Well, I . . . "

Rubén smiled at his guest's reply and said, "Yes, she is a beautiful woman, and as you may have noticed her aunt and the women that attend her have discouraged contact with you. After all, you are a man who seems to have fallen from the sky."

With a nervous laugh, Frank added, "Yes they have and your three vaqueros too. Especially Jose."

"Ah yes, Jose. Well, as I said, Victoria is a beautiful woman, and Jose has not failed to notice this fact."

"But, I am making a point that is relevant to our conversation, Pancho, my strange friend. Many people here know of your peculiar circumstances, and are dealing with the knowledge as best they can.

Paco, for example. Paco actually *saw* you fall from the sky. His wife does not believe him, but he says that he did. He makes an extra prayer each day for everyone's well-being, and particularly for that of himself, I suspect. Of all the people here who know about you, only one seems to accept you without concern. That is my daughter, Victoria, who assures all of us that all is as it should be."

Sensing that Frank was about to interrupt, Rubén held up his hand again.

"All of her life my daughter has been exceptionally calm and happy, as a child and as young woman. She has a sense about her that says all is well, and has always been a comfort to people around her during difficult times."

Rubén choked up a little and stopped speaking. Frank noticed the old gentleman's eyes watering slightly as he composed himself to continue.

"Pancho, I must tell you. Manuela, my wife, died just minutes after Victoria was born. As she passed away, she told me that we had a special child that she knew would be with us both forever because the child had told her so." Rubén swallowed, squinted his moist eyes, and added, "Manuela died peacefully and her happy face made me know that what she said was true; she was aware of things that cannot be discussed."

"I don't know what to say," said Frank.

Rubén responded with a little shrug of his shoulders, then gathered himself and got back to what he wanted to say.

"You see, Dr. Jensen, Paco had no usual reason to be out on that dry lake where you were found. Victoria sent him to get you. She was expecting you, though for the rest of my days here at Rancho Soledad I will never understand why. But I also know that I will not worry about it because my daughter tells me that it is right."

Frank, confused and slightly embarrassed by the things he was listening to, wanted to tell Rubén of his own developing feelings of long familiarity with the man's daughter. But he could not bring himself to do so because he himself did not understand.

So, he simply said, "Señor, Hidalgo, I have met your daughter only formally, as you say. But I too am aware that she is a special person, perhaps the most remarkable I have ever known."

"Yes, well, I am nevertheless quite puzzled by my daughter's attitude toward you. She is even more adamant than her overly protective aunt that she must not be left alone with you, yet she seems to be able to talk of nothing else but you. When she speaks of you it is as though she knows you very well, and in her eyes I can see that she is happy that you are here."

Again Frank felt the sense of disorientation that had taken hold of him often in the past few days. He wondered if he was destined to remain permanently at Rancho Soledad. Clearly, he had no choice in the matter.

But then Frank got his answer.

"Dr. Jensen—Pancho—please do not think me an improper host when I tell you this, for in my heart you will always be my friend. But your visit with us is over."

Adios Soledad

Frank had been shocked to hear that he would be leaving Rancho Soledad, and uncertain, even a little frightened, because he had no idea how he would leave. Yet at the same time he was hopeful that perhaps his peculiar circumstances would be resolved.

"My daughter herself has told me that you will leave us tomorrow," said Rubén. "I think she would prefer that you remain, but she says you are leaving. Please do not ask me why. Like your arrival, your departure is beyond my ability to explain."

"What will happen to me tomorrow?"

"Well," said Rubén with a quiet laugh. "I can't very well ask Paco to drive you back to that dry lake. He has troubles enough with his wife already, and does not need to watch you 'climb back into the sky' as my daughter assures me that you will do."

Frank thought immediately of his Cessna that had evaporated into nothingness when he and Paco left that vast, white, salt flat when he arrived at Rancho Soledad.

"So, my friend, I will drive you to your destiny tomorrow. It will sadden me greatly to do so, for you are a friend to whom my country owes a great debt."

***

The next morning Frank was treated to a festive breakfast shared by all the people he had come to know during the short time he had visited Rancho Soledad. As usual Rubén occupied the head of the table with Frank to his right. An empty chair for Victoria was to Rubén's left.

35

The table was set with bouquets of both white and violet colored lilac blossoms. This was a pleasant surprise to Frank for their fragrance immediately made him feel closer to Victoria who had not yet arrived. He had not seen any lilac bushes anywhere on Rancho Soledad, and knew that they were not common in Northern Mexico. As he was about to ask where they came from Victoria entered the room, causing Frank to immediately forget about his question.

Frank stood up and said, "Good morning, Señorita Hidalgo and good morning to you too young lady." He had noticed little Lupita, peeking from behind Victoria's wheel chair, shyly watching Frank.

"And a good morning to you, Señor," said Victoria. "I hope you had a nice sleep. And, you must call me Victoria, for you and I are better acquainted than you know."

"Victoria," said Frank politely, his heart warmed by the puzzling comment.

As a servant removed the empty, straight-backed chair at the table, Victoria pulled Lupita closer to her and whispered directly into the child's ear, then rolled her wheel chair up to the table. The bright-eyed little girl in her spotlessly clean, white dress skipped around the chair occupied by Rubén and went directly to Frank's side.

"Lupita would like to kiss you good-by. Apparently even the young ladies find you irresistible," said Victoria, grinning happily as she spoke.

Frank caught the little flowerlike child in his arms as she planted a smacker on the side of his neck, then he kissed her lightly on her forehead. Lupita then hopped down and ran out of the room the way she had come, blushing shyly as only a little girl can.

"I am specially grateful to you," continued Victoria, "You have been of great service to my uncle and to my country."

"Uncle? I don't understand."

"Ah, let me explain," said Rubén. "As I told you yesterday Manuela, Victoria's mother, left us in childbirth. This was the great loss of my life. It was also a tragedy for Benito, the man who was recently your patient. For Manuela was his sister.

"My God," muttered Frank. "Benito Juar—"

"Yes, the President of the Republic of Mexico is Victoria's uncle," said Rubén with a smile. "And, by preventing his premature death, you have changed as yet unwritten pages of my country's history, for the better, I believe."

"As we all believe," said Victoria. "Is that not so, Señor Jensen?"

Was Victoria asking him to comment on what he thought about Mexico's current situation, or did she know that he could do much more than speculate on their future if he chose to? Still much confused and a little frightened by the bizarre circumstances he found himself in, Frank decided to be cautious.

"I think that if one's heart is in the right place then all will be well in the long run." Frank looked at Victoria as he spoke, realizing that he had used a lot of words to say almost nothing.

Victoria smiled and said, "I am happy that you think so, kind sir, for it is that long run, the *very* long run, that matters most for each of us in his own way."

Then Victoria sipped from a glass of water and looking hard into Frank's eyes and speaking in a voice so soft that Frank was not sure anyone else could hear, said, "Through good times and bad never forget that there is much more to life than any of us realize, and that for each and every one of us existence is wonderful beyond our wildest dreams."

Thinking of her emphasis on "the very long run" Frank had to mentally shake his mind out to bring himself back to the more general conversation as he heard Rubén continue.

"You see, as was my Manuela, Benito is a pure blooded Indian. He is the author of great changes in our government for the benefit of the working people who are struggling to live off of the land."

Suspecting that Frank did not really understand what turbulent times were upon them all, and knowing that Rubén was proud of the work that his brother-in-law was doing, Victoria said, "Father, please tell our guest more about these changes."

"Well, you see, for many years Mexico has been run by representatives of the Catholic Church, not as desired by God and for the benefit of those who believe in Him, but for that of Church officials here and in Rome, and for the convenience of several European countries.

"So Benito—El Presidente—stopped payment of taxes to the church and gave ownership of much land back to the Indians to whom it belonged. This, however, was not satisfactory to governments and foreign businessmen in Europe. This is why they sent us the hated Maximiliano. Thus the Mexico you see is struggling under conflict between a president chosen by its citizens and an emperor imposed upon it by outside interests.

"Ah," continued Rubén as he sat back more comfortably in his chair, "such subjects are not good for the breakfast table and the start of a new day. Let me conclude by assuring you that Benito's quarrel is not with God but only with the oppression of the poor by European governments, the church, and by the soldiers of Maximiliano."

Then, looking at Frank, Rubén added, "As we say grace before our meal let us add a word of thanks that God, whatever he may be, chose to send you to help Benito with his struggle through the dark clouds of Mexico's future."

Frank, himself unsettled by Rubén 's somber words, could feel the emotion and honest anxiety in the older man's thoughts. As he listened he took it all to heart, but his eyes were locked on those of the lady seated across from him.

While still maintaining eye contact with Frank, Victoria said to her father, "There is no more reason to fear the future than to fear the past."

Immediately the somber mood of the room disappeared and Frank felt her words engulf him like a soft, warm blanket wrapped around a swimmer who has just come out of a cold lake.

Throughout the meal Frank made small talk with Victoria and her father and through it all he knew he must have looked like a love struck schoolboy, for he was totally captivated by the lady's presence. When Victoria spoke, even just a short sentence, she always seemed to give the conversation an air of calmness and sense that all was well. Even when Enrique and Jose turned the subject to the possibility of Maximilano's soldiers coming farther north, with a few words Victoria made the problem seem unimportant.

Frank felt Victoria watching him, always with a smiling, contented expression on her face. He knew that she was happy and that she wanted him to be, too.

At the end of the meal, Rubén spoke.

"Well, my friends, it is time for our guest and me to go for a little ride. It seems that he must leave us now."

These words brought sadness to Frank's face, and Victoria noticed it immediately. With her lively eyes sharply focused on his, Victoria spoke quietly to Frank.

"Do not be sad, Señor. Remember these words:

There are crystal bells that have not yet been rung
and tiny songs that have not yet been sung."

Frank sat basking in the softness of Victoria's voice as she spoke words she obviously thought important to him. Then she added, "Though you may not understand, just know that this moment is an important, even happy, occasion for both you and for me."

The nearly soundless little rhyme, spoken with the movement of lips as delicate as rose petals, reached deep into Frank's heart and memory.

***

Half an hour later Frank and Rubén rode quietly as the older man drove the nicely appointed, two-wheeled vehicle away from the walled courtyard on Rancho Soledad. Frank was looking around trying to remember details about the little road that ran between the dry lake and the house, for he knew that if it were possible one day he would return. And he hoped he might catch a glimpse of Victoria riding her white horse, Mariposa, nearby.

"Are you a religious man, Pancho my friend?" asked Rubén.

Frank swallowed, thinking about his answer and wondering what a "religious man" might be to the old gentleman.

"Señor Hidalgo, I am not a member of any church for I do not put much stock in ceremony and ritual. But I too believe that there is much more going on around us than simple birth, life, and death. I have a faith that any of us who deals with his world in a manner that is considerate of those around him can take comfort that whatever the future brings is well intended, and my visit here has only strengthened my belief that there is grand order in all that lies around us."

Neither man spoke for a couple of minutes as the black mare clopped along the rocky track.

"Ah, Pancho, let me ask my question in a much different way. If you remember, a few days ago I found you holding a particular book that had caught your attention in my library. Do you remember which it was?"

"Indeed I do. It was Newton's Principia, a title one doesn't often find in personal collections."

"Yes, a remarkable book. One in which Mr. Newton demonstrated genius as a mathematician, as I presume you are aware."

"Yes," replied Frank. "He and Mr. Leibniz invented the calculus, probably one of the most important advances in all of mathematical history, right up there with the discovery of the number zero."

"Aha. You know the man's work; I presume you know what else he has done?"

"Sure. He laid out his famous three fundamental laws that explain all of mechanical motion—even the motions of the stars and planets in the sky."

"Indeed, that is so," replied Rubén. "Apparently you have studied the sciences, mathematics and philosophy as well. And you realize the intellectual power that lies in the scientific method; am I correct?"

"Well, yes, indeed I do."

"Then, my friend, that makes you a scientist. And you undoubtedly know something of mathematical logic, and philosophy as well."

"Well, yes, a little bit anyway," replied Frank, wondering where Rubén was going with such a strange discussion, considering Frank's peculiar visit to Rancho Soledad. As he spoke Frank felt a little guilty because he knew that his statement about Newton's Laws of Motion was not strictly correct. It would fall to Albert Einstein, later in the coming century, to show that Newton's work needed a little "tweaking up" as do most theories as science progresses. But to try to explain this to Rubén? Well, that would just further complicate a situation that was already beyond explanation to either man.

Rubén reined in the mare pulling the chaise in order to concentrate more directly on their conversation. As he did so he looked Frank in the eye and asked another question.

"My friend, I am sure that you realize that all of the results from the scientific method, all the great works of philosophy, and all the world's religions have one thing in common. Can you tell me what that is?"

"Hoo, that's a big question. Apparently you and I have a lot of interests in common, because I have also thought about such a comparison, and I think I have an answer. Any serious student of those three different fields would know that each requires the assumption of a given set of ideas from which to start. They may be either simple postulates, inviolate thought processes, or edicts from a superior being, but in all three cases these ideas cannot be proven; you must just accept them and start from there."

"Yes, yes, that is what I was hoping you would say," said Rubén, obviously happy that he and Frank could share such thoughts. "I think that being a philosopher or scientist requires one to accept some basic principles as an act of faith, just as does any religion. You see, my friend, you have answered my first question. I think that you are also a religious man, just as I am."

"I guess you are right," said Frank. "But now let me suggest, respectfully, that there is one way in which one of those intellectual fields differs from the others."

As Frank spoke Rubén raised an eyebrow in obvious interest.

"All of the three try to provide comfort to human affairs by explaining the past and, more importantly, by predicting the future. Religions all do so with pat statements about what will happen to each of us humans—statements that cannot possibly be verified within this world. Philosophy provides answers that are always clouded in human nature. But science, that is, the fruits of the scientific method, provide tools that can—in some limited cases—predict the future, and do so with great accuracy and reliability. It leads to predictions that are the backbone of all the vast technological development of mankind."

Rubén said nothing for a time, clearly deep in thought, and then replied.

"Yes, my friend, I would have to agree, and yet at the same time point out that science is much more limited than we all would like. It is easy to pose situations where science can not predict all events or provide the sort of answers that are of real importance to the human mind." As Rubén spoke Frank knew that the man was right, and understood why the old gentleman had started such a deep conversation.

"I think my presence here at Rancho Soledad is such an event, not so?"

"Yes indeed, and more to my point, the existence of my daughter's special relationship with this world is also not explainable by any human thought that I am aware of." As he spoke Rubén gave the mare a gentle flick of the reins to start the little chaise again on its way.

"My friend, I think that, yes, you are a religious man and perhaps something of a scientist as well. Neither of us has any real idea of what is going on in this vast universe of time and space. Nevertheless, I share your idea that as long as one is considerate to those around him then whatever the future brings is well intended. One of those ideas that, as you say, cannot be proven; it must just be accepted."

After a few quiet moments, Rubén added, "I am sorry to see you leave. I think we could have many interesting conversations and something tells me that we could learn much from each other."

Frank did not reply for they had just reached the crest of a hill and could see the dry lake. Since the sky was overcast and the sun had not warmed the land yet, there was no mirage on the white surface. Frank could see his airplane sitting just as he had left it.

Rubén, not as timid as Paco had been, drove right up to the Cessna, stopped, and sat staring in wonder at the machine. "This is your conveyance?" he said.

"It will be if the engine starts," said Frank. But as he spoke he was sure the airplane was ready to fly. He was thinking of offering Rubén a short ride when a gentle breeze brought to him a wonderfully familiar scent. Lilacs, strong and clear, much more so than the faint scent he had noticed when he first arrived on the dry lake.

Frank quickly searched the skyline in all directions, hoping that Victoria was nearby, but could see nothing unusual. He was about to speak to Rubén when the old man handed him a package.

"This is for you; it is from my daughter."

Surprised, Frank muttered, "What is it?" as he took the package which was wrapped in violet colored silk.

"A gift from a lady who is not usually concerned about material things. She asked that you open it only after I have gone. So, my friend, I bid you farewell, with the hope—nay, the firm belief—that we will yet have many more conversations, sometime, somewhere."

Then, as they stepped from the chaise, Frank took the man's offered hand, and the two hugged each other and shook hands yet another time in the *abrazo*, the traditional Latin gesture of hello or goodbye.

With a wave of his hand, Rubén said, "Adios, Pancho," then turned back to the cart.

Frank placed the package and his medical bag in the cockpit and stowed his suitcase in the Cessna's luggage compartment. Looking up he saw the little two-wheeled vehicle heading back to Rancho Soledad. He smiled at the sight of the same bobbing motion of the horse between the large, thin wheels. The picture was much clearer now than it had been with the mirage on the desert floor so many days earlier.

Moments later, as he unwrapped the package, he was sure that he heard again a faint, tinkling sound like that of distant, glass wind chimes or tiny silver bells. His gift was the small book he had often seen Victoria hold in her lap and that he had presumed to be a little prayer book of some kind. Its page size was like that of a paperback novel but the volume was far thinner. Exquisitely bound in some sort of soft, red colored leather, it appeared to be new with no signs of wear. But somehow Frank could feel that it was old, perhaps ageless.

"Wow," muttered Frank aloud to no one as he examined the thousands of minute, hand tooled indentations that decorated the soft, leather cover of the little book. Frank touched the book's cover with its image of a pair of lilac blossoms. One was textured differently than the other to suggest white and violet, the two common colors of lilacs. Immediately the cockpit's airplane smells of oil, fuel, and electrical equipment were replaced by a gentle, evening breeze and the faint scent of Victoria's favorite flower.

Slowly opening the book, Frank got yet another surprise. He found that it contained only three pages, all completely blank except for a few words on the first page. Obviously done with a quill pen, in Spanish, and in truly elegant handwriting, was the inscription,

"Now is my time; your time and
our time have yet to come."

Slowly Frank closed the little volume and laid it on the seat to his right. As he looked out his left window he saw the departing chaise far in the distance. Then, perhaps a hundred meters away, he saw Victoria, clad in her black riding habit and seated on Mariposa, her splendid white Arabian mare she called by the Spanish word for butterfly. Even at such a distance, sitting motionless in the saddle, Victoria appeared to be a supremely competent caballera, as her father had said. Frank's eyes filled with tears when she took off her large, black hat and waved it at him, then turned and rode away.

Frank shook his head, trying to get back to reality. He performed his usual walk around inspection of the airplane, pulled the propeller through a few engine revolutions, and the familiar tasks helped. True to his training as a pilot, even in this remote location Frank called the warning "CLEAR" before attempting to start the engine. With his feet holding the Cessna's toe brakes, he set the mixture control to full rich, held the yoke back, turned on the ignition and starter, and in seconds the Continental engine was running as smoothly as it ever had.

Minutes later Frank had the Cessna in the air, just a couple hundred feet above the ground. He turned smoothly toward the little road that Rubén had taken to return to Rancho Soledad. In vain he searched for the road, for the buildings he had known as Rancho Soledad, and for the little valley with the creek he had visited. Though he found stone fences and what was probably the creek, it was dry, and the trees were gone. He could see no sign of buildings anywhere. Sadly, the pilot began climbing to a proper cruise altitude and took up a compass heading for home.

More Travelers

Just as he did every day, the lone jackrabbit visited his favorite prickly pear cactus patch near the wagon road south of Rancho Soledad, and again he had to duck into the security of a dense patch of brush as he watched another group of riders pass by.

Much like the small procession of men that had approached Rancho Soledad several days earlier bearing the country's elected president, more armed men had ridden onto the land of Rancho Soledad. Like the earlier visitors, these men were also caught up in serious events. But this group was different in one striking way. They rode in formation, two by two, and all wore colorful green and blue uniforms with bright red pants. The two at the front of the little procession wore elegantly plumed hats held in position by polished, black leather chin straps, bore gold tassels on their shoulders, and carried formal dress swords at their belts. Even the bridles and other tack of their two horses, embellished with some simple silver decorations, clearly bore an impractical, ceremonial flair. Behind the two officers, the soldiers and their sergeant rode straight in their saddles, like the captain in charge demanded that they should. He insisted that they look every inch to be a proper example of a European military unit. But all were uncomfortable and sweating profusely in the hot, desert climate that was so much different from their native France.

Though the Jackrabbit couldn't know about such things, and would not have cared anyway, the common soldiers and their two officers were uncomfortable in the inappropriately heavy uniforms they were required to wear. Their wool, and somewhat baggy pants would have looked strange to any Mexican.

On a hill not far away Enrique Mendosa Martinez, sitting with his arms folded across the wide horn of his saddle, watched for approaching visitors just as he did every day. He carefully counted the eight riders in the group. Then, with an unpleasant tightness in his stomach and a heavy heart, the vaquero turned his mount around and headed back to Rancho Soledad. Señor Hidalgo and Jose must know about these visitors as soon as possible.

***

At the front of the little column, Sous-Lieutenant Courant grumbled a little about the heat, unhappy with what he regarded as the nuisance assignment he and his captain had been given. "What are we, errand boys?" he mumbled.

"One order is the same as any other, Lieutenant," replied Capitaine Jaques Le Bec, straightening up from just the faintest tendency to slouch in the saddle on the hot, Chihuahuan summer afternoon. "This man is no more than a simple farmer, but he has violated the emperor's orders by harboring a rebel leader."

"Well, mon capitaine, it will be easy to arrest him."

"It will be indeed, Lieutenant, because our order says to bring him in alive or dead. After our long trip in this damned desert heat I am of no mind to put up with any resistance."

"Oui, mon capitaine. I suppose a dead prisoner is less nuisance than a live one."

The two royal officers returned to the boring task of demonstrating proper appearance to no one in particular as their mounts plodded on toward Rancho Soledad. With the unfamiliar noises made by the little military detail several minutes out of earshot, the jackrabbit cautiously went back to one of his favorite prickly pear plants.

Home

Frank Jensen sat in the left seat of his Cessna 180, listening to the steady drone of the Continental engine as he neared the huge, Mexican city of Ciudad Juarez. He was still thinking of his strange forced landing that had occurred either an hour or a century earlier, and was not able to reconcile his thoughts. Finally, realizing that he was nearing the international border, the pilot called the El Paso Air Traffic Control Center to request a customs inspection at his home field in Las Cruces, New Mexico, and his request was granted. He then asked the controller for a time and date verification. Hesitating slightly at the unusual request for a date verification, the controller responded with "2114 Zulu, March 22, 1960."

No longer surprised by anything, Frank made a quick mental calculation and found that he would land at his home field in Las Cruces within half an hour of the time specified by the flight plan he had filed in Ciudad Obregon just three hours earlier.

As Frank saw the Rio Grande Valley approaching on the horizon he busied himself with preparations for his landing, and the required customs inspection. It felt good to be absorbed by the familiar routine of an aviator arriving at his home field.

Minutes later Frank slowed his Cessna to taxi speed after landing on runway 26 at the airport in Las Cruces, New Mexico. Then he taxied to the center of a yellow circle painted on the tarmac, shut down his engine, and stepped out of the Cessna's cabin. As required by regulations for an aircraft arriving from an international flight, he remained within the yellow circle, waiting for a Customs and Immigration inspector.

Immediately an officer, whose nametag read L. Ramirez, walked toward Frank's plane from the nearby terminal area.

"Hey Doc, I see you made it back again," came the good-natured greeting from Officer Ramirez.

"Hi Lalo; yeah, it's sure good to be home."

Because of Frank's frequent trips and his well-known reasons for visiting Mexico, the two men were well-acquainted. While making a trivial inspection of Frank's baggage compartment the officer asked, "Hey Doc, you have a decent flight?"

"Oh yeah," said Frank. "A little more turbulence than usual."

"Well, I won't hold you up any longer. You look pretty tired; I know you want to get home."

"Yeah, I really do. Thanks Lalo."

"No sweat, Doc. Keep up the good work!"

As the officer returned to the terminal Frank started his engine and taxied to his hangar. Caught up in familiar settings and conversations, Frank began to feel that Rancho Soledad was just some peculiar memory, like maybe a week old television drama.

But then, as his eyes fell on the leather book lying in the seat next to him Frank felt a sense of loss, almost loneliness. Gently he ran his fingers over the embossed floral design on the leather cover, noticing once again the scent of lilacs. Emotionally drained, Frank picked up the little book and put it in his medical bag. He was home.

***

Frank prudently decided not to tell anyone about his bizarre engine failure incident. Not even his brother Karl, or Karl's little girl Susan, who were all the family he had. After arriving home just about on his originally planned schedule, he found it difficult to accept the idea that he had known the people of Rancho Soledad. As the days passed he found the idea less and less credible, even to himself, and began to think of his memories as a peculiar kind of hallucination. But he knew that the disturbing little book was still there in his medical bag.

Late one evening after a day that had made heavy use of the supplies in his medical bag, Frank reluctantly took out the book to examine it more closely. Immediately, he could feel that it was special, and pleasant to hold and yet a perplexing enigma for Frank. He sat in a comfortable chair near his fireplace and just held the little volume in his hands.

"The whole memory could be a dream, a mind trick," thought Frank. "But this book is real; it's here, now."

As Frank stared thoughtfully at the fire he noticed that someone had entered the room. He started to put the book away, but Susan Jensen was too quick for him.

"Hey, whatcha got, Grandpa?" said the little girl as she ran to Frank. Years earlier a five-year-old Susan Jensen had felt sad when she found out that she had no grandfather; he had died just before she was born. Though really her uncle, Frank had promised to be her grandfather too, and thus the name "Grandpa" was all Susan ever used.

"Ooof," wheezed Frank as his niece jumped into his lap. "You're growing too fast, getting too heavy for me. Or I'm getting too old and feeble!"

"Fooey, fifty-five isn't old. Besides, the older you get the smarter people think you are—cool huh?"

"Yeah, maybe so. Anyway, where's your dad?"

"He's out in the truck. Sent me in to get you; we're going to eat out tonight, remember?"

Frank had forgotten about the date with his brother and niece, but he often did things like that. But this time it worried the physician in him, just a little. "Could I have picked up this book someplace and forgotten where? Maybe down in La Paz before I flew home?" wondered Frank. Again his thoughts turned to peculiar memories of a place called Rancho Soledad. He started again to put the book away.

"Hey, cool," exclaimed Susan as she snatched the book from Frank's hands. Their relationship was a good one and it included lots of good-natured horsing around.

As Susan held the book she noticed the finely tooled cover, and seemed aware that it was something special.

"Wow, where'd you get this?"

Frank didn't answer. He could see that Susan's playful attitude had become more serious as she held the red colored, leather volume in her two hands for several quiet seconds. Then she gently opened the book and saw its two blank pages and the one with writing. Slowly Susan read the Spanish words and, with some help from Frank, translated them.

"I don't know what that means," she said. "But it's beautiful, the words and the handwriting. It looks old and new all at the same time."

As Susan handed the book to Frank he noticed a more reflective manner in her actions. He put the leather volume back into his medical bag.

"Let's get a move on before your dad goes to chow without us, Hey?"

A minute later Frank, with Susan walking at his side and holding his hand, walked out to the pickup truck where Karl Jensen was waiting. As Frank continued to wonder what explanation was really behind the strange book, Susan looked up at him and quietly said, "I've never seen a book like that, Grandpa."

***

The following weekend Frank decided to make a trip back to the salt flat in Mexico and look more carefully for Rancho Soledad. He got out the World Aeronautical Chart that he had used on his flight from La Paz on the day of his peculiar dream. Frank liked the word dream better than hallucination. Carefully marked on the chart was the location of his forced landing on the white salt flat of the dry lake. That is, if there had even been a landing.

When Susan found out about his plans for a one-day flight she insisted that she and her father should get to go too. She loved flying. At first Frank said no, thinking that maybe he was having mental problems and perhaps should not carry passengers as he flew. But he had made several other recent flights to locations in Mexico and done a lot of local flying and was sure all would be well. So, he decided to catch Karl as he was picking his daughter up after school and invite both to go along.

"You bet, Grandpa," was Susan's immediate response to the invitation. "But I get the right front seat so I can fly some, OK?"

Karl, however, declined.

"You two go without me," he said. "You know I'm a boat man. Airplanes are too scary for me."

"Aw, c'mon, dad. You'd like it."

"No no," said Karl, feigning fear of flying. "I can flap good enough to swim, but not enough to fly." He added an elbow flapping motion to imitate a barnyard chicken.

Frank and Susan laughed, both knowing that Karl always enjoyed riding with Frank, but was just too busy that weekend with his work as a general contractor.

The next Sunday found Frank and Susan in Frank's Cessna headed southwestward from the city of Juarez, Mexico, where they had made an intermediate stop to pass through Mexican customs. Ahead Frank could see the white expanse of the salt flat he remembered. He concentrated hard, trying to recall details of his peculiar experience, particularly on the trip he thought he had made with Paco in the horse-drawn chaise.

Frank dropped to an altitude of about 200 feet above the desert surface and reduced his speed to 85 knots. Doing his best to search the area he finally found what he was sure was the little grassy stream he had visited on horseback. There were some dead or nearly dead trees, but no visible water. From there he turned to where he thought the buildings of Rancho Soledad must have been.

Frank searched for another half hour without saying anything to his passenger. Noticing that Susan was getting uncomfortable with the warm, bumpy, afternoon air at low altitude, he finally opened the throttle and climbed back up. The cooler, and much smoother air higher up felt better to both fliers. As he reached 9,500 feet Frank trimmed out the airplane for straight and level flight, and headed for home.

"OK, Ace, you've got the airplane," said Frank as he ceremoniously folded his hands in his lap.

Susan, who had been hoping for a chance at the controls, took the steering yolk and focused her attention directly ahead of the plane, intent on keeping the wings level. She had handled the yolk before, and, like most non-pilots, thought that she had complete control. But Frank still had his feet on the rudder pedals and his right hand near the throttle. In this way he let the little girl make gentle turns and changes in altitude as she "flew" the plane.

Half an hour later Frank contacted the El Paso Air Traffic Control Center and arranged for permission to fly directly to Las Cruces and pass customs there, just as he had done when he flew back from the dry lake a few weeks earlier. His thoughts were on the search he had just made. Though he hadn't said anything to Susan, he had seen traces of the old rock fences and what looked like the faint remains of building foundations and eroded adobe walls that might have been part of the main house of the hacienda at Rancho Soledad.

After Frank landed in Las Cruces and put his airplane in its hangar, Susan asked a question.

"We didn't go anywhere special down in Mexico. How come we just flew around?" A question Frank had hoped wouldn't come up, and one which he had no way of answering honestly.

"Well, you know me, Ace. I like to look at the land as I fly and see new places."

"I don't know, Grandpa, . . . seemed like you were looking for something."

Frank changed the subject to an offer of lunch at a downtown restaurant that was Susan's favorite.

One Bad Day for Rancho Soledad

The group of elegantly attired soldiers approached the front gate of the courtyard surrounding the hacienda at Rancho Soledad. Leaving his men just outside the gate, Capitaine Jacques Le Bec and his Sous-Lieutenant rode into the courtyard where they were met by Rubén and Jose. Before Rubén could speak or inquire about the visitors' business, the captain spoke, in formal, official tones, in crude Spanish with a heavy French accent.

"I am here to place Señor Rubén Hidalgo Cantenera de Silva, and any other members of the Hidalgo Cantenera family, under arrest as ordered by Emperor Maximiliano. The charge is harboring a revolutionary—"

"I deny that charge, Sir, as I have never been involved with any revolutionary at any time. I have only given aid to a sick man who happened to be the elected Pres—"

Immediately the French captain pulled an awkward looking Lefaucheux 12mm revolver from his tunic and shot Rubén directly in the chest.

"This is no time to argue over such matters," said Capitaine Le Bec. "I have had enough of this wasteland and heat."

Jose stood for a moment in shock as the two French officers began backing their well-trained horses toward the gate behind them. Unfortunately for the two, Emilio and Enrique, well-armed as usual, were standing inside the courtyard wall behind the French officers. "There will be no argument, *Franchute*," muttered Emilio as he killed the French captain with a single shot from one of the Walker Colts Frank had noticed earlier during his visit.

At the instant of Emilio's shot the French lieutenant, reaching for his own revolver, charged his mount toward Emilio who fired again. The lieutenant fell to the ground, dead, as Jose immediately ran to Rubén's fallen form and gathered the slightly built, old man into his own arms.

At the sound of shooting, the six mounted soldiers just outside the gate immediately charged part way into the courtyard. Sergent Louis Letounier was caught off-guard, having not expected any significant resistance from what he considered to be simple peasant folk. He and his five cavalry soldiers found themselves in a short but fierce fight with Emilio and Enrique, where he himself was wounded in the right abdomen by Enrique's Henry rifle. As he ordered his men to get out of the courtyard, another shot from Enrique broke the front knee of the sergeant's horse, causing the man to fall to the ground, with his saber drawn.

"Die, *cabrón*," yelled Enrique as he tried to use his Henry one more time on the French sergeant, only to have it misfire. Swinging the rifle like a bat he charged the French soldier, all the while screaming like an Apache.

Sergent Letounier, realizing he was now the only living Frenchman in the courtyard and terrified of the charging Mexican, fired his muzzle loading rifle once in the general direction of Jose, dropped the single shot weapon and turned to run toward the courtyard gate, clutching both hands to his bleeding abdomen.

"No *Franchute*, you will stay right here with us," yelled Enrique as he jammed his Henry rifle between the Sergeant's legs, causing the man to fall to the ground where he would have been Enrique's captive had not one of the French cavalrymen who had taken cover just outside the courtyard gate fired a single shot that hit Enrique.

"Tres bien, Vous avez—"

Thinking he had killed Enrique, who he called a filthy dog, the French soldier's satisfaction lasted only seconds before a single ball from Jose's Colt revolver destroyed the man's head. Struggling to his feet, and realizing that the French Sergeant's wild shot had hit him in the right thigh, Jose looked around the courtyard, only to find that, beside the *Franchutes*, he, Emilio, and the badly-wounded Enrique, were the only people left alive in the bloodbath that had been Rancho Soledad. A peaceful place to raise ". . . the best beef cattle in Mexico . . ." Rubén had often called it.

Then, still holding Rubén in his arms, Jose realized that the French sergeant was nowhere to be seen. Carrying Rubén in spite of his own leg wound, he hobbled toward the hacienda's front entrance. There his worst fears were confirmed; he saw drops of blood on the tiles at his feet. The vile *Franchute* was inside—with Victoria!

Jose burst into the front room of the hacienda, with Emilio just in front of him. There they found the French sergeant lying on the floor with his revolver wobbling unsteadily in his hand. As the dying man tried to point it toward Emilio his hand fell to the floor. Emilio quickly kicked the weapon out of the way. *"Pinche Franchute,"* he yelled and with a second, well-placed kick to the head, finished off the Frenchman.

As Jose carefully laid Rubén's weak form on a nearby couch he saw Victoria come into the room in her wheelchair. He immediately brought her chair directly to her father's dying form, where the young woman scooped Rubén's grayed head into her lap and without words began to cry.

"Emilio! You watch them, help Enrique! Paco is in the stable with the wagon." Jose then limped outside where he saw that Enrique, using a marble fountain as cover, was doing a good job of keeping the remaining Frenchmen out of the courtyard. But he knew that one man could not stop the remaining Frenchmen for long. "Enrique," he yelled. "Get inside; help Emilio." Then he went to the stable where he knew that Paco had prepared a wagon for use by those who were to leave Rancho Soledad.

But just then the remaining four French soldiers burst through the gate, and a volley of shots left Enrique and one of the soldiers dead. But the three remaining Frenchmen were busily setting fire to the hacienda's outbuildings.

Jose saw that Paco had gathered his own family, the only remaining workers on Rancho Soledad, and was preparing to leave. He ordered Paco to take the wagon to the rear of the hacienda, quickly.

Relieved, Jose was glad to see Victoria's mare, Mariposa, in her stall, with the silver mounted saddle on its rack, as it should have been. He quickly bridled and saddled the mare, then tied the reins to Paco's departing wagon

As he left the stable, Jose, clutching his painful leg wound with one hand, saw the three soldiers with torches, clearly trying to set fire to Rancho Soledad's outbuildings. Jose was able to stop one with his revolver, but stumbled to the ground in the process. As he got back to his feet he realized that he was getting weak because of his bleeding leg wound. After trying to make a makeshift tourniquet from his shirt, he wobbled back into the hacienda.

"Emilio! How many are left?"

"There are just two and they are trying to burn us out," yelled Emilio as he rose up to see better out one window of the hacienda. "Ah, here they come!"

Emilio rose up again to fire at one of the French soldiers and caught a bullet directly in his neck. Jose, who was at Victoria's side, saw that Rubén had passed away, and, as he turned to Emilio, Jose could see that he was now the only man left to defend Victoria and Paco's wagon. He had not yet realized that some Frenchmen had managed to set fire to the house itself.

***

Minutes later Victoria sat in her wheel chair, her eyes red from tears at the realization of her father's death and almost choking from the smoke from the fires burning just outside. Her right hand lay in her lap. For a fleeting moment Jose noticed that the little leather-bound book that Victoria always had in her lap was not there. Immediately he unceremoniously gathered Victoria in his arms and headed out the back of the building.

"How many children could you find?" Victoria asked as she was carried by the no-nonsense man she'd known all her life.

"Señorita, there are two children in the wagon, and Paco and his wife." said Jose, speaking as he hurried as fast as his leg would permit, carrying Victoria outside. "There is food and water, and one spare horse. And your Mariposa is here too." With that comment Jose set Victoria in the saddle of her beloved white horse.

"Jose, who is left? What is—"

"Señorita, you must go now. I am all that is left of our people. The *Franchutes*, there are three, no two of them left, Señorita," said Jose,

"*Pinche Franchutes*" said Jose, almost spitting out the slang word for the hated French soldiers. He then quickly apologized to Victoria for his profane language.

"Then quickly Jose, we must all go—"

"No Señorita, *you* must go, with Paco. If I leave now the two will follow. I must stay here and see that they do not."

"Jose—"

"Si Señorita?" Jose stood directly by the left side of Victoria's Mariposa, partially supporting himself by hanging onto the horse's bridle.

Victoria took out the white, silk handkerchief she always carried in the breast pocket of her riding clothes. "This is to tell you, Jose, that all is never over, that there are better times to come." She then reached down and with her right hand gently caressed his dark, weather-beaten face, leaving the handkerchief in his hand that had reached up to hers.

"Go Victoria," said Jose as he slapped one of the wagon team horses with his hat and gestured to Paco to get moving—fast.

In a glance Victoria saw the single tear on the dust-stained face of a man who had clearly taken a gunshot wound during the fighting, and meant to finish the fight alone. She also knew that the sadness in his eyes was not from the pain of wounds, not at all. For never in her life had the handsome vaquero ever chanced to call her by her name as he had just done.

Victoria turned Mariposa and followed the departing wagon, knowing that her own name was the last word she would ever hear from the vaquero who had always been her friend and had wanted to be so much more.

***

Returning to the main room of the hacienda, Jose saw that the two remaining soldiers were trying to enter the front door, hoping that all within had been disposed of. The first stuck his head inside, and Jose's Walker Colt taught the *Franchute* that he had made a mistake. But it was clear to Jose that the remaining Frenchman had set fire to the building. Stepping outside one more time, Jose was lucky enough to catch a glimpse of the other *Franchute* trying to see in one window.

Staggering from weakness in his legs, Jose carefully aimed his Colt at the man and brought an end to the attack on Rancho Soledad by the soldiers of Maximiliano.

Jose then turned to see Paco's wagon, with Victoria and her white mare Mariposa, about to pass over the crest of a distant ridge. Though nearly a kilometer away, Victoria stopped and turned in the direction of Rancho Soledad, and Jose thought he saw her wave one last time at what had always been her home. Then she turned Mariposa back and followed the wagon that was disappearing over the ridge.

***

Minutes later from far away, Victoria saw smoke from the direction of Rancho Soledad behind her, and she knew that Jose was giving the survivors of Rancho Soledad all that he had left to give. She took heart in her knowledge that for her father and for the brave vaquero, and all the other people of Rancho Soledad life, *real* life, had only just begun.

Riding Mariposa, Victoria glanced at little Lupita in the back of the wagon behind Paco and his wife, who were sitting on the bench seat. The bright little face with its dark eyes and white teeth exchanged a knowing smile with the caballera; for Victoria had told her that all was well and as it should be.

***

Now suffering badly from loss of blood, Jose wobbled into the hacienda again in spite of the flames that nearly engulfed the building, and made his way to the lifeless form on the couch. Just as he had promised to Rubén a few days earlier, Jose had given his all to protect Victoria. He then fell to the floor of the smoke-filled room where his eyes slowly closed as he began to lose consciousness. Then, thinking of Victoria's words, "This is to tell you that all is never over, that there are better times to come," Rancho Soledad's last survivor and finest vaquero passed away, with Victoria's white handkerchief clasped in both hands at his chest.

A Visit to Rancho Soledad

Two weeks after arriving home in New Mexico, Frank spent three days in Chihuahua City in Mexico teaching classes as a guest lecturer in a medical school. He had decided that on his way back he would make a side trip to his dry lake again, but this time on the ground. So, Frank found himself alone in a borrowed Ford pickup traveling across the white expanse of salt flat. He was glad that he had chosen a cool day in November for the trip. He wouldn't have to contend with the shimmering mirage he remembered from long ago.

Doing his best to follow the direction he thought Paco had taken, Frank drove across low hills covered with greasewood, cholla cactus, and yuccas. Occasionally he thought he found what might have been a track or the remains of an old road, but he couldn't be sure.

Finally Frank stopped the truck on top of a ridge overlooking a broad, shallow valley. It fit the image in his mind, and he became more excited as he headed down to what should have been the buildings of a hacienda.

An hour later Frank sat in the truck eating a beef burrito and thinking about what he had found. Just a few building foundations nearly hidden in the dry grass, many glass fragments and small pieces of metal junk, along with a few weathered timbers that had once held up a magnificent ceiling. Not far away were the rusted remains of a wrought iron gate with an elaborate letter "H" built into its headpiece. Frank knew where he was.

But for Frank the discovery was not only perplexing, but disturbing for another reason. The rooftop vigas were badly burned, the iron decoration was mutilated beyond usability, and nearby he had found a single, copper, .44 Henry rim fire cartridge case, old and blackened with age. With a heavy heart, Frank left the little valley and headed back home. Clearly, Rancho Soledad had met a violent, fiery end a long time earlier.

Mariposa

During the last year Karl Jensen had noticed a change in his brother Frank. A few years earlier Frank had had a rapidly developing mainstream medical practice going, but a distinct change had taken place. More and more Frank was devoting his time to treating patients who couldn't afford to pay and to repeated trips to Mexico where he helped out by teaching personnel in local clinics.

Karl was concerned about this peculiar change in his brother and decided to bring it up while they were having lunch at a restaurant in the old town of Mesilla near Frank's home.

Frank had watched the arrival of his brother's order of enchiladas covered by two fried eggs and a dollop of sour cream.

"You know that stuff's a cholesterol nightmare don't you?" said Frank. His own order consisted of a bean burrito and some coleslaw.

"Hey bro, us Jensens didn't send you through medical school just to have you join the diet police. I get enough of that harassment from Susie. She makes us eat better at home." Karl was proud of his fourteen-year-old daughter's precocious talent for cooking and her efforts at keeping herself and her father on a healthy diet. Then Karl took a good swig from his bottle of Corona beer and prepared to tackle a subject that had been bothering him.

"Ah, Frank, have you been feeling OK lately?" Then, a little embarrassed, he added, "You know, you seem kinda different these last few months. Like something's bothering you."

"Heck no, I'm fine. Just been working hard, that's all."

Karl was thinking again of Frank's more frequent trips to Mexico. He also knew that Frank had a reputation as a good teacher among the medical community and had received offers to join the teaching staff at medical schools in both California and Texas.

"Bro, I've noticed you been flying to Mexico a lot. Seems like you spend more time there than on your practice here. Maybe you ought to think about some of those snazzy job offers you've been getting."

"Teaching positions?" replied Frank. "Actually, what I do in Mexico is teaching, among other things, and there the help I give has a more immediate effect. I can see results every trip I make."

"Yeah, well, OK man. If you want to miss the big bucks I guess that's your business. Still, seems like you ought to get out more and have some fun. Chase some nurses or something, like we used to do."

"Look who's calling the kettle black," said Frank. "You haven't been dating at all since Anne died, and that was a long time ago."

Then seeing in his brother's eyes that the loss of his wife was still a sensitive subject, Frank apologized for his slightly sarcastic remark.

"Aw that's OK Bro; I guess we're both headed for old codger bachelorhood the way things look." Then, to change to a more lighthearted subject he added, "Hey, it's about time to pick up Susie. I gotta take her down the valley to a friend's house in Canutillo. A birthday party."

"OK, guy, tell the little gal hello for me."

"Hey, I got a better idea. It will only take an hour or two. Come with us."

"I don't know, I need to get back to the office and—"

"C'mon Frank, don't give me that too busy crap, and you know how happy a surprise visit from her grandfather would make my little girl."

Frank chuckled at Karl's use of the term "grandfather" and gave in. Susan never quit calling her uncle by that term and it had become second nature over the years. Susan had a rare gift of perpetual optimism and her charm always magnified life's little pleasures for everyone around her. She was one of the real joys in Frank's life.

Minutes later in Karl's pickup truck the two men pulled into the school parking lot. They got out and Susan ran up and, tossing her books to her dad, jumped onto Frank for a hug as he caught her in his arms.

"Hey Grandpa, when we gonna go flying again?" asked the bubbly little girl.

"Oof," said Frank, feigning strain under the child's weight. "We may not be able to if you keep growing so fast. An airplane can only carry so much you know."

"Yeah, well, that Cessna of yours had better get used to me, 'cause in another year or two you are going to have to teach me to fly it for real!"

Karl beamed at the two, a proud papa. Then the three, with Susan in the middle holding tightly to both men's arms, walked to Karl's pickup for the trip down the valley.

Karl chose to use the old highway that ran down the Rio Grande Valley to El Paso knowing it would be practically free of traffic. All three travelers were enjoying the ride and noticing the springtime freshness of the trees, the growing chili fields, and the richly colored blossoms that covered cotton fields like thousands of bright yellow roses. A much more pleasant drive than they would have had on Interstate Highway 10, a parallel route a few miles away.

On a long, straight stretch of highway, Frank was vaguely aware of a car approaching in the other lane, but gave it little thought. He was engrossed in the happy banter going on between Susan and her father as they discussed the "house rules" that were to be imposed on the young girl who was making plans for her first formal school dance the following Friday evening.

"Ten o'clock? I have to be home by *ten*? Gad, it's probably still light out by then."

"Oh c'mon now, that's way after dark and you are only fourteen," argued Karl. It would be his first experience as the father of a young girl who was actually out on a date.

"I bet Cinderella's wicked stepmother would have given her a better break than that," replied Susan.

Frank felt proud of his family as he listened to what he knew would eventually result in a modest compromise in the direction of Susan's request to stay until midnight.

Frank noticed the car, closer now, was driving somewhat erratically, and slowly. He glanced at Karl and saw that his brother was watching the road ahead, so he gave little further thought to the on-coming vehicle which appeared to be pulling over to the side of the road.

"Fourteen isn't old enough for dating anyway," said Karl.

"Oh Dad, it's not a *date* date. It's just a school party!"

Susan knew that her mother and father had grown up together as childhood sweethearts and probably hadn't dated anyone except each other. After a moment's thought Susan asked a question that had been on her mind for some time.

"OK Dad, how old was Mom when she first started going out with you?"

"Thirty," came Karl's reply, as he looked at Susan with a grin.

"Oh Dad," said Susan as she playfully tickled her father's ribs because of his answer.

As the father and daughter horsed around slightly, Frank looked again at the approaching car that was getting quite close. He didn't even have time to open his mouth in panic as he saw it wobble toward Karl's pickup. Frank lost consciousness in the explosion of shattered glass and crushed steel in the nearly head-on collision.

A few seconds later Frank regained awareness of what was around him and realized that a wreck had occurred. He could hear almost nothing except creaking metal and could smell hot anti-freeze from a ruptured radiator. His first thought was about the possibility of fire, and he checked to see whether or not he could get out of the vehicle.

He couldn't. His left leg was trapped under the crumpled wreckage that had been the dashboard of the pickup. He could feel Susan's body shoved up against his, and knew that she was breathing. He squirmed around to see what had happened to Karl, and was horrified by the sight of his brother's hopelessly crushed body. Frank had a fleeting thought that Susan was probably unconscious and might not have to see that sight.

Frank's medical training immediately took over and he began to assess Susan's injuries as best he could. At first he found nothing obviously wrong, but then his heart sank as he saw her left foot.

The girl's foot was smashed under the same dashboard that had pinned Frank's leg. He saw the pulsing flow of arterial blood coming from Susan's foot and using his left hand immediately grabbed a pressure point near her knee and found that he could stop the bleeding.

A minute later nausea and wooziness threatened Frank. He knew that he might be slipping into shock and that if he passed out, relaxation of his left hand would cause Susan to bleed out from her wounds.

As the minutes passed Frank fought to maintain consciousness by talking to himself about other matters, by yelling, by listening intently for sounds of sirens, and by focusing on his own pain. Surely someone would discover the wreck soon. Frank tenaciously held his grip on Susan's leg.

As the injured physician felt himself slipping closer to unconsciousness he imagined he could hear sirens. Frank yelled, hoping for the sound of a human voice, but got no answer. Then he stayed quiet trying to hear the distant sirens. As he did so, he realized that there were no sirens, just some strangely attractive, almost musical sounds. He also noticed the scent of flowers, the same scent of lilac that he had known long ago in a place far away. The comforting memories of Rancho Soledad came flooding back, reducing his anxiety, and preventing his lapse into shock.

For half an hour Frank focused intently on keeping pressure on Susan's leg and realized that his own left arm, in an awkward position, was getting weak and numb. He felt panic building again because of his fear that he would pass out.

But then the scent of lilacs became stronger, and Frank noticed a motion just at the edge of his field of view. A single, white butterfly fluttered into the wreckage, flitted about Susan's face, then landed on Frank's arm and sat there facing him inches from his eyes

A common cabbage butterfly, pure white, fresh and delicate amid the twisted wreckage. As Frank's attention focused on the tiny visitor, one any Mexican would call a *mariposa*, the scent of lilacs grew strong, driving out the acrid smells of blood, hot radiator fluid and sweat. He was reassured by faint, almost musical sounds, like chirping of fledgling songbirds. In the blackness that surrounded Frank he felt as much as heard happy children's voices in some unknown song, carried to him ever so faintly on the wind from far, far away. The ethereal melody consoled him, and he felt that somehow Victoria and her splendid white horse, Mariposa, were with him.

"In this world each of us gets only a glimpse of what life really is," her voice seemed to say, and those words enveloped him like a warm, soft blanket on a cold, winter morning. Then the scent of lilacs overwhelmed him as the blackness became a vision of little Susan, a tiny child playing with one single red rose, in a field of violet and white flowers everywhere, safe and secure. Frank knew that all was well. He need only hang on a little longer.

Minutes later Frank realized that the butterfly and the scent of springtime were gone and that the heavenly sounds had slowly changed to those of real sirens and people's voices. When Frank saw that an emergency medical technician that he knew personally was attending to Susan, he let himself drift into unconsciousness.

***

Hours later Frank awoke in a hospital bed in El Paso and mashed the call button on a cord nearby.

"Ah, Dr. Jensen, you're back with us I see," said a middle-aged woman with a tag on her white uniform to indicate that she was a licensed practical nurse named Nelson. "How are we feeling?"

A little annoyed by the use of the word "we" Frank said, "I'm fine, but how is my niece? Where is she; is she OK?"

"She's here in the same hospital, in intensive care after her operation. She's doing fine."

"Operation? What operation?" Frank wanted all the details.

"According to your chart, Doctor Jensen, you are just fine, except for a wrenched left knee. It'll stay sore for awhile, but you have no serious injuries."

"But Susan, how is she?"

"The little girl has had a difficult time but she's in pretty good shape, considering," said Nurse Nelson.

"Considering what, damn it! What happened to her?"

"Now calm down Dr. Jensen, don't tear out your IV."

Frank glared at the nurse.

"I hate to have to tell you this Doctor, but your niece had a badly damaged left foot. She will have some deformity, but otherwise she is just fine."

Frank slumped back against the bed's collection of pillows.

"And my brother, What about Karl?"

"I'm sorry Dr. Jensen; he's not here. He didn't make it."

Frank then sank into a state of despair. He'd seen Karl's crushed torso in the truck and had known what to expect, but hearing it from Nurse Nelson hit him hard. Now the little girl with an injured foot was all that was left of his family.

"I'll see if we can get you another sedative so you can—"

"No, no, I don't need that," said Frank. He had remembered the calming feeling he had experienced just before the ambulance arrived, and knew that the single butterfly he had seen had kept him conscious long enough to keep Susan alive.

"Where is my bag, my medical bag!" Though not a common practice for modern physicians, Frank always carried a small bag of emergency items when traveling and it had been with him in the wreck. "It was in the truck with me! Please have someone find it and get it to me!"

Nurse Nelson walked to a small closet containing Frank's clothes and other possessions. Looking around she found a small, black, leather bag, and picked it up to show Frank.

"This it?"

"Yes, yes, let me have it."

The older woman handed the bag to Frank and said, "Gosh, I haven't seen one of—"

She thought better of what she was saying when she saw what a comforting effect it was having on her patient. Then she remembered that it would undoubtedly contain several drugs of one kind or another and that she didn't know Frank at all.

"Ah, Dr. Jensen, the staff here will take care of your medication; you really don't need anything in there do you?"

Frank laughed a little at her concern, then opened the bag and removed his little leather book.

Smiling at Nurse Nelson he said, "This is all I need," and handed the bag back to her.

Seeing what she presumed to be a prayer book, the woman, herself a practicing Catholic, smiled and put Frank's bag back into the closet.

"I won't need that sedative, ma'am. I can sleep just fine now."

"OK, we'll be in to check on you. If you change your mind, just use the call button again."

Frank waved affirmatively, and the nurse left him alone.

For about fifteen minutes Frank lay on his back holding the book against his chest, running his fingers over the finely tooled leather image of lilacs on its cover. Then he slowly opened it and read the first page, the one he had first read down in Mexico long ago.

Then with a trembling hand he turned to the next page, one he had always known to be blank. Immediately he noticed the familiar scent of lilacs as he read the elegantly flowing handwriting that he found there.

"Now is your time. My time has passed,
and our time is yet to come."

A pleasant smile crept over Frank's face, and his contentment would have been complete except for his thoughts of his brother, and of a little girl with a damaged left foot who was all that was left of his family.

Doctor Rodriguez's Patient

Several years later on one of his visits to Mexico, Frank was talking with a hospital orderly in a corridor of a clinic in Ciudad Delicias, just south of Chihuahua City, Mexico.

"Boy, there is one sturdy old gal."

"Oh?" said Frank

"Yeah, that's the old woman from one of the *ejidos*; she's older than Methuselah, they say". The orderly was referring to a nearby communal settlement.

"Oh yeah, I've heard of her. She the one who's well past 100?"

"Yeah," said the orderly. "Way past, nobody knows for sure how far."

Frank looked down the corridor toward the nurse's station where he saw a tiny, frail woman standing with the aid of two crutches in front of a wheelchair. The lady was involved in an animated conversation with several of the nurses. Curious, Frank decided to stroll by.

As he approached the lady had returned to her wheelchair, the conversation apparently resolved to her satisfaction.

"Hello Dr. Jensen," said a nurse with the name Sainz on her uniform tag. Another physician, whose nametag read Dr. Rodriguez, and, using the Mexican familiar form of Frank's name, said "Hey Pancho, good to see you back here again. Let me introduce you to my favorite patient. This is Señora Guadalupe Esperanza de Gomez."

Frank looked at the ancient, wrinkled face and saw two dark eyes that sparkled with life as the lady met Frank's gaze with both intelligence and interest. Frank knew he was looking at an example of a mind that had far outlasted the mortal body in which it resided.

Dr. Rodriguez continued with "And Lupe, this is my American friend Pancho Jensen."

As Lupe heard Frank's name, a change came over the elderly lady's expression. She was obviously in deep thought. After a few seconds her eyes narrowed and focused sharply on Frank.

"You are a doctor too—Doctor Jensen," said the feeble, nearly unintelligible voice. But weak as her words were, it was clear that the lady did not mean them as a question.

"Yes, ma'am, I am a doctor. And I am proud to meet you, Lupe."

After a few seconds the ancient voice continued with the Spanish words, "Pancho Jensen, Francisco Jensen—*El Medico Milagro del Soledad!*"

Clearly the elderly lady was becoming a little agitated, but not frightened, just excited.

"Lupe is going back to her bed now Pancho," said Dr. Rodriguez. Then quietly as an aside to Frank he added, "We gotta clean some fluid out of her airway, then get her some rest."

Lupe was willing to be wheeled away by a nurse only after repeated reassurances from both physicians that Frank would come and visit her.

As the nurse took Lupe away, Dr. Rodriguez looked at Frank and said with a laugh, "Wow, the "miracle doctor" she called you. Do your own patients find you that charming?"

"Only the ladies," answered Frank, returning the comment in kind.

But Frank had seen sin the clear, dark eyes, and was much more taken with the word *soledad,* Spanish for solitude, in the lady's comment.

As Dr. Rodriguez left to attend his patient, Frank stopped at the Nurse's station to ask a question.

"Excuse me, Maria." said Frank after reading a name tag. "That elderly woman, where is she from?"

"Oh Lupe? She's so sweet. Just a minute and I'll look that up."

After a minute of record searching Maria had an answer.

"It says here that she is from Meoqui. That's another town not far from here. Then there's a note that says '*Ejido de Tres Milagros*'."

"Where's that?"

"Probably near the town of Meoqui. *Ejidos* are communal farming villages set up by the government. There are a lot of them along the river around here. If you want to know where it is for sure you could ask Lupe's granddaughter. She comes here almost every day at about six in the evening."

Frank thought again about Lupe's comment "The miracle doctor from Soledad," and muttered "Yeah, thanks. I'll do that." He had promised to visit her, and the haunting thought that perhaps her word "*soledad*" might have referred to the old ranch would not leave Frank's mind.

Several hours later Frank passed by the door to Lupe's room and noticed that she had a visitor. Hoping that this was indeed the granddaughter, Frank decided stop by. He stepped into the room and noticed that Lupe was sitting up in bed and had apparently just finished a small bowl of some sort of pureed food.

"Excuse me, ma'am," he said to Lupe's visitor. "I am Dr. Jensen."

"Ah ha," said the gray haired woman who herself appeared to be quite old, "my grandmother has talked about you for the last hour. You must have a super bedside manner, doctor."

"Well, I don't know about that; I just met Lupe this morning." Then to the elderly lady herself, Frank asked, "How are you doing this evening?"

"I'm fine, thank you—Marta, the miracle doctor! It is him!"

As Frank stepped nearer to the bed Lupe took hold of his hand and held it tightly in both of hers. Even as a practicing physician Frank was surprised at the appearance of the lady's hands. Little more than bones wrapped in thin, translucent skin, a few dark veins, and little else held Frank's large paw as the dark eyes looked up with obvious admiration. Frank had the feeling that if he moved too fast, the frail, old hands might fall apart.

Gently, in his best comforting manner, Frank laid his other hand on Lupe's forehead and noted that her temperature was normal—the physician in him automatically evaluating her overall condition. In doing so he could not help but notice the emotion in the lady's clear, jet black eyes. Eyes that brought to mind the little girl who said her name was "Lupita" as she walked with him for a few steps on the day that President Juarez left Rancho Soledad.

Remembering that he was really only a visitor, Frank stepped back just a little and turned to the granddaughter whose name was apparently Marta.

A little embarrassed, Frank said, "I don't know why your grandmother seems to know me. We have never met before this morning." But as he spoke Frank felt uncertain about his words, and he heard Lupe say the single word "*Dios*" as she attempted to cross herself with one stick-figure arm.

"Marta, I want to ask some things about your grandmother. I would like—"

Frank was interrupted by a nurse's aid who bustled into the room and immediately took Lupe's hand and felt for a pulse. Laying the hand down again, the young woman smiled and she too touched Lupe's forehead, sincerely interested in her patient's well-being.

"Lupe is our favorite patient here," she said with a smile, while making some notes on a chart attached to the foot of the bed.

"What is her condition?" asked Frank.

"Oh Dr. Jensen. Isn't she your patient?"

"No, no, I'm just a friend."

"Well, she's just fine. We were concerned that she might have been developing a little pneumonia, but that is all under control. Dr. Rodriguez says Lupe will outlive us all."

"Good, nice to hear," said Frank as the young woman disappeared as quickly as she had come.

Frank then turned his attention back to Marta.

"Your grandmother is from a place called Tres Milagros I am told. Has she always lived there?"

"Dr. Jensen, my grandmother's body is frail with her many years, but her mind is as clear as yours or mine. You can ask her. She will tell you when she is tired."

"Of course," said Frank, again slightly embarrassed. He had an uncomfortable feeling asking questions that he knew were not motivated by concern for the patient's well-being.

"Lupe, where is your home?" he asked.

"*Tres Milagros del Rancho Soledad*," was the reply from the frail, child-sized form lying on the bed.

Frank's heart nearly skipped a beat as he heard the full name of the collective farm community Lupe was referring to. She had called it "Three Miracles of Rancho Soledad." Rancho Soledad! This was the first time Frank had heard that name since his strange visit to Mexico many years earlier. Rancho Soledad, and a *caballera* named Victoria.

"Rancho Soledad," said Frank. "Did you live there, Lupe? Do you know where it is?"

"It is no more," said the quiet, soft voice. *Lo siento mucho*, it is gone with the *Federales*."

"*Federales?*"

"Yes, *Federales* and Maximiliano's soldiers destroyed it. My mother told me that."

"Your mother—"

"We don't know for sure whether my grandmother was born at Rancho Soledad or in Tres Milagros interrupted Marta. But her mother was definitely one of the people from Rancho Soledad."

"Benito gave us Tres Milagros," added Lupe.

"Benito? Who was Benito?" asked Frank.

"Ah," said Marta. "We know that a big ranch where my family came from was destroyed during the revolution and that the rancher was a good friend of President Benito Juarez. Because of the tragedy, President Juarez designated a tract of land as a permanent place for the people from his friend's ranch to live. It became an *ejido* back in the '30's. It's not far from here."

"It is *Tres Milagros del Rancho Soledad*," came a soft, but emphatic voice from the bed.

"Yes, *del Rancho Soledad*," conceded Marta with a smile.

Frank was scheduled to return home the next day, but he knew that on his next visit to Mexico he would see Tres Milagros, and that his next trip would be much sooner than he might have otherwise planned.

The Padre of Tres Milagros

Two weeks later Frank and Susan returned to Mexico in his Cessna. Since Susan had recently finished training and had passed the exams for her commercial pilot's certificate two days earlier, Frank let her do all the flying.

"Hey *hey*, young lady. That was a nice crosswind landing!" Frank was impressed by the skill Susan displayed in landing the extremely skittish Cessna 180 in difficult wind conditions.

"Yep. We're both alive, anyhow," joked the proud pilot. Though she had not yet told Frank, Susan had decided to go for a career in aviation. Then she added, "Now, on this trip *I'm* the pilot and you're the ground-pounder, so you gotta drive the rental car!"

After a two-hour drive south from the airport just north of Mexico's Chihuahua City, Frank drove into a small village in a broad valley.

"Well, here we have it, the village of Tres Milagros," said Frank as he began hunting for a place to park their rented Ford Taurus. He found one, not far from the large park near the center of town.

"Let's look around the plaza some," he said as he shut off the motor. The two then walked across the street to the public square, a rectangular, tree-lined, grassy area with concrete sidewalks on all four sides. Each sidewalk had several cast-iron benches facing inward toward a gazebo-like bandstand in the center of the square.

"Hey, a neat place," said Susan, who was not familiar with the interior of Mexico.

"Yep, the plaza," said Frank. "The heart of any Mexican town, big or small. Notice that the church is right across the street." With his hand Frank indicated a small chapel made of stuccoed adobe across the dirt street at the narrow end of the plaza.

Frank had a sincere respect for Mexico and was enjoying showing some of it to Susan, who always soaked up new experiences like a sponge.

"You are lucky to be here at just this time," said Frank. "Soon it will be Saturday night in beautiful downtown Tres Milagros."

"Ah-ha," said Susan. "This is where the action is, Hey?"

"Yep, always has been. Note that the benches face inward from the street. Sitting on any one of them you can see what is going on everywhere. Long ago, in a less modern world, (at this point in his discourse Frank feigned a frown at his niece) this was the 'boy meets girl' part of town. On Saturday night after the week's work was done, young ladies would wear their best clothes and walk together around the square, taking in the evening air you might say, but all of them walking in one direction.

"In the other direction came the local young bucks, shined up some themselves, also in small groups, chatting among themselves.

"In this way all the girls met and passed by all the boys, and each was free to smile, blush, push a nose in the air, or just ignore anyone they wished to. Sort of a place for formalized and supervised flirting. And choosing partners for a little dancing that might occur later in the evening, also under adult supervision."

"Supervision?" said Susan.

"Yep. Note the benches again, facing inward. That's where the old folks sat, keeping an eye on everything. At least that's how it used to be."

Susan had noticed that many benches had filled up—a couple of men here, another group there, and an occasional woman or two accompanied by several children running about or climbing on the bandstand. And, there were groups of teen-age girls walking around the plaza.

But only a few of the boys were walking around. Most were circling the plaza in pickup trucks, some in the cabs, and some in back. Occasionally boys and girls both rode in the back of the trucks.

The trucks might have been a modern addition to the scene, but the old game was still the same. Cocky teen-age boys strutting noisily about with teen-age girls trying to simultaneously attract and snub them, and everyone chattering with everyone else. On the benches were older women with their best tisk-tisk expressions on their faces, and old men ignoring it all.

"You know Gramps, there's three, maybe four generations of people here" said Susan.

"Yep, this is rural Mexico at its finest," said Frank. "Lots of these folks have lived here all their lives."

Susan singled out a particular elderly man sitting quietly alone on a bench on the opposite side of the square. She wondered, "Did he play on that bandstand as a little boy too? Did he meet his wife walking around this patch of grass? How many evenings has he sat here with his family or friends? Lots of them are probably gone now."

Susan's thoughts were interrupted by an energetic boy of about twelve years carrying a shoeshine box. Clearly, the boy was soliciting business.

"Shine shoes, lady?" asked the young entrepreneur.

Laughing because she was wearing white Adidas jogging shoes, Susan pointed at Frank's feet and said "*Sí.*"

Frank lifted one foot and placed it on the iron footrest on the top of the boy's wooden box. Immediately Frank's shoe was subject to a vigorous scrubbing with a small brush and soapy water. A fingertip tap on the ankle was the signal for Frank to change feet on the box. After another round of scrubbing, this time the shoe got a coating of black dye. Then a change of feet and more black dye. Next came applications of black wax, heavily brushed in, followed by elaborately theatrical polishing with a long, soft cloth that popped in the air as it whipped across Frank's boot. In minutes the leather took on a finish that rivaled polished ebony.

"Wish I could get a shine like this at home," said Frank as he handed the boy several coins.

"Gracias, Señor."

"What's your name son?" asked Frank.

"Miguel."

"Well, Miguel," said Frank with a nod of his head toward the little church. "Do you know the padre? Could you find him for me?" He handed Miguel another coin.

"Si, Señor. I know him. He is not far away." Miguel picked up his box and ran toward the other end of the plaza.

Frank told Susan that he had sent the boy on an errand, but not what the errand was, then sat back on the iron bench and watched Susan continue to take in the sights and sounds of the Mexican culture. She was intently focused on five musicians dressed in tan colored *mariachi* costumes who were tuning up their instruments near the bandstand. One had a violin; there were two trumpets, several guitars, and a huge base violin.

"You were right," said Susan. "This is where the action is."

Shortly Frank pointed out to Susan a man dressed in dark blue slacks and wearing a *guayavera*.

"Hey, sharp looking shirt," said Susan.

The man's shirt, though bearing much embroidered decoration, was all solid, light blue in color, and hemmed evenly at the bottom for wearing outside the belt. Always white or some single pastel color, such shirts were a common form of casual, but stylish, dress in Mexico.

Frank, however, knew Susan was probably more interested in the shirt's owner who was walking toward them from the far end of the plaza. Of good build and athletic-looking, perhaps thirty years old, the man clearly knew everyone around as he walked with lighthearted confidence and purpose along the sidewalk.

Susan watched the man approach, and noticed the boy Miguel prancing along at his side. The pair stopped about fifty feet away and Miguel pointed toward Frank and Susan. The man took note, waved toward the Americans, and Miguel ran to rejoin his own youthful social set which included an impromptu soccer game. Apparently Miguel's business hours were over for the day.

"*Hola,* Señores, I am Martin Garcia Rivera, at your service," said the man, changing to English as he offered his hand to Frank.

"Frank Jensen, and this is my niece Susan Jensen."

Martin took Susan's hand and with a slight hint of a bow, said, "Very pleased to meet you Señorita."

Then, looking past Frank's shoulder and seeing an elderly man waving at him a short distance away, Martin added, "Excuse me for a moment, I see that I am called. I will only be a moment." With that the strikingly handsome young man stepped over to a nearby iron bench to speak with the older man.

"Wow," said Susan. "Jack Scalia with a Spanish accent and no wedding ring! I may move to Mexico!"

"Hold it, girl, don't throw a lash fluttering your eyes at the man." Frank always enjoyed teasing Susan about the false eyelashes she wore. Then he added, "He's the local priest."

"Hoo boy, it's like they say, the good ones are always either married or gay or—"

"Priests," said Frank, finishing her sentence and enjoying her slight embarrassment and noticing that the padre had returned.

"Miguelito has told me that some *Norteamericanos* wanted to see the priest. Well I am he. What can I do for you?"

Noticing that the young clergyman found the use of English awkward, Frank changed the conversation to Spanish, after a suitable apology to Susan who had only a rudimentary grasp of the language.

"Well you see, Padre, I have become acquainted with a lady named Guadalupe Esperanza de Gomez in a hospital in Ciuadad Delicias—"

"Ah, Lupita, my oldest and dearest parishioner, I know of her visit to the hospital. Is she well?"

"Oh yes, yes indeed. She is recovering nicely from a slight bronchial inflammation."

As he spoke Frank felt a twinge of awkwardness at his automatic physician's choice of words and added, "She's a fine lady."

"Indeed she is," said Martin. "She is our town's oldest citizen and is known and liked by everyone everywhere."

"Padre, Lupe told me something of the origin of your village, and of the people who first came here. Those people are of personal interest to me. I hoped that you could tell me more about them."

"Ah, yes, Señor. Come, let me show you something of which we at Tres Milagros are quite proud." Martin then led the way to a marble statue about eight feet tall set in a large open area of the plaza.

Frank immediately recognized that it was a statue of President Juarez posed to accent the man's Indian facial features, not an uncommon theme throughout Mexico's northern states.

Martin directed Frank's attention to the inscription on the statue's pedestal. *El Presidente Benito Juarez Garcia, un hombre verdadero del pueblo de Tres Milagros del Rancho Soledad.* "A true man of the people of Tres Milagros del Rancho Soledad," said the inscription, and Frank's pulse quickened at the full name given for the town.

"Padre, it says the town's name is Three Miracles of Rancho Soledad; it is this Rancho Soledad that interests me. I know—Lupe told me—about the old ranch that was destroyed by soldiers nearly a hundred years ago. I know that President Juarez created this town as a place for the survivors of Rancho Soledad. What can you tell me of those people? What are the miracles?"

"Yes, it is true that Presedent Juarez founded this town, and many of its original citizens came from a place called Rancho Soledad. There are burial records for our church cemetery that speak of Rancho Soledad. And my predecessor, who was himself an extremely old man, mentioned it from time to time."

"Padre, could I trouble you to help me look for some names in those records? Just a name or two?"

"Yes, of course. But I would prefer that we do that in my office tomorrow, after the services. You see, this evening is a *quinceañera*, a special time for a young lady and her family. I have preparations to make, and there will be celebrations in the plaza. This is not a time for cemeteries and graves, Señor Jensen."

"No, no, of course not. I am glad that my niece and I have had the good fortune to be here on such a happy occasion. She has not seen such a ceremony."

"Ah, well then, you both will be my guests this evening. Perhaps you can explain the *quinceañera* to the lady. I think my English cannot do that well."

Frank did indeed explain to Susan all about the "coming out" ceremony that marks the fifteenth birthday for a Mexican girl. The afternoon ceremony and the evening's festivities soaked up Susan's rapt attention.

***

On the next day Frank and Susan visited the padre in his rectory, just a tiny office cubicle at the rear of the small church.

"Good morning, Señorita and Señor Jensen," said the Padre as Susan and Frank entered. "It was nice to have visitors at mass this morning. Thank you for attending."

"Good morning, Padre. There's no better place to be on a Sunday morning, and we enjoyed listening to you. I can see that you have a good relationship with the people of Tres Milagros."

"Without earning the respect of my parishioners I wouldn't be worth my keep, now would I?" said Martin with a smile.

"I have given some thought to your request about names of people who came here from that old ranch long ago. Is there anyone in particular you are interested in, perhaps some particular family?"

Frank swallowed and cleared his throat before he answered.

"Yes, Padre, I'm curious about a man named Rubén Hidalgo, of the family Silva," said Frank, remembering the formal name he had heard who knows how long ago. "And perhaps the name Victoria Hidalgo too."

"Ah, the name Hidalgo I have seen." Martin then lifted an old leather bound record book with pages as large as those of a newspaper from a dark mahogany cabinet. "Let us see what we have here."

"Wow, how old is that?" said Susan.

"It goes back to the beginning of Tres Milagros and to early days of this parish. Here births, marriages, and deaths are recorded."

Martin opened the ancient volume carefully, and after turning two pages, ran his finger down the right hand page to an entry he thought significant.

"I think you are in luck. The name you asked about is a prominent one in the old records, as is the location of last remains."

"Last remains?" said Frank.

"Yes, of course, Señor," said Martin with a slightly puzzled expression.

Frank had felt an emotional tug at the words, and had to remind himself that these people who were important acquaintances to him must all have died long ago. He glanced at Susan and wondered if she knew what he was thinking.

"Señor Hidalgo is buried here?" said Frank.

"According to church records Señor Hidalgo and several others from Rancho Soledad were originally interred on the ranch. Years later, when Benito Juarez founded our community, the graves were moved to our church cemetery. I can show you the exact resting place of the Hidalgo people if you would like. I am familiar with it."

"Yes, I would like that. And, Padre, the other name I asked about?"

"Ah yes, that was Victoria Hidalgo, was it not?" Martin then perused his huge ledger for a few seconds and looked up.

"No, I see no mention of that name or any similar one in the list of graves that were brought here from Rancho Soledad. Our records are done quite carefully, Señor, and the only Hidalgo name listed is that of Rubén. There are ten other names, all apparently ranch workers or relatives not of the name Hidalgo. Only three are women—Maria, Pilar, and Constance."

No mention of Victoria, thought Frank, not knowing whether he was disappointed or not.

"Could I ask a question?" ventured Susan.

"Yes, of course, Señorita."

"Yesterday you said you would tell us how the town got the name *Tres Milagros*. That means three miracles, doesn't it?"

"Ah yes, the name. That is a name that was chosen by an elderly lady who was part of the Juarez Garcia family, a relative of Benito Juarez Garcia himself. It has to do with a folk tale that made a big impression on the Juarez family. It seems that, according to legend, three miracles occurred at Rancho Soledad. I caution you that these are not miracles in the sense of the church—they have not been sanctioned in any way."

"What miracles—"

"This elderly lady," interrupted Frank. "Do you know who she was? Or what happened to her?

"Well, as I have said, she was part of the family of Señor Juarez, that is clear in our records. She came to the newly formed village and brought with her several children who had been quite young at the time that Rancho Soledad was destroyed when it resisted the emperor's troops. She did not remain here, and there is no further record of her or her name."

"But what were the miracles? You said she named the town after three miracles."

"Ah yes, the tale from which our *ejido* eventually got its name. Let me explain a little of my country's history to put some of this in perspective. You see, during the last years of the existence of Rancho Soledad, Mexico had two governments. One was the legitimate one of Emperor Maximiliano. The other was an unofficial one headed by Benito Juarez Garcia who called himself the President of the Republic."

Frank smiled slightly as he listened to this summation of historical events from the Catholic Church point of view.

"These two groups had difficulties with each other and the result was that travel was dangerous, especially for prominent people. Now Benito Juarez was, in the eyes of Maximiliano and his French military supporters, a revolutionary. This made travel quite dangerous for supporters of Señor Juarez."

"But Juarez was President, he was elected by the people," said Susan. This resulted in a nudge from Frank's elbow.

"That was at a time in Mexico when the people were not capable of choosing a proper leader. The man Juarez was not familiar with how nations were run at that time and thus had much difficulty with leaders of other nations, particularly in Europe."

"And in Rome," added Frank, not able to resist commenting.

"Yes, Señor Jensen, Señor Juarez was not popular with the Roman Catholic Church." Frank immediately regretted his comment. Both he and the padre knew perfectly well that Juarez was an enemy of the Catholic Church, and this was part of the reason that a European Emperor was forced upon the country. But this was not a time to bring out historical dirty laundry.

"But the miracles, what *were* they?" pressed Susan.

"Ah, it seems that Señor Juarez was traveling in the State of Chihuahua and became ill. What his particular malady was, no one seems to know. But while he visited Rancho Soledad—some people say that Señor Hidalgo was a relative of his—three things happened. First, a man, apparently a physician, fell out of the sky and came to Rancho Soledad; second, this man immediately fixed whatever was bothering Señor Juarez; third, the man then disappeared back into the sky.

"In any case, Mexico was a quite primitive country back then, and still is to some extent today. Folklore such as the story of three miracles is pretty common."

"Apparently President Juarez took this bit of folklore seriously enough to found this village," said Frank.

"Yes indeed, that is so, and seriously enough to have the remains of the people of Rancho Soledad brought here. Perhaps it is time that I show you their final resting place."

Minutes later Frank, Susan and Martin stood looking at an old part of the graveyard just behind the church. They saw a small area separated from the more modern graves by a low chain link fence. Inside were a few mounds, barely recognizable as graves, surrounding a single granite monument. There was no grass, just dirt burned dry by the desert sun.

Walking carefully toward the monument, which was wider than it was tall, Frank and Susan looked for an inscription. The weathered marble was worn and battered by the ravages of time, but the embossed words were still barely legible.

One row of large letters said, *La Gente del Rancho Soledad, Pasada Y Futura, 1868.*

"The people of Rancho Soledad, Past and Future," translated Martin for Susan.

Susan stepped closer to the rose granite marker and rubbed her fingers on another inscription in smaller letters and below the first. This one needed no translation:

There are crystal bells that have not yet been rung
and tiny songs that have not yet been sung

"It's a beautiful thought," said Susan. "And it's in English!"

"Yes, that is a little unusual," said Martin. "But there were many people in Mexico who spoke English, even then. Perhaps the use of a foreign language seemed more likely to be remembered. Or it may have had special meaning for someone."

Frank said nothing. For he remembered those same words spoken almost soundlessly by Victoria on his last day at Rancho Soledad. And one more time he recognized the fleeting, but unmistakable scent of lilacs. All combined to give Frank a euphoric sense that all was well with the world.

Lost in thought, Frank stared at the inscribed message. The wild emotions in his heart told him that they were Victoria's words, and he knew that they were all that he was going to find in Tres Milagros of that lovely woman from long ago. And he wanted to believe that the inscription was in English as a special sign to him.

Realizing that his two companions had noticed his introspective mood, Frank looked up and said, "Hmm, that's interesting."

"Well, since we are on the subject of local folklore, there is one more little piece that may be of interest to you Señor Jensen. As I said, there were several children who came to Tres Milagros with the woman from the Juarez Garcia family. Several of our elderly townsfolk claim that your patient in the hospital in Ciudad Delicias was one of those children. Certainly Lupita herself says that she once lived at Rancho Soledad, but there are no records to verify her claim."

"Wow, little Lupita, It's her!" thought Frank. He had thought of asking the elderly lady about people from Rancho Soledad when he visited her in the clinic in Delicias. But he had not because the frail lady was obviously tired that day. But he knew he would visit again and ask about Victoria.

As he glanced at Susan he saw that she had been watching him closely, and realized that for Frank there was some special significance in all they had seen. Through all the years since his strange visit to Rancho Soledad Frank had never spoken to anyone about his extraordinary forced landing on that dry lake. Even though Susan had occasionally seemed a little puzzled about his interest in Mexico and remembered flying with him as he searched for Rancho Soledad by air several years earlier, she had never pressed the subject.

In Susan's eyes Frank could see that she knew that their current visit had something to do with the profound changes that had come over Frank back then, but still she wouldn't pry. He realized that he owed an explanation to this one person closest to him in this world.

But what would that explanation be? Well, he could at least describe the events as he believed he experienced them and trust that Susan would understand. So, Frank decided to tell his story.

As they left the village of Tres Milagros, Frank used most of an hour to tell Susan about his remarkable forced landing in that vast, white, dry lake in northern Chihuahua. When he finished, some time passed before either of the two spoke.

"Well, what do you think? Have you been hanging out with some kind of nut all these years?"

Seconds more passed in silence before Susan spoke.

"Grandpa, I think we ought to stop by that little clinic so you can visit that elderly lady one more time. You should ask her what she knows about your Victoria."

"Yep. I'v been thinking about that ever since I realized who she was—who she was in my old visit—that sweet, little, dark-eyed child."

***

Later that day Frank and Susan visited Lupe in the clinic in the city of Delicias. Frank chose a time late in the day hoping that the elderly lady's granddaughter, Marta, would also be there, and she was.

As soon as Frank entered the room Lupe immediately recognized him. "Ah, the *'medico milagro,'* has come." Miracle doctor, Lupe had called him. Frank was immediately uncomfortable with the remark, hoping Lupe would not be expecting him to perform now, on her behalf. But after a few minutes it was clear that the title was simply one of respect that Lupe had remembered all through her life as she told people, most of whom didn't believe her, about the three miracles of Rancho Soledad.

"May I ask you some questions about Rancho Soledad, Lupita? When did all the people leave there and —"

"*Los pinche Franchutos,*" muttered Lupe as she then drifted off into unintelligible muttering. Frank was a little shocked to hear such coarse language come from the lady he was idly thinking of as a tiny, little girl in a clean, white dress.

"My grandmother has told me a little about leaving Ranch Soledad, Doctor Jensen, but she was only five years old at the time," said Maria.

"Did she tell you anything about other people who were there? Did she mention a lady named Victoria?"

At hearing the name Victoria, Lupe brightened up and spoke again. *"La Señorita del Rancho Soledad. Y su Mariposa."* then drifted back into nearly incomprehensible muttering.

"And her butterfly?" Clearly Marta didn't understand the remark.

"That was the name of Victoria's white Arabian mare," replied Frank.

"Heh? You know the name of the old lady's horse?"

Immediately Frank realized he had to be more careful, and confine his efforts to asking questions, not offering comments. And he found it uncomfortable to hear Marta refer to Victoria as an "old lady."

"Do you know who Victoria was?" he asked.

"Oh yes, she was an elderly lady who brought my grandmother and several other people from Rancho Soledad to Ciudad Delicias long ago. She became known as a superb caballera, a horsewoman, and was famous for the work she did teaching young people the art of riding horses. They say her work helped many young people get better starts in life during the bad times that came just after the turn of the century.

Frank realized then that Victoria had not only lived through the bad times of one revolution in the nineteenth century, but she had also faced another in 1910.

"What happened to her?"

"No one seems to remember. Some old timers say she died about the time of the great depression, but no one knows."

"Marta, can you ask your grandmother now; does she know?"

"Victoria and Mariposa, they just went away," muttered Lupe who had been listening attentively.

Frank could see that Lupe was getting tired, and did not look as sturdy as she had been the first time he had seen her. Fearing that thoughts of such old times, bad or good, might be too much for her, he decided it was time to leave. Stepping close to Lupe, he put his hand on the frail bits of bone and skin that were her left hand, remembering a time when it was the tiny hand of a beautiful child in a world they had once shared for just a short time. He then kissed her gently on the forehead, much like he had done more than a hundred years earlier.

"Gracias a Dios," said Lupe, with smiling eyes that looked to Frank just as beautiful as they had been in a child's face so long ago. He turned his head to the side so Marta would not see the tears welling up in his own eyes, and as he did so he noticed one more time the faint scent of lilac blossoms in springtime air.

It was only two weeks later when Dr. Rodriguez at the little clinic in Delicias sent word to Frank that their oldest patient had passed away. Frank's heart was heavy as he thought of the lady he had met only for a few moments at each end of a lifetime that for her had been more than a century long.

Susan

Ramon sat in the left seat of the Cessna 152 with both hands on the control yoke and straightened the airplane out from a gentle left turn.

Susan, his instructor in the right seat next to the 15-year-old boy, smiled, noticing her student's intent focus on what he was doing. No macho swagger now, no belligerent shell to present to the world. Now Ramon was caught up in the satisfaction of meeting a challenge that, though he would never admit it, had frightened him. A challenge he couldn't meet with attitude or tough guy bluster. And he was doing it by learning new skills. Ramon was actually flying an airplane!

"A-ha, nice turn, Ramon. I think you have some natural talent there," said Susan as she put her hands back on the dual controls of the Cessna trainer they were flying. "Now, keep your hands on the controls, just lightly, and follow me through. We'll head back to the field and see if we can land this thing."

"OK," was the enthusiastic response.

Minutes later Susan had the plane set up on a long final for runway 26 at the Las Cruces airport, and Ramon was intently focused on the approaching runway. She picked up the microphone to make a radio call, and knowing that there was no other traffic in the airport's landing pattern, she decided to expose Ramon to the radio.

"Here Ramon, you do the radio call." She handed the mike to the boy.

"Heh? Me?" Ramon held the microphone like it might bite him.

"Sure; why not? Just use the phrases I taught you. Our aircraft number is right there on the panel."

Ramon pushed the button and said, "Ah, Las Cruces, ah, were land—ah, we're N159RJ—a Cessna—and we're landing on final for the runway."

Susan chuckled a little as she put the mike back in its bracket on the panel and Ramon concentrated on the approaching seven thousand foot long strip of asphalt pavement with its big white number "26" at the near end.

"Ok, not bad for a first shot. You need a little polish, but with practice we'll have you sounding like an astronaut.

"Ok, now we ease back the power some; see, we're settling down, and that big number isn't moving up or down, its just getting bigger, right? That's the way we like it.

"Now we take off a little more power, ease the yoke back just a tad, . . ."

Seconds later Susan had the little airplane flying just inches above the pavement and noticed that Ramon was using his hands and feet to follow all the motions on his half of the dual controls.

"Now, we cut the power, and try to keep flying as long as we can, . . ."

Gently, the plane settled onto its main landing gear.

"Now, we hold the nose wheel off as long as we can, . . ." Susan moved the control yoke back slowly until the plane had slowed so much that the nose had to come down even with the yoke all the way back.

"OK, when we can't keep the nose wheel off the pavement any more, we put the yoke all the way forward to hold the nose down. Helps with steering."

Under Susan's careful watch Ramon taxied the plane to its tie-down spot, and following her instructions, shut down the engine.

"Well, that's your second lesson. What do you think?"

"Wow, Ms. Jensen, I can do this stuff!"

Susan was pleased with the boy's honest enthusiasm. Like always, the result of another of her free flying lessons made her feel good to be alive.

"Ok, Ramon. Think about what you did today, what you learned. And about how much farther you can go. These days with rockets and space ships, the sky isn't even a limit anymore. Think you can get yourself ready for another lesson one of these days?"

"Shi—Ah, yeah, you bet. Yes ma'am!" Ramon was a little embarrassed by his near slip of language.

"All right fella. Just keep your act clean and stay with the program and we'll make an ace out of you yet."

"Ah ma'am, can I ask you something?"

"Sure Ramon, shoot."

Ramon turned and pointed at a beautiful little Great Lakes biplane sitting on the parking ramp. It was painted pure white with sky-blue trim and matching blue leather upholstery in each of its two open cockpits. With its front end tilted upward because of its tail-wheel design, the immaculately maintained aerobatic biplane looked ready to jump into the air as it sat gleaming in the sun. Ramon knew that Susan often flew the plane, practicing aerobatic flying. Though she didn't know it, he had watched her many times as she flew loops, rolls, spins and other precision maneuvers in the little craft.

"That's your airplane, isn't it? I seen its name right below the front cockpit. Mariposa, you call it. That's butterfly. How come you to pick a name like that?"

"Oh that's a secret between my grandpa and me. He met a special butterfly once long ago."

"Huh. Weird. But I guess that makes you kin to another kind of flyer, right?"

"Yeah, I guess it does," laughed Susan. She had guessed that Ramon was getting interested in more than just flying from here to there in a Cessna. "Tell ya what, fella. You get through the program like we talked about and I'll take you up in it. OK?"

"Christ—ah, wow, you bet, ma'am. Wow, open cockpits and all! Can we fly upside down and—"

"We'll see fella. But first you gotta learn to fly right side up, OK?" Susan could plainly see that Ramon's world was opening up; he was realizing there was a lot more to life than the local gang membership he had been aspiring to.

Minutes later as Susan watched Ramon walk away from the aircraft parking area toward his waiting ride, she noticed that the boy's deliberate swagger was coming back. But she knew that now it was caused a little less by streetwise, macho attitude and a little more by pride in accomplishment. Another reward to Susan for her efforts.

***

"Hey Sue, did ya see the paper?"

Susan had just stepped into the airport's lounge when Jerry Stern, the airport manager, waved a local newspaper at her.

"Awright everybody, listen up," he said indicating all the dozen or so people in the pilot's lounge. "It seems that this week marks ten years of service to the youth of our fair city on the part of our gorgeous and intrepid pilot here, Ms. Susan Jensen."

"Gad, any opportunity and a politician will try to talk to a crowd," said Susan, with a smile. She and Jerry had been bantering good-naturedly with each other for years.

"Yes, Indeed," continued Jerry in imitated Stentorian tones. "Let me quote our local scandal sheet here," and he began reading.

"As part of the 'Challenge for At Risk Teens' program administered jointly by the Dona Ana County Juvenile Court, the District Attorney's office, and the Office of the Airport Manager (extra emphasis on the latter) Ms. Jensen has given flying lessons to twenty-seven young boys and girls who might otherwise have continued their socially counterproductive life styles."

"Geesh, Jerry. That sounds like something you would write," said Susan.

"OK, OK, I will summarize. It seems that practically all of those twenty-seven young folks have left their scuddy ways, dodged the drug scene, and become productive citizens. It seems that two of those boys are U S Navy pilots, one young woman is flying right seat for an airline back east, and four more, including another young woman, are flying helicopters in the Army. Many of the rest have private or commercial pilot certificates, and everybody's been staying clean and out of jail."

Jerry handed Susan the paper with a "How about that toots! We're all proud of ya, ain't we folks?" Then from behind a counter he produced a large bouquet of red roses which all of Susan's friends knew were her favorite flowers. This was followed by a round of congratulations from the local flying crowd and some soft drinks from the nearby machines.

As she was about to leave, Marge Kendall, who worked the desk at the little airport and was a close friend of the lady pilot, gestured to Susan.

"Well?"

"Well what?" answered Susan.

"Sheesh girl, what's the matter with you. That poor guy's been after you for months, and—"

"Not again. He just isn't my type." Susan knew Marge meant the handsome, successful, and highly eligible Airport Manager.

"Ha. Don't be silly. A guy with all that goin' for him, he's anybody's type. And you've pushed past thirty, in case you haven't noticed!"

"C'mon Marge. Give it a rest. I'm really happy with the way things are, and I'm just gonna see what the future brings. I'll see ya tomorrow for lunch, as usual, OK?"

As Susan started to walk to the parking lot door, Marge caught her arm and gently stopped her.

"Seriously, girl. All your friends are married now—including me and my lunk I wound up with. And guys keep taking you out now, but the field will dry up soon. Isn't it about time for you to get serious?"

Realizing the sincerity in Marge's comments, Susan took her aside and quietly said, "Marge, I'm doing just fine right now. This is my time for just me. Don't worry about me. I know that when life decides the time is right, then I won't be alone —ever."

Marge became quiet, having noticed the serious tone to Susan's comments.

"Hey, you're my best buddy," said the lady pilot. "I know you worry about me and I love you for it. But I'm OK. Really. Deep inside I know that there's a guy, someone special for me, but our time has not yet come." As Susan spoke, thoughts of her grandpa's little book popped into her mind.

Susan drove home feeling good about the business of living and about her personal choices in life. She knew that she couldn't really explain her remarks to Marge, even to herself. She took a deep breath and the fragrance of the fresh, red roses in the confined space of her Volkswagen strengthened her feelings that her life was a grand adventure, stretching out forever.

As Susan drove, the little book, with its three pages, came into her thoughts again and again. She realized that just thinking about it was somehow comforting to her. Thinking of putting the fresh flowers into a particular vase she always used for roses, the young lady was happy with her favorite blossoms that always symbolized soft, good times for her.

***

One day three weeks later, Susan Jensen came home from work, looking forward to seeing Frank, her "Grandpa," as she still called him.

"Grandpa, are you sleeping?" asked Susan as she stepped quietly into Frank's study. She could see that he was in his favorite chair, wearing his spectacles and holding a book in his lap. She knew that even if he was enjoying his customary nap in the afternoon sun, the old man she loved so dearly would always awaken happily at the sound of her voice.

"Grandpa, are you OK?" she asked, this time with concern in her voice, for Frank had not responded.

With a tightening feeling in her chest Susan approached the old man's chair.

"Grandpa?"

Still no response.

Susan's eyes began to moisten as she knelt beside the chair and looked into Frank's face. In the age-wrinkled and weathered complexion she saw all the strength, wisdom, and compassion that had made her love her uncle for all of her life. She knew that the best friend she would ever have had passed away, and would have broken down in tears were it not for what she saw in Frank's face. There was a peaceful expression of contentment that flowed from the old man into the young woman's heart to help protect her from the sorrow that was coming.

Susan reached slowly for Frank's hand that was resting on an open page of the small leather bound book lying in his lap. A book that had always been in Grandpa's medical bag as long as she could remember, one he had always treated as reverently as one might a Bible. Softly she took the finely tooled, maroon colored volume from the lap of this man she respected more than any other. She wanted to see for herself what had been the last thing he ever read.

Through tear-filled eyes Susan saw that the book was open to page three, one that she knew had always been blank. But it was not blank now. In elegantly flowing handwriting were the words,

> *"My time and your time have passed,*
> *and now our time has come."*

Susan read again the three completed pages, then softly closed the book. As she did so she noticed that in spite of having been carried daily for many years in a physician's medical bag, the leather bound volume still appeared to be brand new. The finely tooled impression of two lilac blossom clusters seemed so sharply detailed that Susan felt that she could almost see them waving softly in a spring-time breeze. Carefully, she placed the book back under Frank's lifeless hand. Gently she kissed the old man's forehead, stood up and left the room to tell the world that her grandfather was gone.

***

Frank's funeral was attended by hundreds of people of modest means as well as by dozens of his colleagues in the medical community from both the United States and Mexico. On the day after the funeral Susan and two attorneys sat in an office in downtown El Paso. No one had even thought much about the possibility that Frank would have a will. He had no family except for his niece, and no significant property other than the small office that he owned and from which he had carried out his medical practice.

"Well, Ms. Jensen, this shouldn't take long," said a rather disinterested lawyer in a business suit. "Your uncle has made arrangements for his office building to be sold. The proceeds are to be used to supplement the retirement of his office nurse-receptionist and to pay off the mortgage on the home in which the two of you have been living."

"Oh, Mrs. Weatherbee, Grandpa's nurse? That's great. She's too old to find another job, and she worked hard for him all these years," said Susan.

"Yes, well, be that as it may, the last part of the will is a bit peculiar. It refers to you. I will just read it, verbatim."

"It says the following: 'My life has been rich with treasures beyond count. They are the friendships I have known, the conversations and experiences I have shared, and the memories I have collected. Since I have taken all of these things with me they are not the concern of this document. However, there is one material object that has been my greatest treasure of all. It is my little leather book. I leave to my niece Susan my "Book of Three Pages" in the hope that she will find it to be as important in her life as it has been in mine'."

"Miss Jensen," continued the attorney, "there is no indication of where this book might be."

"I know where it is. It's here in my purse. It has been since before the funeral."

"Ah, I see. Then I presume we can all consider the matter before us to be concluded." The lawyer offered his hand to Susan who took it, and then he began gathering his papers.

***

Half an hour later Susan sat in a nearby park in the shady solitude of a great, old, mulberry tree. From her purse she took the maroon colored leather book, noticing that, as always, it appeared to be brand new in spite of its considerable age. Immediately she saw that the intricately tooled cover had an image of two flowers. Not the lilacs that had been there for so long, but a pair of rose blossoms. As she gently ran her fingers over the finely detailed contours she felt that she could detect just the faintest scent of her favorite flower. Susan realized then that the tiny leather volume was telling her that life stretched far beyond the few years she would spend in this world.

Susan opened the little volume, slowly examined each of its three pages, and with a sad heart gently closed it again. Holding it against one cheek she closed her eyes and thought about how little anyone knows about what life really is. Experiencing sights and scents like being in an elegant garden of multicolored roses, the lady pilot, with one deformed foot, was overwhelmed with a sense of eternal well-being. For even though each of its pages was now completely blank, she knew that the little Book of Three Pages was destined to play a profound role in her life.

The End

THE WATERHOLE

Summer, 1992, State of Arizona

"Right over there on the far side of that draw," said Jack."That's where I found it. We have to walk from here."

"Yeah, OK," said Lou. "Sure makes you wonder what happened out there. What made ya come lookin' here, anyway?"

"I'd seen the place from the air."

Lou knew that Jack, being an amateur prospector, often flew a light plane about the desert looking for unusual land features.

"Last year I noticed the peculiar color of the rock out there and thought I'd like to see it on the ground. So, last month I hiked over to that flat spot on the far side."

"Looks from here like a place tryin' to be a lake, but can't quite make it" said Lou."

"Yeah. It probably collects a little water when a thunderstorm dumps its load in the right place. Might even have been a spring there back before the water table dropped so much."

"Let's head out," said Lou. "No tellin' what else is there."

Jack crunched his gray, cowboy hat down on his head as he got out of the truck, then picked up his day pack and wiggled it onto his back. Next he checked his pockets to be sure he had the keys to the Chevy pickup, looked around inside, picked up a stray Baby Ruth bar, then locked and closed the doors.

Lou had finished getting his own equipment together, but his was different. His fascination with the Arizona desert was the search for artifacts. So, in addition to a similar pack with lunch and water, Lou had brought along a modern metal detector capable of finding objects buried in the ground.

The two men began their hike across the low, basalt ridge, each thinking of Jack's remarkable discovery and eager to see what else they might find.

Winter, 1861, Territory of New Mexico

It was barely daybreak as the six-year-old Apache boy heard the two women in their rough shelter make the noises that meant the beginning of another day. Wrapped in the worn cowhide he used for protection against the cold night, he wanted to be unnoticed as long as possible as he lay on the hard ground. For as cold and uncomfortable as his night had been, he knew that soon he would be sent to fetch firewood, and it was a lot colder outside.

It had been a bad winter and the worst was not yet over. Even as toughened as it was by generations of living in a land that was either too hot or too cold, and always too dry, the little band of Chiricahua Apaches was smaller than it had been the previous summer. The scarcity of game and the cold, windy winter had taken away one child and two old people.

That's why most of the men were gone on this particular morning. Nearby ranches had cattle that would not be guarded well in the bad weather. For the little group of families, the hazard of raiding nearby ranches was less important than the starvation they were facing.

"Chato!"

The boy was startled by the call, even though he expected it. With only his name and a swing of her arm, the old woman had ordered the boy to get after his part of the preparation for the new day. As he lay for a few moments more in relative comfort, little Chato thought of the cold rocks and frost outside, and the dead branches of mesquite he would search for.

Chato was getting to his feet when he heard distant voices mixed with the sounds of men on horseback. Were the men of the camp returning? No, they had not had horses when they left two days earlier.

Chato stood up and stepped outside. There wasn't the normal feel of dawn in his Apache camp. No sound of yapping dogs. They had all been eaten long ago. But there were sounds, lots of them, and Chato knew they weren't right. He heard horses, saddle leather, and harness noises mixed with loud explosions. Men were shouting too, but the words had no meaning.

Suddenly Chato was pushed aside by his mother's sister as she came outside. Then, to his amazement, the woman fell to the ground with blood flowing from her back.

As Chato shouted in fright at what he had seen, he felt his mother grab him roughly and pull him to her side just as a dark object filled his vision. A horse, steaming with sweat and breath in the cold air, lunged to a stop almost on top of the mother and boy. Chato could see the leg of the horse's rider, the light blue uniform pants, and something else too.

The rider's leg had a bright yellow stripe running its full length. The yellow striped leg, the saddle, the excited horse, the shouted, meaningless words, and many explosions overwhelmed Chato, and he threw his frail arms in front of his face. He felt himself held harder against his mother's side as she faced the mounted soldier.

Little Chato wondered why anyone would have such a long knife as the soldier swung his cavalry saber at the two Indians. Then Chato felt himself being pushed to the ground by his mother. And the little boy saw his mother's head lean sideways, partly sliced from her shoulders as she fell. Chato screamed in a long wail that ended only when his young lungs were empty.

Chato knew the blood now covering himself and his mother had been caused by the strange, long knife in the hands of the rider on the huge horse. A man with a beautiful, golden stripe down his leg. Like a rising flame, the yellow color grew in the boy's mind, overwhelming his thoughts until he fainted and fell to the ground in the pile of death that had been his family.

Half an hour later Chato raised up and, revolted by what he saw, ran into the shelter. Slowly sticking his head back outside, he yelled for help. There was no reply—only the sounds of a cold wind like the breath of death itself. The boy went to his cowhide bed that had seemed so secure a short time earlier and curled up to get as warm as he could.

***

The next day Chato heard more sounds outside the shelter. Suddenly the entrance flap was thrown open and the form of an Apache man was silhouetted against the gray sky. The boy had never seen this stranger before and tried to speak as the man picked him up, carried him outside, and handed him to another man on horseback.

In this way Chato was taken away by another band of Apaches. He had no way of knowing that his father, uncle, and two cousins had been killed as they attempted to raid a nearby ranch. Soldiers had backtracked the raiders and cleaned out the camp that had spawned the raid. The confused young boy was the only survivor of his little Chiricahua band.

May, 1862, Hartford, Connecticut

As young Billy Winthrop held a small piece of high carbon steel in his hand, he savored the sounds and smells around him. The hum and flapping noises from the various wide, leather belts driving the arrangement of jackshafts near the ceiling of the shop and the odor of burned cutting oil coming from the grinding wheel surrounded the boy as he attempted to sharpen a lathe bit.

Barely twelve years old, Billy had been spending time in the shop for years and was now beginning serious lessons in the machinist's trade. He knew he must take his newly sharpened bit to his grandfather for inspection. He hoped he had done the job well, perhaps well enough to get a chance to try it on a piece of scrap metal in the lathe.

"OK Grandpa, how's this?" the boy asked as he took his latest effort to a gray-haired man wearing a leather apron.

"Well, let's see what you have here," said the old man as he pushed his wire rim spectacles into better position. With much ceremony he examined the piece of metal and pronounced the work satisfactory.

"Could be better," he said, "but satisfactory. After I finish here we'll go see if you can turn some steel with it."

Billy had it made; he would get to operate the lathe! He could hardly contain himself, but knew he must wait for his grandfather to finish straightening the rifle barrel he had been working on.

The old man peered through the newly bored rifle barrel at the open sky visible through a distant window. He rotated the barrel several ways and studied its interior with great care, looking for reflected light patterns that weren't quite right.

Next the rifle barrel was laid with each end on a lead supporting block and a third block, controlled by a heavy, mechanical press, was poised to push the middle of the barrel downward. Slowly and carefully the man pulled a lever and the barrel was bent—ever so slightly—by the force of the press.

This process was followed by more inspections, realignments of the barrel in its blocks, and more bending. Finally, the man stood back with his hands on his hips, and said, "Well, what do you think?"

This was the boy's cue to look through the barrel for a few moments, and with all the wisdom of his 12 years say, "Looks pretty good, Grandpa." Billy couldn't really interpret the subtle reflections within a newly machined rifle barrel, but he knew that few men anywhere knew the art of straightening a rifle barrel, and that one day the skill would be his.

"OK, lets see if you can chuck some steel in that lathe. Then we'll see how badly this bit of yours tears it up!"

The proud old man put his hand on his grandson's shoulder as they walked toward the lathe. They both believed that some day Billy would be a master gunsmith, just like his grandfather.

September, 1866, Territory of Arizona

A frail man, an eleven-year-old boy, and two animals were making slow progress across an open desert basin. They were returning home from a visit where the man had traded clothing made by the two women in his household for the old horse he was riding.

Wuj, as the old Apache was called, sat on his mount, hunched over by the burden of the more than 60 winters he had survived. The horse, a worn out cavalry pony, was bent low by the rider's weight, and by its own years of sparse, desert grazing. The boy was sitting on a burro that mindlessly followed the broken-down horse.

As they approached the ridge of low hills at the east end of a shallow valley, Chato noticed that the impatient burro was pressing the horse to pick up the pace. But, feeling the need to relieve himself, Chato stopped the burro, slid to the ground, and stepped toward a nearby yucca.

"Chato!" shouted the old Apache. "The burro is leaving!"

The burro was indeed trotting away toward the damp earth and vegetation it could smell somewhere ahead. Chato made a halfhearted attempt to catch the animal without success, but he wasn't concerned. He knew they would find the burro drinking from a spring not far away. This suited the boy just fine since he was thirsty too.

Surprised, Chato watched Wuj urge his tired mount forward in an effort to catch the burro, but this too was futile. Turning to Chato, the old San Carlos Apache delivered a profane scolding that the Chiricahua boy only partly understood.

Sometime later Wuj stopped his horse and Chato, who had been following on foot at his side, stopped too.

"See what you have done," said Wuj. His weather-beaten face was the color of saddle leather and contorted with anger as he indicated the distant scene in front of them.

Chato could see a juniper tree and some scrub oaks, enough to mark a good spring. And the burro was standing there too. The boy still didn't see much cause for concern, and started toward the burro and the water.

"No!" shouted Wuj.

"Why not? There's water, and the burro——"

"No! The burro is dead. We don't go there."

Again, Chato did not understand. "Why not?" he asked.

"See that place," said Wuj. "Remember it. It looks good but it is not. It is a place of bad spirits who do not like animals or men!"

"Can't we get the burro?"

"No. The burro is dead! If you go there and take anything you will die. The burro has taken water and grass. The burro is dead!"

Chato looked at the burro standing in the grass. It didn't look dead. But that is what the old man said, and the boy believed that it was so. The burro was dead.

The two turned and resumed their trek across the desert. A few minutes later Chato looked back again at the burro and saw that the animal had fallen to its front knees with its hindquarters still in the air.

"So that is what a dead burro looks like," thought Chato. He looked again at the grassy draw and its surrounding hills. He would remember this place of bad spirits, just as he had been told.

June, 1870, San Carlos Reservation, Territory of Arizona

Chato, in his fifteenth year, hoped that none of the soldiers would notice him as he left the San Carlos reservation. The young Apache walked quickly, his thoughts full of wonder and excitement at what lay ahead, for he had reached his time of vision.

Chato trotted into the nearby hills until he reached a high ridge that felt good to him. He began talking to the spirits he was sure were nearby and singing songs that had been taught to him for this purpose. Occasionally he built a small fire and burned some of the dried plants he had brought with him. Breathing the smoke was difficult at first; it caused much coughing. But the smoke was important, and he continued to inhale the acrid fumes.

After two days, with no food and only a little water, Chato found that the smoke was good. It helped make the bad feelings in his stomach go away, and it made his reasons for being where he was much clearer. The sky became a richer, more brilliant blue, with billowy clouds so intensely white that they were hard to look at. He felt that he could reach out and touch the scrub oak trees in the valley below, or put his hand into the clouds in the sky above. He had become one with the entire world around him.

Late in the afternoon of the last day, Chato burned all of his remaining medicine leaves, fell to the ground, and experienced his vision.

Chato thought he was awakening as his body writhed with convulsions and shivered. In spite of the early summer weather he was cold, and could feel the frozen ground of a winter he had known long ago. Nothing was warm but the nearby bodies of two Apache women.

Suddenly, like an explosion of darkness, a huge horse appeared in front of him with a giant rider in the saddle, a rider whose sky-blue uniform leg had a brilliant yellow stripe. The young Apache groaned in horror at the vile scene that seemed so familiar.

Feeling rage as he had never known it, Chato reached out to the yellow-striped leg and grabbed it with his own two hands. Like floating leaves caught in a whirlpool, the sky and horse spun about as he jerked the rider from the saddle. Now the horse did not seem so big, and the man was smaller too, and yet Chato's hands were very big, and growing bigger. His arms felt powerful, and his shoulders felt good as he gripped the yellow-striped leg.

Chato smashed the rider to the ground, beating him against the rocks as a man might kill a freshly caught fish. His enormous hands whipped the man against the ground again and again, until all that was left was the bloody leg.

Chato raised the leg high above his head and screamed from the depths of his soul, just as he had once done on a cold winter morning long ago. He looked up and saw that the object clutched in his powerful hands was so soaked with blood that the yellow stripe had turned to dark red. Then the young Apache noticed that his powerful hands had turned yellow in the light of the setting sun and looked beautiful against the brilliant blue sky.

***

The next morning Chato walked unsteadily into the San Carlos encampment, his normally lean frame more emaciated than usual because of the fasting he had undergone. Though none of the white men knew he had been gone, his own people knew why he had left the camp. They took him to see a man known throughout the Apache people as having the gift of understanding spiritual experiences like that which Chato had just been through.

The shaman listened as Chato described his vision. He asked about the young man's feelings and about what was in his heart. Chato answered, describing the mixture of horror and beauty that he had seen.

With his eyes closed, the old man sat thoughtfully for several minutes, his body rocking forward and back, and then he spoke, his raspy voice frail with age.

"Keep this with you," he grunted as he handed the boy a rounded, light-blue stone. "It is a piece of the sky where your hands fought the bloody leg. It will protect you from that enemy."

Then the old man told Chato that his name was gone. He would have a new one. The young Apache would now be called Yellow Hand.

Clutching his blue stone and weak with hunger and thirst, Yellow Hand walked feebly out of the older man's presence onto the dusty road where he met a single soldier riding a gray mare. As the white man passed by, he spat a wad of chewing tobacco toward the young Apache's feet. Yellow Hand realized then that he could no longer stay at San Carlos, or on any other reservation.

April, 1874, Camp Smith, Maryland

Lieutenant William Winthrop sat in a wicker chair in a room furnished like that on any other military post—functional and basically dull. A staff sergeant, trying to look busy with two or three papers, sat at a simple desk. Billy had been waiting for less than a minute when he heard a voice mutter something from the next room through a partially open door.

"The cap'n will see you now, Lieutenant," said the sergeant.

Billy stood up, straightened his uniform, and with his hat under his left arm walked into the next room. This room, also dull, had a single desk not much different from that occupied by the sergeant outside. Billy walked up to the desk and came to attention.

"Second Lieutenant William Winthrop reporting as ordered, sir."

The man behind the desk stood up, offered his right hand across the desk, and said, "At ease Lieutenant. Glad t' meet ya. Pull up that chair and have a sit."

Surprised at the officer's lack of formality, Billy hesitated.

"Hey, come on fella! Sit down. If we could get outta this office I'd buy you a beer."

"Thank you sir" replied Billy as he took a seat.

"Don't look so surprised, Lieutenant. I'm just real pleased the way you decorated the scoreboard up at the Walnut Hill shoot. You made us infantry look good by beatin' the whiskers off them horse soldiers and civilians."

The captain was referring to a recent Massachusetts Rifle Association tournament in which a few infantry and cavalry soldiers had participated.

"I should have done better" replied Billy.

"Yeah, sure. I know about your score. If that one shot had been a hair's breadth closer t' center you'd of had a perfect 400—joined the 400 club. But you beat the best of 'em by three points anyhow!"

"It was my privilege to represent the United States Infantry sir. Are you also a competition shooter?"

"Yeah, I've won a few shoots with the service carbine, but I ain't in your class. I favor shootin' the Colt, myself. Hey, let me see your weapon, if you don't mind."

"Yes sir," said Billy, as he stood, opened the flap on his holster, removed his revolver, and handed it butt first to the captain.

"Hey, just as I expected. Standard issue cap and ball, well cared for, clean as a gnat's ass. Well, I got a bit of a surprise for ya. But first tell me about the rifle you used up at the shoot. You really built it up yourself?"

"Yes sir. With a lot of help. My grandfather worked for the Sharps Rifle Company in Hartford. He learned barrel making from August Zischang."

"That the German feller who builds them nice target rifles?"

"Yes sir, it is. I grew up hanging around the shops and picked up some of the gunsmith's trade."

"Well, gunsmith or not, you're about the best rifleman t' come out of The Point in a long time. Accordin' to your service record, your habit o' winnin' shoots is what got ya into the Academy."

"Hey," continued the captain, "I'd sure like t' see that rifle of yours. Heard you built it up from one of them new Sharps Creedmoor actions."

"Yes sir," responded Billy. "I would be glad to bring it by your office at your convenience."

"Good, any time. Oh hey, I told you about a little surprise. Here, take this paper over t' Sergeant Stevens, the quartermaster." Reaching across the desk, he handed the paper to Billy.

"Yes sir. May I ask what it's all about?"

"You'll see when you get there, Lieutenant. And good luck at your new post."

"Thank you sir," replied Billy. "About my new assignment. I was expecting orders today."

"Hey, I forgot. That's what you came by here for, ain't it?"

Opening a desk drawer, the captain took out another paper and handed it to Billy.

"Looks like you're goin' to a place called 'Soldier's Farewell.' Way t' hell out west somewhere."

Billy looked at the paper with considerable interest. Like any young man with adventure in his soul, he wanted to share in the excitement of his times. He had missed the Civil War by being too young, which was probably just as well. That thing had been a mess. But he had dreamed about the taming of the west and knew that the menace of the savage Indians had not yet been completely cleaned up.

Billy had worked hard to get an assignment out west—hopefully along the Mexican border. He knew that being an ordinance officer attached to the infantry would be a handicap. Most units in the Arizona and New Mexico territories were cavalry—the "horse soldiers" the captain had referred to. But Soldier's Farewell? Billy had never heard of the place.

Before he could finish examining the orders the captain interrupted. "Don't look so concerned. You're going out t' the territories just like you asked. And you're gettin' your damn transfer to the cavalry. Why the hell you'd want to do that, I don't know. But anyhow, on your way I've arranged a little side trip."

Billy raised his eyes inquisitively, saying nothing.

"It seems, Lieutenant, that out there they're gonna have a little shootin' match. Some damn celebration or some such. A tournament with local military boys shootin', even some Mexican Army fellas too. Can ya believe that?"

Billy listened, with growing interest.

"Before you get to your new post and quit bein' a honest foot soldier you're gonna be the only infantryman in the whole shoot. Me and other folks at this here post are lookin' forward to hearin' how you shot the socks off all them horse soldiers, whichever side of the border they come from."

Embarrassed by the flattery, Billy replied, "Thank you sir. I will be proud to represent the U.S. Infantry one more time."

At that point the captain stood up and Billy quickly followed his lead. The two officers shook hands as the lieutenant stepped backward and saluted. When the captain returned the salute Billy turned toward the door.

"Oh hey Lieutenant!"

Billy stopped and turned back around.

"Don't forget to bring that rifle by."

"No sir, my pleasure, sir."

***

Billy inquired at the sergeant's desk about the location of the post armory, and then stepped outside into the warm sunshine, his thoughts full of the promise of adventure that keeps men young.

Minutes later Billy stood at a wooden counter looking at a brown, cardboard carton that Quartermaster Sergeant Stevens had handed to him with a touch of pride and fanfare. The note Billy had been given had simply said, "This here's the guy," and bore the captain's signature.

From its size and weight Billy knew instantly what was in the box that the quartermaster handed him. Like a little boy at Christmas, he felt the wonder of new things as he opened the carton.

Inside, wrapped in waxed paper, was a new issue Single Action Army revolver chambered for the .45 Colt cartridge. The weapon was a modern technological breakthrough, much superior to the cap and ball revolver that currently graced Billy's uniform. Using self-contained cartridges, the new Colt was far faster to reload, and more reliable in bad weather. Eventually the Army would be completely switched over to the new weapon, but at the moment such prizes were usually issued to officers of higher rank than second lieutenant. Feeling a little guilty about his coming defection to the cavalry, Billy mentally thanked the enthusiastic captain.

After turning in his older sidearm and supporting accessories, Billy left the armory with the new Colt and an issue of 100 cartridges. Much like a little boy with a new toy, he headed toward the post small arms range to begin the pleasant task of mastering the new weapon.

August, 1874, Territory of New Mexico

Sergeant Andrew Broxton walked out of the adjutant's tent at the dusty village of Soldier's Farewell. Not a real army installation at all, the office was just a temporary camp to handle the recent rifle competition. Originally established as a station on the Butterfield Overland Stage route, the town had been a convenient location for American and Mexican military units, along with a few interested civilians, to gather and compare marksmanship skills.

After carefully checking the wind, the old sergeant fired a wad of tobacco juice in the general direction of the road, then hitched his belt higher against the ample belly of his stocky frame. It seemed that Army clothing was always built for skinny men.

Sergeant Broxton had just been assigned a dull, but not unexpected, detail. He was to take a supply wagon, now mostly empty, back to Fort Huachuca. A few days of drudgery accompanied by one of the troop's less promising new recruits. This kind of work was mostly what the Army was all about now. The exciting days of the Indian wars were pretty much over. But this was only part of what annoyed the sergeant this day.

Sergeant Broxton had been informed that on the trip he would be under the command of a Lieutenant Winthrop. Having an officer along was annoying enough, but this officer was the *infantry* lieutenant from back east who had beaten all comers at the recent shooting match—all of the contestants, including Sergeant Broxton, who considered himself to be an expert with the Springfield carbine.

"Jenkins! Get your butt over here," yelled the sergeant. "You and me gotta drive that damn wagon back t' the fort. We're leaving soon's I find that red-legged lieutenant we gotta take with us."

Like a surly schoolboy the young cavalry private walked over, saying nothing.

"Get the wagon together, fill them water barrels," said the sergeant. "Draw us ca'tridges and rations for ten days. I'll hunt up the damn passenger."

Private Jenkins noticed the odor of alcohol and snuff on the sergeant's breath as the older man spoke.

Billy was waiting at the stage depot, taking in the sights and sounds of the frontier culture. Winning the shooting match hadn't been difficult since it had been conducted in a somewhat rustic attempt at tournament style shooting. This emphasized precision marksmanship at longer ranges, not the fast and ready combat shooting most of the local men were used to. Still, one Mexican corporal and a couple of cavalrymen from Billy's new duty post had demonstrated considerable skill. One had been the sergeant Billy saw approaching from across the dusty road.

"Sergeant Broxton, reporting for detail, sir."

As the sergeant spoke he stared at the maroon colored ordinance officer leg stripe on Billy's infantry uniform. Billy noticed this, but was used to it by now. He knew he stood out as a stranger among the cavalry soldiers whose leg stripe was yellow. But that would change as soon as he reached his new post.

"Hello Sergeant. I understand I am to accompany you to Fort—ah, to the fort." Billy wasn't sure how to pronounce the name of the newly established Fort Huachuca spelled out in his orders.

"The word's wa—chu—ka, Lieutenant. Y' kin skip the 'H' at the front."

"Huachuca," said Billy, pronouncing the name correctly. "Thank you, Sergeant. Incidentally, I noticed the good job of shooting you did yesterday."

"Not as good as you done, sir."

"I also noticed that your men call you Andy. With your permission I will too."

"Suit y'self, sir."

"Well Andy, you seem to be a first rate carbine man. Maybe you can show me how a working soldier uses the old Springfield!"

Surprised by Billy's friendly manner, Sergeant Broxton relaxed some, and thought about maybe shooting that rifle he'd seen the lieutenant use. Maybe the trip wouldn't be so bad. Still, here he was, a sixteen-year veteran Indian fighter in the Arizona Territory, stuck under the command of a gold bar infantry officer who'd just seen his first cactus. Andy wondered if he could find a way to get a quick drink before they left.

***

The next day the little detail was making slow progress, with men and horses feeling the midday heat. "Pull up there on that flat spot," said Andy to Private Jenkins who had been sharing the supply wagon's wooden seat. "You can give them animals some water while I take a piss."

The younger soldier brought the two-horse team to a stop and stepped down to fetch the canvas bag he would fill from one of the wagon's water barrels and use to water each animal in turn.

"Be a mite more comfortable on the wagon Lieutenant, if you're tired of that saddle," said Andy.

"No, that's all right Sergeant, I'd rather stay mounted."

Billy was riding a cavalry horse that as an officer he had been issued for the trip to the fort. Sensitive about his impending transfer from his current infantry status, Billy was not going to arrive at his new cavalry post seated in a horse-drawn wagon. Removing his hat and wiping his sweaty forehead with his sleeve he stepped to the ground to water both himself and his mount.

"Man it's hot," muttered Billy "How can anyone make a living out here anyway? You can't farm this rock and sand."

"Well, ain't much farmin'," replied Andy, "but lots of ranchin'. Beef and horses, in the valleys they's some vegetables."

Billy, used to the streams and green valleys of the eastern part of the country, was still uncomfortable in the desert. "A man could die in a day out here without these water barrels we carry," he muttered.

"An Indian wouldn't. They's always water out here someplace and them damn 'paches always knows where it's at."

"Lordy, how can they feed themselves in a place like this?"

"They ain't nothing but bones and leather, get what they eat by grubbin' around the ground, or stealin' from honest folk," said Andy as he fired tobacco juice at a nearby saguaro cactus.

Knowing that Billy had never seen an Apache village of any kind, Andy continued. "When ya see one'a their camps someday, take a look at what them squaws feeds their men. Rabbits, squirrels, snakes, dog meat—any kind of damn root they can grub up. Them camps stink t' high heaven."

"OK Sergeant," said Billy, remembering that he was officially in command of the little group. "We have a few more hours before sunset. We had better make good use of them."

Andy caught Private Jenkins's attention, and both soldiers climbed onto the wagon and started the team on its way. Billy mounted his pony, thinking about what life must be like for the primitive savages.

***

Two hours after daybreak the next day the warming air and lack of breeze promised another hot day.

"Too bad we all ain't on horseback," said the old sergeant.

"Why is that?"

"Just off to the west there, across them hills a short day's ride they's a good road comes down from the north. Be a lot shorter trip."

Their route, clearly marked on the map Billy had been given, had to make a considerable detour around the south end of the ridges that lay to the west.

"What's the country like over there, anyway?"

"Well don't go t' thinkin' you could take this wagon across. They's some lava rocks out there we'd never get through. That's why the road's where it is."

After another shot of tobacco juice, Andy added, "But saddled up like you are, you could do it easy."

Andy knew that Billy could never leave his little command just to take the short cut but the thought was a pleasing one anyway. The veteran cavalry sergeant was not looking forward to arriving at Fort Huachuca sitting on a wagon, and being under the command of a lieutenant wearing red striped infantryman's pants.

"Well, we ought to be there by tomorrow night anyhow," said Andy.

***

A few minutes later the little group was crossing a rougher area, heavily covered with greasewood and mesquite. Billy had moved his mount up near the left side of the wagon to make it easier to talk to the sergeant, who was seated on the left side of the wagon bench. Private Jenkins sat to the right, half asleep, while tending the team.

A flicker of motion was the beginning. Billy saw something move at the edge of the road near the wagon team. An Apache hidden in the brush fired one rifle shot directly into the head of the left hand horse. The animal died instantly and collapsed to the ground.

At the same time, Billy heard a hideous scream and saw another man rise up, right near the forequarters of his own mount. The horse shied to the right and came back on his haunches, startled by the noise and sudden appearance of the nearer Apache. Billy lost his seat and slid from the saddle, but grabbed his carbine as he fell. As Yellow Hand had jumped up beside Billy's mount, hoping to upset the rider, he had also released an arrow that found its mark a scant ten feet away, deep in Andy's chest.

But Andy, already in motion, scooped up his own carbine and fired directly into the head of the first attacker. A fraction of a second earlier and he would have saved Private Jenkins's life. But the Apache had fired again, his second shot of the day, and put a fatal bullet through the younger soldier.

Yellow Hand realized that Billy's horse now had no rider, and in a moment he himself was mounted. In a few seconds more, he and the horse were gone.

As he regained his footing, Billy caught Andy by the shoulders as the wagon, sluing badly because of the fowled harness and the uneven ground, rolled onto its side.

Minutes after the attack, Billy had made the wounded man as comfortable as he could in the shade of the overturned wagon box. He looked at the wooden shaft stuck deep in the soldier's chest.

"Should we try to get that thing out?" asked Billy, unsure about what he should do.

"Leave me alone! I seen enough arrow holes to know you ain't gonna fix this one. Just leave me be."

The wagon had been pulled by the bay mare the first Apache had killed and a smaller gray which was struggling to stand up. White, splintered bone stuck out from the gray's left foreleg which had broken when the bay fell and tangled the harness. The gray's eyes were round and wild with pain and panic.

With his new Colt revolver in hand Billy walked closer to the struggling animal. Choosing a spot on the animal's forehead, Billy took aim. With an explosion of fire and smoke, a 255 grain lead slug solved all the problems the gray would ever have in this world.

Billy then turned back to his wounded companion, frustrated and embarrassed because there was nothing he could do.

Andy slowly raised up on one elbow and said, "Looky. There's that damn 'pache, sittin' on your horse." After a bit of coughing, Andy continued. "You're the fine-assed infantry shooter; get 'im!"

Billy saw the Apache sitting quietly in the saddle several hundred yards away.

***

Yellow Hand was watching the wrecked wagon, safely out of range of the .45-70 carbines he knew the soldiers carried. He was now alone, his only ally dead. He had lost his bow while mounting the horse and the rifle the two men had shared was gone. He was mildly curious about the shot he heard come from the wagon, but was more concerned about something he had seen during the attack.

While upsetting Billy's horse, Yellow Hand had noticed the rider's leg. A sky blue leg with a blood red stripe instead of the yellow stripe other soldiers wore. The enemy from his vision years ago!

Clearly Bloody Leg was there because he expected Yellow Hand's attack. The Apache, feeling that he was now about to be tested by a fearsome old enemy, took comfort from the blue stone he wore in a leather medicine bag around his neck. As he summoned all his nerve to fight back, Yellow Hand felt encouraged because he had gained his enemy's horse, a great accomplishment. Now he would try to get a rifle from the wrecked wagon.

***

Thinking about Andy's demand, Billy realized that the savage was not as far away as he thought. So he dug through the jumbled wagon wreck and found a long, slim box made of finely finished walnut and fitted with polished brass corners, hinges, and latches. On the top was a brass plate that read, "William B. Winthrop, Hartford, Connecticut."

Opening the case, Billy removed its contents. As he held the target rifle in his hands, he thought of the pleasant hours of patient machining and woodworking he had put into building it. His grandfather's shop seemed far, far away.

Billy looked again at the savage and estimated the distance to be about three hundred yards. He held the rifle to his shoulder and sighted at the distant target. He carefully compared the apparent size of the horse and man to his memory of the standard black disk shaped paper target at which he had last fired the rifle. After careful thought he judged the distance to be closer to 400 yards.

Next Billy arranged a roll of bedding from the wagon as an improvised rest, and laid a single brass cartridge beside it. After getting himself into a comfortable position with the rifle to his shoulder and supported by his arm across the improvised rest, he gave thought to the wind. The last time he had fired the rifle there had been a distinct crosswind from the right, one that he knew was good for about three inches of drift at the 200 yard range at which he had been shooting. His sights were adjusted correctly for this condition. This meant that he should expect the rifle to deliver its lead slug to a point about six inches to the right and about eighteen inches below his point of aim at the more distant range of his new target on this hot, windless, day.

After thinking through all his preparations, he took a deep breath, let some of it out, and took careful aim at a point just above and to the left of the savage's body. Slowly he increased his squeeze on the trigger, with only the muscles of his right thumb and index finger doing the job, until he heard a distinct click.

This was just what Billy had expected. No motion of the sights or his body. His experience as a precision marksman told him that had the rifle been loaded, the shot would have been right.

Billy opened the action of the rifle and loaded the bright, brass .44-100-550 cartridge into the rifle's chamber, thinking of the time when he had loaded the primer, black powder, and paper patched lead bullet into that cartridge case. A new, experimental, target cartridge he had been helping to develop. It seemed a long time ago.

Billy repeated his process of lining up on his target, which still hadn't moved, and began carefully increasing the squeeze on the trigger. This time he felt the familiar kick of the rifle as its muzzle exploded in a cloud of white smoke.

***

Yellow Hand had been sitting in the saddle watching the wagon when he saw the puff of smoke. During the next second his mind started to register surprise that the soldiers would fire at him at such a long range. But a fraction of a second was all he had before he felt a sharp pain in his right leg as his newly acquired horse buckled and slumped to the ground. The agile Apache was off the horse and on the ground himself before the crippled animal could roll over on him. Billy's bullet had clipped the large muscles in the Apache's thigh and hit the pony in the spine. Since the range was even longer than Billy had estimated, his shot had been low.

Yellow Hand, familiar with a yellow leg stripe on all the other soldiers he had ever seen, thought of the blood-red stripe he had noticed on Billy's leg. He felt a surge of fear, realizing again that this was the soldier from his vision four summers earlier. And this enemy, Bloody Leg, had been given special power in the form of a strong rifle that could be used at great distances. Realizing that he was about to be tested even more severely, the Apache again took comfort from the blue medicine stone he had been given on his name day long ago.

The wounded horse was whinnying in fright, slashing at the ground with its front hooves, trying to stand in spite of its paralyzed hindquarters. Yellow Hand paid no attention to the stricken animal. Of no further use, it would die in time.

Using a strip torn from his shirt and staying low and almost out of sight, Yellow Hand tied a thick bundle of grass tightly to the wound in his leg. Ignoring the pain, he thought about his problem. "Could he fight Bloody Leg and get the strong rifle? Was that what his vision had meant?"

***

At the wagon Sergeant Broxton knew, even in his pain-clouded mind, that killing the Apache at that range was unlikely, but it had felt good to demand that somebody try. With fading vision he had seen the horse collapse and the Indian slip to the ground, apparently unhurt.

"Christ, Lieutenant, you're gonna be some kind of cavalry man. First y' fall off your horse, then you shoot the damn thing!"

Billy knew that Andy was attempting a little humor, in spite of his pain.

"Thanks for tryin'. Damn good shot anyway at that dist—"

Andy coughed up some blood, then continued. "Guess you 'n me ain't gonna' do no more shootin' together. Wanted t' show ya how a horse soldier uses a carbine. . . ."

A quiet minute later Billy realized that he was now completely alone—except for one Apache warrior.

In the still, desert air under the hot, morning sun, Billy walked over to the attacker Andy had managed to kill. Ragged clothing covered a small, lean body. The man probably didn't weigh more than 130 pounds. The dead man's tanned skin was like thin, wrinkled leather. Billy noticed the thickly callused feet and hands with dirty, broken nails.

The man's rifle lay nearby, a beat up old Henry rim fire carbine, in such poor condition Billy would not have bet it could fire. But fire it had, with unfortunate effect. Billy smashed the rifle against a nearby rock to make sure it would not be available for any further mischief.

After looking over the wrecked wagon, Billy found that he had several rifles and his new revolver, but little else. The wagon had crushed the water barrels when it rolled over, and Private Jenkin's canteen had been nearly empty at the time of the attack. Sergeant Broxton's canteen held only a little whiskey, and his own was up on the ridge with his dying horse in the possession of the very live Apache.

Realizing that he might not survive at the site of the attack long enough to be found on the relatively unused trail, Billy made plans to walk through the hills to the west. If Andy had been right, one day's walk would bring him to the more traveled wagon road.

Except for his revolver and one carbine, Billy disabled all the firearms including his match rifle which was too heavy to carry. With tools from the rifle's case, he removed part of the rifle's trigger assembly. He did so reluctantly, thinking of the hours he had spent fine-tuning that precision mechanism. But he could not risk letting any operable weapons fall into the hands of other savages.

As Billy began his trek he looked about to see what the Apache was doing. To his surprise, he saw that Yellow Hand had himself already started walking toward the hills to the west.

"He has to have water too," thought Billy, remembering what Andy had said. He decided to try to keep the savage in sight. The man might be headed toward water, and anyway, there might be a chance for another shot. So, the eastern born soldier, new to the southwest, set out in the midday sun to follow an Apache warrior across the hot, black, lava flows of the Arizona Territory.

Yellow Hand was not looking for water. He had Billy's canteen. He was moving to a better location for a new attack. But when he saw Billy start following him he was surprised by this aggressiveness. This frightened Yellow Hand, but he knew he had to fight Bloody Leg to get the strong rifle. So, without a plan, he continued across the desert toward the hills to the west.

***

Two hours later the heat of the afternoon sun and dry air had taken their toll. Billy was suffering from dehydration and in danger of sunstroke when ahead he saw his own canteen lying in the sand. Though he knew it would be empty, he ran to it and with trembling hands shook it from side to side anyway. It sloshed! After jerking out the cork, he shoved the canteen to his mouth only to find the stench of warm urine. Revolted with disgust he fell retching to the ground, weak and a little dizzy. After a few minutes he got to his feet, wobbling like a drunk for the first few steps, and began again to follow the vile Apache's footprints in the sand, realizing that the savage knew he was being followed.

Yellow Hand was trying to keep ahead of the evil thing that was following him, but found himself weak, unable to escape. He did not understand that this weakness was caused by loss of blood from the wound that had opened anew in his thigh. He was sure he could feel Bloody Leg reaching out to pull him back.

Approaching the low hills, Yellow Hand realized where he was. He remembered being there long ago with the old man Wuj and a burro that had died while quietly eating grass. Just beyond the ridges of black rock were some trees and a water hole. The Apache knew what would happen to anyone who tried to take anything away from that place.

Yellow Hand fell to his knees and begged the spirits of the water hole to help him. He assured them that he himself would not take anything away. He was only asking for protection from what was following him and maybe a little help in fighting the evil thing that had destroyed his family—if the spirits would choose to do so.

After watching the water hole for a while, Yellow Hand decided that it looked inviting and that as long as he took nothing away he would be tolerated by the spirits who controlled it. He began walking apprehensively toward a big juniper tree thinking of Bloody Leg, the vile thing that he knew was behind him.

Near total collapse Billy saw that Yellow Hand was heading toward a bunch of trees—toward water! Pleased with his decision to follow the savage, Billy felt some hope.

Yellow Hand walked to the edge of the water hole and knelt down. He saw that the water was clear and clean—much too clean. No animal tracks, and no sign of the usual water bugs that would be in a desert spring. This was not right. The spring was a treacherous place, as old Wuj had said. So, Yellow Hand stood up and walked away from the spring, in the direction he and the old man had taken earlier. As Yellow Hand walked, he could feel the spirits of the water hole say, "Don't go far—Wait and see." So he stopped near some rocks he felt would protect him from the strong rifle and watched Bloody Leg approach the water hole.

Having seen the Apache leave, Billy hurried to the water hole and saw the clear water. Not much, just a puddle a few inches deep and a few feet across, but more water than any man needed. He plunged his face into the pond and drank until he noticed that the water had an unpleasant, metallic taste.

Like a tired old dog Billy crawled to the shade of the juniper tree and collapsed against its rough trunk. Surprised that he was still carrying it, he laid his carbine at his side. He no longer cared about the Apache and could not have tracked the savage further anyway in the rocky lava ridges beyond the water hole. Hoping to recover strength, he lay in the shade of the tree. But he wasn't feeling better. His stomach had developed an ache that was turning into pain.

Looking around at the hills near the spring Billy realized that the strikingly colored rock was highly mineralized. Obviously there was copper and manganese present, and undoubtedly salts of other metals. Slowly he realized that the water probably contained salts of arsenic or some other poisonous metal. Minutes later he became violently ill and knew that he would never see his cavalry post at Fort Huachuca.

Remembering the Apache, Billy reached for his new Colt revolver and found comfort in its walnut grip. He wanted desperately to destroy the savage but had little strength left. He knew that if the Apache was watching, he would know Billy was dying and would come back for the guns. This gave the rifleman with the gunsmith's training an idea.

Billy reached for the carbine, opened the action, and removed the single .45-70 cartridge. Holding it by its copper case, he bit hard into the lead bullet and wrenched the cartridge apart. He then set the powder-filled case aside and jammed the lead bullet into the chamber of the carbine as far up the barrel as he could.

He then repeated the process of tearing apart two more cartridges and poured this black powder into the chamber too, behind the bullet. Then he put the original case, itself full of powder, into the chamber and closed the carbine's action. The carbine was now loaded with the usual lead bullet, but with three times the normal charge of black powder.

Next he unloaded his revolver and threw the cartridges as far as he could from the shade of the tree. He then buried the new Colt where he hoped the savage would not notice it. With dirt and mud he filled as much of the carbine's barrel as he could from the muzzle end. Finally he cleaned all signs of mud from the weapon and collapsed onto his back, holding the rifle across his chest. Then Billy relaxed as much as the pain and nausea would permit, and let himself slide into unconsciousness from which he would never recover.

***

Yellow Hand was indeed watching the water hole, hoping for signs that he had successfully gained the cooperation of the spirits of the little valley. He had seen Bloody Leg take water from the spring, and was pleased to see the violent sickness his enemy was experiencing. Yellow Hand waited patiently, long after any sign of movement near the juniper tree. His hopes mounted, for it appeared that the spirits had indeed decided to help him and soon the strong rifle would soon be his.

The sun had nearly reached the hills in the west as Yellow Hand approached the water hole. Surely the spirits of the valley had dealt with Bloody Leg. Clutching his medicine bag with its blue stone against his chest, he decided that the spirits would not object if he took away the strong rifle. It had not belonged there anyway. As he stood by the tree Yellow Hand could see that Bloody Leg was dead. And there was the strong rifle lying across the soldier's chest.

Yellow Hand grabbed the rifle and, feeling its power in his hands, held it up to the sky. In the golden light of the setting sun his hands took on a brilliant, yellow color against the deepening blue of the sky. His hands grew big and strong, and his shoulders felt powerful, just as in his vision long ago. With a howl of triumph Yellow Hand cocked the rifle and pulled the trigger.

Summer, 1992, State of Arizona

Having crossed the basalt ridge, Lou was working the flatter land he and Jack were crossing, swinging his metal detector carefully from side to side. It takes patience to search for things buried in the sand, and Lou had developed a good routine.

Jack, anxious to reach the place where he had made his discovery, had hurried to a familiar open spot.

"Here's where I found it. Right here."

"OK," said Lou as he stopped his immediate activity and caught up with his friend.

"I'd been walking down the draw, and just as I came across this low spot right about here a peculiar object caught my eye. I kicked it and it sure wasn't a rock. It looked like an old piece of pipe." Lou stared intently at the dried mud hole as though it had profound importance.

"I started digging and saw that it was the muzzle of a revolver!"

"Yeah, what luck," replied Lou. Then he began a slow, systematic search of the area, beginning at the spot Jack had pointed out.

After about 20 minutes and numerous false alarms, Lou's instrument gave a beep that was more encouraging than any he had yet come across. He swung the round antenna back and forth over the spot a few times until he was sure he had something real, then turned off the instrument and began to dig.

"Bingo,!" he shouted. In his hand he was holding a brass belt buckle.

Handing his find to Jack, Lou said, "This buckle once held up somebody's side arm, maybe even that old Colt you found."

"Let's hope that whoever owned it had just knocked off a bank," replied Jack, with a grin.

"Nope, not likely. This thing's U.S. Army issue, 19th century vintage. If that old Colt you found and this buckle came out here together, they were probably strapped around some soldier's butt."

After another half hour of searching, Jack announced, "I'm about ready for some chow, how about you?"

"Yeah, me too. I'm going to sit over by that juniper stump, and kinda think about things while I eat." Squatting down in the sand, Lou opened his pack, and took out a sandwich.

The two men ate quietly for a time, enjoying the unspoiled countryside, the pleasant, springtime weather, and their companionship. Then Jack took the old revolver out of his day pack and held it thoughtfully in his hands.

"Hey, you brought it along!" said Lou.

"Yeah. I thought it would be nice to see it out here again." He handed the somewhat rusted artifact to his friend, who had of course seen it before.

"Seems odd that it wasn't loaded. No fired cases, either."

"Probably didn't get lost in a battle of some kind then."

"Yeah, but something peculiar happened," replied Jack. "People don't just throw their gear away in a place like this."

"Well, I'm gonna get back at it," said Lou as he stuffed the remains of his lunch into his pack. "I'm gonna work around this dead tree some. Must of been more water here when it was alive—maybe made some shade. Somebody else might of thought it was a good place to sit, like we did."

Lou got up, and resumed his search of the area, beginning around the old stump. Just a few minutes later, still not far from the dead juniper tree, he was rewarded by a signal much stronger than any so far that day.

"Whoa, I got somethin' with a little size to it here," shouted Lou. Laying the metal detector aside, he began digging. Jack knelt beside Lou and together they dug up the source of the signal. It was a little rusted, but easily recognizable.

"Jesus! A rifle! This thing's an old Trap Door Springfield!" Lou could hardly contain his excitement at what he had found.

"Yeah, but look at it," exclaimed Jack.

The breech end of the barrel was split open, with jagged ends of steel bent sharply outward. Clearly the mechanism had failed to contain the explosion the last time it had been fired.

"I'd hate to have been the poor bastard who fired that thing last," muttered Jack. "Like having a small hand grenade go off in your face. Looks like some soldier got his out here a long time ago."

But even though they continued their search, the two friends never found the few fragments of dried leather and the sky-blue turquoise lying just below the surface at their feet. The remains of a medicine bag that had once hung on a thong around the neck of an Apache warrior.

The End

TIMETANGLE IN TALAVERA CANYON

New Mexico State University, March, 2007

As he sat at his desk in his office, Professor Miguel Anaya's left hand trembled as he read the photocopied document he was holding, so he laid it down beside the unopened letter. As an expert on military history, he had examined hundreds of similar copies of musty old papers from government archives, but discovering this one had made him doubt his own sanity.

In his right hand he fondled a small, brass object, worn shiny by countless hours of such almost subconscious treatment. It had never been far from Miguel's person at any time since his accident—or whatever it was—more than twenty years earlier.

After staring absently at the brass twenty-gauge shotgun shell in his hand, he rubbed his thumb one more time across the head stamp indicating that it had been manufactured by the U. S. Army's Frankford Arsenal in the year 1882. Miguel had always told himself that he had experienced only momentary mental confusion, an aberration brought on by shock from the careless hiking accident that had crippled his leg. But then, shaking his head in frustration, Miguel squeezed the brass object tightly in his hand, because he knew he had been right there when Abner fired that old shotgun shell— much more than one hundred years earlier.

Miguel's attention was drawn one more time to the unopened letter lying in the center of his otherwise clear desktop. Addressed in pencil, it was heavy enough to show that it contained something more than just a letter. He was almost afraid to open the envelope because it could contain certain proof that his hallucination had been no such thing.

New Mexico's Mogollon Mountains, Springtime, 1984

Miguel Anaya was miserable, lying in the patch of brush with his shoulder shoved against a prickly pear cactus. He wasn't moving at all;

he was just assessing his situation and mentally chastising himself for the careless misstep of the last few seconds. The cactus hurt his shoulder, but not as much as the single Spanish Dagger plant that had jabbed his rump. These things were painful all right, but not nearly as important as the damage to his left leg.

The young assistant professor slowly managed to stand up on his good leg. One attempt at walking told him that he had twisted his leg badly, maybe even broken something. With many hundreds of miles of hiking experience in New Mexico's mountains and deserts, Miguel should not have made the careless misstep that caused his fall down a twelve-foot embankment. With the shame of the foolish mistake hurting his ego nearly as much as his physical injuries, Miguel cursed himself as he stood there. He realized full well that because he was alone in the Gila Wilderness miles from any human contact, his damaged leg was a serious, even life-threatening, problem.

Ten minutes later Miguel had crawled back to the little used trail he had been following and was relieved to find that the cactus injury, though painful because of all the tiny cactus spines he could not remove from his shoulder, was not important. And he had been lucky with the Spanish dagger plant. He had fallen on only one of the sharp, sturdy stalks and the resulting wound, though painful, would not cause much difficulty. But the damage to his leg was serious business.

Miguel had been careless, but he wasn't a fool about getting along in the wilderness. His pack contained plenty of dried food, enough water to last three days more if used carefully, and he had lots of adhesive bandage tape for just such eventualities as sprained joints. Using some of the tape he managed to tie three sotol stalks together into a crude sort of crutch, and found that he could hobble along, slowly.

About an hour before sunset Miguel Anaya had progressed only a few hundred yards along his chosen route to a ridge top that he knew would take him to the head of Talavera Canyon, and a few miles down the canyon was where he had left his truck. Clearly Miguel was going to have to spend an extra night in the mountains.

Miguel wondered about his chances of meeting another hiker, or hunter, and getting some help. As he rested, standing on his good leg thinking about such things, he heard a noise that immediately got his attention. Gunfire. Far away, but distinct, and quite a lot of it. He thought he could almost hear some yelling or howling, faintly, mixed with the shooting.

Miguel thought of his own Glock handgun that was in his pack, and considered trying to signal by firing three fast shots, something that was a universal emergency signal among hunters, at least in years past. But the gunfire had been faint, a long distance away, and upwind from him. He knew that there was no chance that those folks, who had now stopped their shooting, would hear his pistol. It was better to save his limited ammunition in case some better signaling opportunity arose. With that thought in mind, Miguel rearranged his pack and put the Glock inside, right on top where it was easily available, and continued hobbling along the ridge. As he did so he wondered what would cause someone to do a whole bunch of shooting in just a minute or so, and then stop altogether.

Light was fading fast, so Miguel worked his way into a stand of pines and found a reasonable place to spend the night. After eating a little chow from his pack and taking some water, he chose a large pine tree with its bed of needles and got as comfortable as his injured leg would permit. His damaged leg would not permit him to get into his sleeping bag, so he just wrapped it around himself as best he could, then lay still until he drifted off to sleep.

New Mexico Territory, June, 1884

Master Sergeant Charles Anderson stood in the middle of the group of men for whom he was responsible as they used the last hour of daylight to prepare for the night. The little detail of four cavalrymen and their sergeant had been sent on a mission that Master Sergeant Anderson was still not too happy about as he thought back to his commanding officer's words a few days earlier.

"Get your men together and shove off tomorrow at daybreak," Captain Miller had said.

"Jesus Cap'n, why me? I ain't no policeman."

"Sergeant, you are the one man I've got that can get from here to Mogollon and back without getting lost. Everybody else in this outfit is new to the territory."

The captain had been referring to the fact that his United States Cavalry Troop had been expanded with about thirty replacements who had just arrived from the east. Most were conscripts who had decided to stay in the army at the end of the War Between the States. Having served only in the Eastern United States, they had little experience with getting along in America's New Mexico Territory.

As Sergeant Anderson surveyed his men's preparations for the night—the picketing of the horses, assigning guard duty, and a dozen other chores he had to check—he heard a noise not far away. Immediately, with a pleasant grin, he thought he recognized it.

"Shush everybody—quiet!" The sergeant didn't have to tell his men twice; they knew they were in hostile Indian territory and paid immediate attention. "Hey, Serg—ah, Steinmetz, get over here," continued Sergeant Anderson, still in a lowered voice.

Staff Sergeant Abner Steinmetz ambled slowly over to Sergeant Anderson.

"Did you hear that?"

"Yeah, I heard it," replied Abner.

"Them's turkeys! If we could get one or two of them birds it would go a long way toward improvin' our menu for the night, don't'cha think?"

"Them don't sound like turkeys to me—"

"Oh hell, they's turkeys sure enough. They probably jist got a little different accent than those eastern birds you grew up huntin'," said the sergeant with a grin.

Again came the call, just a faint gobble gobble, and both men listened carefully as they looked at each other.

"Steinmetz, you're the fine-assed hunter from Virginia; think you could get us a bird for tonight's pot?" Sergeant Anderson was thinking of Abner's reputation among his eastern colleagues for being a good hunter, especially of wild turkeys.

"How could I do that sarge? I'm unarmed, and—"

"Y' think you could mind yer manners well enough to go get the forager gun and a few shells, see if you could find one 'o them birds?"

"If they's birds, yeah," muttered Abner, still skeptical about the faint call the two men had heard.

"Well, git after it; you'd like roast turkey as much as any of us."

Abner collected the forager gun, a trap door Springfield, and started to leave the camp.

"An' hey, Steinmetz. I said mind yore manners. Don't get cute ideas with that scattergun there. Jist remember that there's nothin' but miles of canyons and 'paches 'tween you and anybody else 'cept us boys right here. You git your sorry ass back within an hour. Be darkinin' by then anyhow."

Abner headed toward the draw where the call had come from, moving quietly and quickly like the skilled hunter that he was. On past the draw he started up a ridge. He knew that those turkeys, if that's what they were, would be well aware of the soldier's camp. He wanted to get on the other side of them, on the higher ground.

Ten minutes later the hunter was moving carefully up the ridge when he heard again the gobble call, much clearer and louder. Puzzled at the sound that wasn't like turkeys back home, Abner stepped slowly to his left to get a better view. And what he saw caused him to freeze in his tracks.

It was a man, one with long, straight, black hair, a red cloth wrapped around the top of his head, dark clothing, and some sort of buckskin leggings. Though the stranger was almost completely hidden by the scrub oak trees he was using for cover, Abner knew he was looking directly at an Apache warrior, less than fifty yards away. Fortunately the Indian's attention was in the direction of the soldier's camp, and the man hadn't noticed Abner.

Immediately Abner's back felt exposed, like a vicious lion could be creeping up behind him. He realized that he was looking at a wild savage, the first he had ever seen. His mind filled with the horror stories local, seasoned Indian fighters had used to dazzle the newcomers from back east. His stomach tightened as he realized how miserably armed he was with nothing but the single-shot shotgun he was carrying.

But Abner, older than most of his colleagues, was a seasoned veteran of Monassis, and other battles in the recent war that had nearly wrecked his native Virginia. He'd been shot at more times than he could remember, and had scars to show he was a combat veteran many times over. But here, in this miserable southwest desert, what could he do? One savage meant that there were undoubtedly more, and they might be watching him just as he was watching the man just below him.

Before Abner could make any decision the Apache stood up and headed down the draw directly toward the soldier's camp. Abner was amazed at how quickly and quietly the fellow seemed to move. Realizing that he had to somehow warn the camp, Abner was about to make a decision when he heard gunfire break out in the canyon below him. Moving toward the obvious fight, the lone soldier got a better view and stopped, shocked by what he saw in the campsite below.

Two of his colleagues were seriously wounded and along with the others were leaving on horseback at full gallop down the canyon.

About a dozen savages were excitedly tearing through the camp, noisily looting anything they could find. Several others were busy catching the abandoned pack horses.

Realizing that there was nothing he could do to help, Abner headed on up the ridge he had been following, moving fast and carefully, expecting to be attacked any second.

After about an hour of cautious scurrying through the unfamiliar mountains and draws, Abner realized that nightfall was coming. The ridge top, covered with sparse piñon pines and junipers, was too open for a good place to hide. But the frightened soldier found a little draw that had a nice stand of pine and other trees. Just a little way down he crawled under a big juniper that was growing in a clump of scrub oak.

Catching his breath, and a little nauseous from the surges of adrenaline he had experienced, the eastern born soldier, new to the southwest, tried to collect his wits. As he felt his heartbeat come down to something more normal, he realized that he was alone in a wilderness of mountains and canyons full of wild savages, without food or water, and felt like a pincushion full of pain from the cactus spines and other thorny brush injuries he was suffering. As the soldier lay in his miserable hideout, clutching the Springfield shotgun to his chest, he realized that beyond preparing to survive the cold of the coming night, he had one additional, serious problem. Abner had no idea where he was or where he could go.

Getting Acquainted

Miguel Anaya was a morning person by nature. At the first hint of the coming dawn he was awake after a night of fitful sleeping because of pains in his leg. Nevertheless, he gathered his gear, ate two of the granola bars from his pack, and drank just a little water. Just minutes later he had hobbled over to a little draw that he knew was not far from the head of Talavera Canyon. The steeper ground made walking difficult and his crutch of sotol sticks was not sturdy enough to help much.

In spite of the pain in his leg Miguel was doing the best he could when he suddenly heard a dry, scratchy sounding buzz like that of a cicada or perhaps a large grasshopper, coming directly from the ground near his feet. Instantly the experienced desert hiker recognized the sound as the buzz of a rattlesnake and instinctively jumped to one side. Since his injured leg was not able to take any weight, Miguel fell a second time, again into the spiny desert shrubbery that covered all the open ground. With a scream of pain the injured hiker scrambled to a position where he could face the reptile and assess the mess he was in. There, about six feet away was the source of the sound.

Miguel held perfectly still, hoping not to disturb the reptile any more than he already had, and tried to see what variety it was. From the dark markings near the rattler's tail and the lack of the prominent markings one would see on a diamondback, Miguel was relieved to see that he was dealing with a black-tailed rattler. A more timid variety than the feisty and aggressive timber rattler or a diamondback.

After several minutes of holding still, Miguel saw the reptile crawl away into a large clump of prickly pear cactus. This would have relieved a lot of tension if it hadn't been for what else he heard. While waiting for the snake to go away, Miguel knew that when he fell down his yell had caused some other animal, much larger than a snake, to make some rustling noises in the brush about thirty feet away.

***

Staff Sergeant Abner Steinmetz was awakened and startled into alertness by a sharp, loud scream like that of a frightened child. He quickly realized that it was just about dawn and that in spite of the discomfort from having stabbed himself on some sharp plant or bush and annoying cactus spine injuries, he had slept well. But what the hell was that scream? The civil war veteran had heard such yells many times before, but all were the result of injuries during the heat of battle. He regretted having reflexively moved around some when the scream awakened him, and tried to stay as motionless as he could, checking his situation.

Miguel Anaya, in pain from his injuries that were far worse than those of the cavalry soldier, and still pumped up because of the rattlesnake, also remained motionless trying to decide what the short commotion was in the nearby brush. Neither man moved as the minutes ticked by in the little draw just off the ridge top. A gentle, morning breeze, the first light of the sun hitting the taller of several nearby pines, and the clear blue sky promised the beginning of a nice day in the mountainous desert southwest.

Miguel was fortunate in that his fall had left him in a position such that he could see the scrub oak patch where the minor commotion had occurred, and he was watching it, searching for any sign of what was in there. Then he saw what he thought was a familiar object. After a minute more of staring he decided he was looking at the heel of a boot. Not a familiar hiker's boot, but some sort of boot all the same.

Abner hated the desert southwest. In addition to vile plants to deal with there were all sorts of strange herbs and blossoms that triggered his allergies. And what a time to have to put up with an uncontrollable urge to sneeze. Finally, Abner came up with a stifled sneeze, nearly silent, but enough to send a slight tremor throughout his body.

Miguel, still starring at what he thought was a boot heel, decided that it had moved, just a little bit. It had to be somebody, some person, hiding in those bushes. "Kinda weird" thought Miguel, and he thought for a moment about the Glock handgun easily available in his pack. But the need for help from some other human made him choose instead to say a quiet, "Hello."

"Oh Jesus, oh Jesus," thought Abner. "Do 'pache's speak English—say hello?"

"Anybody there?" Miguel repeated his attempt at communication. "Could it just be an old boot with some squirrel or other animal messing with it?"

With that Abner quickly squirmed around, keeping much of his concealment, but getting his Springfield pointed in the direction the words had come from, and at the strange looking man he could plainly see. "Who the hell are you?" he blurted out.

Miguel could now see little more than a gun barrel pointing out of a bunch of commotion in the scrub oak brush, but he knew there was a real, live human being there, talking to him. He was relieved not to be alone any longer, but nervous about the gun barrel.

"Hey, everything's cool. My name's Miguel, Miguel Anaya. I'm sure glad to see somebody else out here today."

"You an Apache? Miguel Anaya, ain't no name like that could be a white man. You sure you ain't no savage?"

"Heh? An Indian—an Apache? What? No man, I'm just a university teacher."

"You don't sound like a savage. Stand the hell up so's I can see you better." Abner wiggled the shotgun barrel twice indicating an upward direction.

"OK, yeah, I'll try. My leg is bunged up; hurts a lot when I stand on it."

Miguel worked himself to a standing position balanced on his good leg, wishing he could get to his sotol stick crutch. As he did this Abner stood up, with the forager gun to his shoulder, looking Miguel up and down.

"Why you wearin' them little boy clothes? What'd you do to your leg, fella? And that hat, Jesus, I ain't never seen a getup like you got." Abner was referring to Miguel's hiker's shorts leaving his well-tanned legs bare, and his wide brimmed, Mexican style sombrero.

"Hey man, I'm just a hiker. These clothes are cool in the summer, and everybody has to have a hat in this sun. And could you please point that gun some other direction? I'm not doing anything."

After a few seconds Abner lowered his Springfield, but kept it handy. "A hiker? What the hell's that? What you doin' here anyhow?"

"Ah—I've been hiking here for several days, just enjoying the countryside." Then Miguel pleasantly asked, "What brings you out here to the Gila Mountains? And your clothes. You look like a soldier dressed up for Memorial Day down at Fort Selden."

"*Look* like a soldier? I *am* a soldier. Was in the War betwixt the States. Was in the Virginia Volunteer Militia, though there warn't that much volunteerin' that I done."

"The war between the—you mean the Civil War?" Miguel was getting convinced he was at the mercy of some real nut case.

"Civil War? Don't know of no war like that. They sure warn't nothin' civil about the one I was in."

Miguel was wishing he had some way to get away from this weirdo he had encountered. Not only was the guy waving a gun at him, but he was physically a huge man. Way past six feet tall, and husky. But Miguel was in dire need of help. He had also noticed that the man was in some sort of discomfort himself and looked to be pretty bushed.

"Look, it's getting hot here in the sun and I've had about all of the standing on one leg I can handle. Lets find some shade and see what's going on for both of us, OK?"

"Yeah, I expect we could do that. Jist you don't move any too fast!"

Almost losing his balance as he did so, Miguel picked up his sotol pole crutch and hobbled about twenty feet to the shade of a great juniper tree as Abner followed a few feet behind, still holding his forager gun at the ready. He too could see that he was dealing with some real uncommon sort of fella. But he had at least decided the stranger wasn't an Apache, and didn't seem to be much of threat, what with the way he bumbled around on that silly crutch he had. Just a bunch of flimsy sticks tied together.

Reaching the shade, Miguel shucked off his pack, squatted on his good leg, and collapsed to the ground on his butt. "Eeych!" yelled the injured man. Though crudely splinted, his leg hurt plenty with almost any kind of sudden motion. Then he pulled his pack closer to himself.

Abner, thinking about what he had been through in the last few hours, still had in mind the wild savages he had seen.

"You alone out here? You seen any 'paches?"

"Apaches? What do you mean? There's a Mescalero reservation maybe hundred miles from here."

"Reservation, what the hell's that?"

"Ah, it's a big bunch of land the government gave the Mescaleros to live on and—"

"What are you talking about? We don't give no land to them savages. What we do is shoot the sons o' bitches!"

Whooee, Miguel was again sure he was in the hands of a lunatic, and one that was armed with what looked like a genuine U. S. Army "Trap Door" Springfield rifle. An antique, but a weapon that could be plenty dangerous if used by some nut case.

"The Apaches aren't savages; they're peaceful folks living on their own reservations. And we sure aren't going to run into any here in the Black Range."

Still looking around furtively, like he expected an attack any minute, Abner kept his shotgun in his left hand. But he could plainly see that the injured "hiker," or what ever he was, was not concerned about any danger. And the man was obviously in need of some kind of help.

"Seems you got a real bum hind leg fella," said Abner. "You still ain't told me what ya done to get it all bunged up like that."

"I fell, damn it. Sprained something bad. I can hardly walk."

"I think you done more than sprain it." Abner had watched Miguel's painful hobble carefully, especially the movement of the bad leg. "It looks broke to me."

"I thought you were a soldier; now you're a doctor too?"

"Don't get smart with me fella. No, I ain't no doctor, but I seen how your pin moves and the way that foot ain't steppin' right with the other one. I seen lots o' busted up arms & legs, and I knows one when I sees it."

"God it hurts," muttered Miguel, resigned to Abner's amateur diagnosis. "I don't know how much more of this I can take." He then laid down on his side, holding the bum leg in both hands. Then he sat upright again and pulled his pack toward him, thinking he might actually need the Glock handgun inside.

Abner, noticing that Miguel had paid special attention to his pack a second time, raised the forager gun back to his shoulder. "Hey, hey, fella. Let's just you keep your hands off that pack awhile more. What you got in there anyways?"

"Ah, just a few supplies. Some water, a little food. A first aid kit, but it isn't enough to fix my leg. Some maps and a compass too." Miguel hoped his attempted inventory would satisfy the nut with the gun pointed at him.

"OK fella. Stick that bunged up leg out where I kin see it better."

The injured man squirmed around some, and wincing with pain, did as he was told. Abner could plainly see that the lower leg was badly swollen and that Miguel's pain was real. Clearly the man was not likely to be much of a threat, at least as long as he kept his hands out of his pack. Abner relaxed a little.

"Y' want me to see if I kin help some? I kin sure splint that leg for ya, ease off some o' the pain. And we ought to fix ya up with a whole lot better crutch, too."

Miguel, looking up at the huge hulk of a man standing just over him, took in the light blue pants with a yellow cavalry stripe down each leg, the dark blue jacket and a similar colored hat, just like those he had seen in museums. "If this nut is a soldier he's about a hundred years out of uniform. But I gotta get help somewhere" thought the badly injured hiker.

"OK, yeah."

With that Abner looked over at a nearby half-dead scrub oak tree, hoping to use a branch to splint Miguel's leg. Then he thought about his six-inch blade belt knife that had been taken away from him by the law back in the mining town of Mogollon.

"I ain't got nothin' much to work with; you got a knife in that there pack of your'n?"

Miguel did indeed have a good Swiss Army knife and wondered about handing it to this screwball, but realized how silly worrying about that was considering how helpless he really was anyway.

"Yeah, I have a knife." Miguel reached toward his pack.

"Hey, fella. Just you do that kinda slow, OK. I ain't sure just what you got in there."

Slowly Miguel reached into his pack, and stopped as his hand touched his Glock handgun. But with the alleged soldier focused intently on what he was doing, he reached just a bit further and slowly took out his knife and handed it to Abner.

"I've got some water in here too, OK?" He then reached back, noticing that his Glock was handy, and then brought out a one-liter bottle of water.

"Incidentally, you haven't told me your name. Mine is Miguel Anaya."

"Yeah, you done said that awhile back. Mine's Steinmetz, OK?"

"Steinmetz—*Steinmetz?*"

"Yeah, fella. Sergeant Abner Steinmetz to you!"

"Wow, that's . . . ." Miguel caught himself and decided not to mention that Steinmetz was his own mother's maiden name. It would be a silly thing to say to such a weird stranger anyway. But still, the haunting familiarity of Abner's eyes and some facial expressions made Miguel curious.

"I think we could use a little drink, OK?" Miguel indicated the bottle he had just brought out.

"You got likker?"

"Alcohol? No man, not way out here"

"Ah, ok, water then, maybe some chow too?" Abner could hardly remember the last time he had had much of either one.

"Enough of both to last a few days. I always carry lots of water, for emergencies. I guess now I've got one, in spades!"

"Heh. Sounds like you're provisioned out real proper, at least for a fella that still wears short pants. But next time ya offer a man a drink make sure ya know what yer talkin' about. Jesus, I could sure use a drink."

Miguel just stared with little response.

"Ain't as provisioned as I thought!," grumbled Abner, quietly.

"What?"

"Nothin'. Just talkin' to myself. Way out here a man ought to have a little likker of some kind—just for them emergencies o' course! Anyhow, lets fix your bunged up pin some," said Abner as he began to examine the knife Miguel had handed him.

"Damn peculiar, this thing you call a knife." Abner was holding the large, bright red, folding knife in his hand, fascinated by the little white cross on one side and the numerous blades it held. "Jesus, it's kinda puny, but this things a tool box. Ain't hardly a knife at all, 'cept this one flimsy little blade."

"That blade is sturdier than you might think, and sharp as hell. If you're careful it can whittle some sticks just fine."

"Woah, a screw driver, a file, even a little pair of scissors. And looky there by damn, a corkscrew! That thing could come in useful, some'ers else from here." Then, with a shrug of his shoulders, he added, "Anyhow, we'll see what me and it kin do for your bum leg."

Forty minutes later Abner knew that Miguel had broken one of the lower bones in his left leg. He had twisted the clearly broken bone back into its proper place, a procedure that caused yelps of pain from Miguel. Then, using two carefully whittled branches and some tape from Miguel's pack, he had done a first rate job of immobilizing the leg. A lot of the pain was still there, but the sharp jabs from any little movement weren't happening. Miguel had to admit that Abner did indeed know what he was doing. The two were resting again in the shade of the juniper tree, and Miguel had taken out some more granola bars from his pack and handed one to Abner.

"You sure you ain't got a little shot or two in there?" said Abner with a good natured grin as he tore the wrapper from the granola bar. "It sure would help just a tad with washin' this stale thing down."

During the whole first aid operation Miguel had been quietly watching Abner's face, with a slightly uncomfortable feeling that he had seen the man before, or someone who looked like him. Abner's eyes, some faint facial expressions, or head position would, for a fleeting instant, remind him of his own mother back before she died long ago.

Miguel struggled to a standing position on his one good leg, then moved the bad one around some and said, "Thanks man, thanks a lot. That's a whole lot better."

"Well, what with me to lean on you ain't gonna need that ole crutch you had."

"Yeah, ah, where are you going, anyway? You haven't told me what the heck you're doing here, being a soldier or whatever you are. You a hunter, or just another hiker like me?"

"Hiker? Consid'rn what you done told me about this hikin' stuff, it sounds a lot like marchin'. Somethin' I sure as hell wouldn't be doin' if I did't hafta."

"Then when are you going to tell me what you *are* doing here?"

With a shrug of his shoulders, Abner gave in and told Miguel about getting separated from his military detail in a scrap with some of the savages that wern't supposed to be around. At the end of Abner's story, Miguel didn't say anything. The two men just sat and stared at each other for a long time. Miguel couldn't help feeling that Abner believed what he was saying, but the story was preposterous. As both men sat in an uncomfortable silence, Miguel watched Abner carefully. The man was continually looking around, sometimes off into the distance, sometimes down into the several draws that ran both ways off of the ridge they were on.

Abner was indeed watching all around, and each time he took a few seconds to look off into the distance all he saw was miles and miles of more canyons, trees, brush and ridges; nothing any different from the ridge top he was sitting on. Finally, he broke the silence.

"They's one more thing," said Abner. "I gotta tell ya, I'm lost."

"Lost? You don't know where we are? Heh. That's—"

"I tole ya damn it! Them savages attacked us, the other fellas got run off, includin' the sergeant. He's the only one knew where the hell we was!"

Abner's shoulders drooped a little as he spoke, and Miguel could plainly see that the man really didn't know where he was. As Abner talked more about his alleged Apache attack, Miguel remembered the peculiar, short bunch of gunfire he had heard the previous day.

"I ain't got no food, no water, nothin' but this damn shotgun. I sure as hell want out of this God-forsaken bunch o' mountains what can't decide whether they's forest or desert. And every damn thing around here's got spikes on it, and they ain't hardly no water nowhere! We're right in the middle o' nothin' but rocks, hot sun, stickers, and savages!" Abner's voice rose as he spoke, and a tremor in his shoulders made him look vulnerable for just a moment.

Miguel realized that the peculiar soldier really believed what he was saying, and was pretty fed up with New Mexico's Gila Mountains. He tried hard to believe the man's story, that he really was a soldier. But the man had no equipment whatsoever, except for that antique gun. The guy sure looked like he'd been through some sort of mess. Maybe he was injured mentally, or something, maybe needed help as much as Miguel himself did.

"Well, *I'm* not lost. I've got the topos and I've hiked all over this place."

"Topos? What're them?"

"Maps, topographic maps. They show the shape of the hills and canyons."

"Kin they tell you how to get us back to the camp?"

"Camp? You mean a military camp? No man, not that. But the state highway is only a few miles away, right down Talavera Canyon. Right where Talavera meets the Gila River, that's where I left my pickup."

"You got maps? Don't know what them fancy map words means, but maps wouldn't help me much anyways what with not knowin' where I'm at. An what the hell's a pickup anyhow?"

"Look, seems to me like we both need some help from each other. I'll show you the way home and you help me with my walking, OK?"

"Yeah, we might could do that. What with me bein' a big fella and you a little on the puny side, we oughta do OK, ya think?"

"Yeah, maybe," said Miguel, feeling a whole lot better than he had in a lot of hours. With that, the two confused, new acquaintances headed toward Talavera Canyon.

***

Two hours later the crippled hiker was hobbling along slowly, using as a crutch a strong arm and shoulder of the strangest soldier he had ever seen. A soldier who seemed to be expecting to be attacked by something or other at any time. Miguel decided that he needed a few minutes' rest so Abner helped him to a sitting position in the shade of a low cliff in the draw they were following. They each took a little more water, just a little.

Then Abner just stood in the creek bottom looking up at the sky.

"What's the matter, man?" Miguel noticed that Abner was staring intently at a brilliant, white streak high up in the blue sky. "You seem pretty nervous; what's bothering—"

"Never you mind, let's just git goin. We could run afoul o' some o' them savages at any bend in this here dried up crick, damn it. I j'st want to get back to the camp afore them savages finds us. The camp's on that there Gila River you mentioned, smack dab in the middle of a big open spot. They's nigh on to sixty men there. Ain't no savages gonna come rippen' and tearin' inta that place like they done to our squad's camp yest'day."

"What is this guy talking about?" thought Miguel. He seems decent enough. Everything he says sounds like he really is a 19th century soldier. Miguel decided to ask a question.

"Ah, Abner, I have been thinking a lot about us—about you and me—and I want to ask a question. It might sound silly, but just answer it anyway, OK?"

Abner just looked at the peculiar fella he hoped could really lead them out of the dried-out mountains, but said nothing.

"Abner, what's today's date?"

"Date? You wanna know the date? Hell, I don't even know what day o' the week it is."

"Not the day, what month, what year is it?" Miguel was apprehensive about the question, knowing that it could sound like he was doubting Abner's sanity.

Abner just dropped his head and looked at the ground between his feet as he sat on a rock ledge and thought about the request. "This damn hiker guy. He ain't no savage, clear enough. But has he got all his marbles?"

"Near as I know it's about half past June. And I ain't never knowed a man didn't know what year things was."

"Please, man, say what year it is," pled Miguel.

"All right. It's eighteen eighty-four, damn it, in case y' ain't never been told before. What the fuck year d' you think it is?"

Miguel slumped down on his side and felt a surge of nausea as his stomach tightened even more under the tension of being in the presence of this peculiar so-called soldier. "I'm not dreaming. A hallucination? Too much heat; is this what dying of exposure after a bad injury is like?" The wretched hiker looked at his hands, at the nearby gramma grass, a big fishhook cactus three feet away, at the piñon pines and junipers surrounding the two men, and couldn't believe it was anything but real.

Then Miguel remembered his wallet and took it out of his left rear pocket.

"Here, man, look at this. My ID." Miguel handed his New Mexico State driver's license to Abner, who took it gingerly, like it was something he had never seen before. "Look at the dates on it."

Abner took the plastic card in his two hands and flexed it a little. "Huh. What's it made of? Ain't paper, or such."

"It's plastic, man. Read what is says."

"It's got a pitchur, a colored one. Looks kinda like you."

"Yeah, it is me. But look at the birth date, the expiration date."

Squinting some, Abner looked at the card. "Bunch 'o numbers, yore name 'n stuff. What d' they got to do with anything?"

"Jesus man. Three, twenty-two, forty-seven. I was born on the twenty-second day of March in the year of nineteen forty-seven. *Nineteen* forty-seven. And today's date is June 14, nineteen eighty-four."

"Don't mean nothin' t' me," muttered Abner." And nineteen forty-seven, that wouldn't make no sense."

"Hey, wait, I've got other stuff here." Miguel pulled a university ID card from his wallet, along with a folded, white sheet of paper that was the fire permit that he had obtained from the US Forest Service before he began his hike. "Here, look at these; see the dates on 'em."

Abner took the offered papers, but just held them in his hand.

"Here. Look at this." Miguel dug further into his pack and pulled out a well worn paperback book. "Look at the title of this"

After a few moments he handed the book and credentials back, unexamined. "Damn it. These ain't nothin' to me." Then, looking to one side, he muttered, "I cain't read; never got no schoolin'."

"My God, on top of everything else this guy's illiterate," thought Abner, as he quietly put his driver's license and the papers away. Then he thought about the book. "The Battle of Midway," said the title, and he read it to Abner. Then he pointed out a little section near the middle that had a few black and white photos of the aircraft carrier Midway, along with a few other World War II ships. And a nice shot of navy fighter planes flying in a tight formation. You could even see the pilot in the nearest machine.

"There ain't no ships like that. And what d' ya mean, ships that kin fly?"

"They're real airplanes," said Miguel. "These here are older and much smaller than the big airliners that make those white streaks in the sky I know you noticed a while ago."

"Yeah, I seen them white lines. Skinny little things. Ain't never seen clouds like them till today. More damn desert stuff, I s'pose." But what d' ya mean, "air liners," why do you folks out here want t' make lines in the sky?

"No, man. Those are airliners, jet planes carrying hundreds of people across the country. See, it's the *twentieth* century, damn it."

"Ya mean like stage coaches, goin' across the sky?" said Abner, sarcastically. "You 'spect me to believe crap like that? I think you been out here in this damn wilderness too long; yer head's got fucked up or some such."

Then, relaxing his shoulders into a slump, Abner muttered, "None o' this makes no sense," Noticing a sad tone to the soldier's voice,

Miguel felt a little sorry for the man who then quietly asked, "What's plastic anyhow?"

Scrunching back to a sitting position, Miguel thought, "No, It doesn't make sense to me either. Nothing does." And again he wondered about hallucinations.

Then Miguel remembered something in his pack. Scrunching around some he fished out a coin, "Look, look at the date on this coin." He handed the nearly new-looking piece to Abner, who took it reluctantly. "See. Look at the date, man. Nineteen forty-seven. *Nineteen!*"

Abner hefted the big, crown sized coin in his hand. "Feels like a dollar, same size. Looks like silver, too."

"Yeah, it's nearly pure silver just like our silver dollars used to be," said Miguel. "Now look at the date on it. It says nineteen—"

"I see it, I kin read numbers, damn it. Don't mean nothin. Ain't no real dollar. Look at the pitchure on it. Some fella with funny hair and earrings!"

"It's Mexican, man. My dad gave it to me when I was a little kid. Its date, that's the year I was born, *nineteen* forty-seven."

Abner stood in silence for a few moments as he turned the coin over. "Jesus. Looky at the back. Some big bird standin' on a cactus tryin' to eat a snake. See, everythin' around here's got either claws, fangs, or stickers."

"That's the Eagle and the Serpent, the national symbol of Mexico. Pretty important to any patriotic Mexican."

"Huh. If this things's your lucky piece it don't seem like it worked much, considerin' the tumble you took. And whose mug is that on it anyhow?"

"Cuauhtemoc, an Aztec Indian chief, hundreds of years ago," said Miguel, annoyed. "But if you can't read, you probably don't know about things like that."

Abner looked up from the coin straight into Miguel's eyes.

Immediately, Miguel regretted his sarcastic comment, and added, "Hey man, I didn't mean to—"

"I know what the hell you meant, damn it. Let's you'n me just get our butts out 'a this place. Fuckin mountains anyway; everthin's either stickers or claws and too damn dry," muttered Abner.

To free his hands to help Miguel get to his feet, Abner dropped the silver coin into his pocket. The two headed down Talavera Canyon in silence for a long time. "Couldn't be much of a lucky piece what with a picture of some old buck indian on it," muttered Abner quietly, thinking about the coin in his pocket.

Later, Miguel chanced to glance toward the southern sky.

"Hey, look there, man." Miguel stopped in his tracks, nearly knocking the tired soldier off balance.

"Keerful, fella. Y' damn near knocked me down. That wouldn't of done neither of us no good."

"No man. Sorry. But look over there at the sky. See that cloud, that long, white streak?" What they were seeing was sharp and clear, a white streak high up in the otherwise cloudless blue sky.

Abner did as told, and just stared for a few moments. "Yeah. Another one o' your skinny damn desert clouds." The white streak that was getting longer on the east end and slowly fading away at the west end.

"That's a contrail, man. See, look close, right at the front end. You can see a little black dot. That's a jet airliner, probably heading from LA to El Paso or Dallas. See, it's *nineteen* eighty-four, man. There weren't any airplanes in *eighteen* eighty-four, damn it."

Abner didn't say anything. He just kept the pair of them shuffling down the rocky, dry streambed.

"You can see it, can't you?" pleaded Miguel.

"Yeah. I see the damn thing; I see it. Let's just git on down t' that there Gila River."

As he spoke Miguel slipped on a loose rock and Abner adroitly caught his weight, and as the two resumed walking, Abner spoke quietly to Mguel.

"I been thinkin' on stuff you told me. Yer con-tails you call 'em, them skinny clouds. Then back a ways you used them fancy map words—top-graphs or whatever you said. Don't make no sense . . ."

With that the pair of new acquaintances continued their trek down Talavera Canyon in silence, each wondering what kind of stranger the other man was. But the confused soldier continued to help with the walking as the injured hiker showed the way. Then, after a moment of silence, in a sad little voice, Abner muttered, "You still ain't told me, what's a 'pickup'?"

Surprises in the Brush

The two uneasy men struggled down Talavera Canyon for another hour without speaking when both stopped, having heard something ahead in the brush.

"Huh!. What was that?" muttered Miguel

"Shush!" Abner let go of Miguel and in a two handed grip pointed his Springfield in the direction of the movement in a clump of scrub oak just to their right ahead in the trail. Catching Miguel again just before the injured man fell, Abner pulled them both to the right side of the creek behind a large fir tree, all the time scanning their surroundings for any other signs of movement.

"Might be more 'paches. Stay quiet and don't move," whispered Abner as he kept the Springfield pointed directly at the bushes where the disturbance had come from.

A few seconds later there was more motion in the scrub oak, and a small fir tree was pushed flat.

"What the hell is that?" thought Abner. "No 'pache is gonna make that much fuss."

Seconds ticked by as Abner kept the two men frozen still. Miguel, getting fed up with what he considered to be nonsense, finally broke the silence.

"Probably just a deer or coyote; Let's go—"

"Shush, damn it!"

Miguel could see in Abner's eyes that the man was serious, maybe even dangerously so. Then, after another few seconds the commotion in the brush increased and Abner stopped his search for other 'paches and gave his full attention to what was obviously a large animal just ahead.

"It's a b'ar."

"A what? What's a b'ar?"

"They's a b'ar in them bushes; I kin smell 'im," said Abner. "I know b'ar smell. Hunted 'em lots with dogs back home."

"Ah, a bear!" Miguel had never in all his time in New Mexico's mountains ever seen one, but he knew there were a few black bears around.

"He'll likely skitter away when he sees us." Abner kept his Springfield pointed in the animal's direction as the two cautiously moved ahead.

134

"Hope he does," added Miguel as he tried to get his Glock out of his pack. But as he fumbled around, standing almost on one leg, he lost his balance and fell to the ground.

"Agh, God that hurts—"

"Gawd a'mighty, what kind'a b'ar is that?" yelled Abner, who had not even noticed that Miguel had fallen; his attention was on the huge animal that had risen on its rear legs, swinging its head from side to side, trying to decide what sort of intruders had entered its territory. Abner was looking at a bear that was twice a big as any he had ever seen back in Virginia. Generally brown in color, the bear's fur was a mix of brown and gray on its back and shoulders, and in spite of his familiarity with bears, Abner felt a shot of adrenalin as he pointed his Springfield in the monster's direction.

"Oh my God, a grizzly!" yelled Miguel, as the color drained from his face and his shaking hands clawed at his knapsack, digging inside. "Kill the damn thing!"

Realizing that this bear's body language was a lot more belligerent than any of the black bears he had dealt with back home, Abner stood his ground, facing the 600-pound grizzly that was standing on its hind legs just 30 feet away. The bear was now focusing its attention on the two men, one standing still, and the other scuttling around on the ground, like a fish out of water.

Still on his hind legs, the bear took a couple of steps toward the two. Abner held his ground with the Springfield at his shoulder and pointed directly at the animal's neck.

"Kill 'im! Kill 'm," yelled Miguel.

"Shut up, damn it," said Abner in a calm, almost soothing voice. "Don't rile 'im none. This scatter-gun ain't nothin' t' face any b'ar with. Leastways not one like that!"

Then Abner was startled to hear several explosions—gunshots—from the ground to his left. In his peripheral vision he saw that Miguel was holding a pistol with both hands and was firing furiously at the grizzly. So many shots that the soldier lost count, but he saw that they weren't particularly effective. Most completely missed the animal; others hit in areas that were sure to do little more than aggravate the huge creature. Freshly fired cartridge cases from the semi-automatic handgun flew in Abner's direction and one landed in the collar of his shirt, slightly burning the soldier's neck.

The bear, taking a dim view of Miguel's shooting, promptly attacked. In little more than a second and charging like nature's version

135

of a wild locomotive, the creature came directly at the two men. Abner, having been surprised by the wild volley of gunfire, had in an instant of carelessness turned slightly toward Miguel, just as the huge animal's forepaw made one swipe at the soldier. But Abner held his ground, and as the behemoth let out an intimidating roar, Abner shoved the Springfield's muzzle right down the animal's open throat and pulled the trigger.

Minutes later both men sat in front of the great bear, neither speaking, and both trying to control their nerves. Abner was embarrassed because he had dropped his Springfield immediately after firing it while he was furiously digging into a pocket to get another cartridge. Realizing that the bear was not moving, he slowly reached out for the fallen shotgun and pulled it to himself. As he did so he shook his back some, realizing that the behemoth had managed to actually hit him once on the shoulder.

The crippled Miguel was sitting on the ground looking at the pistol he held in his hands. Its action was locked open, ready for reloading, having been fired until empty. Abner noticed that Miguel had obviously lost control of his bladder, and was relieved to know that he himself had kept his cool pretty well, except for dropping his weapon as he tried to dig out another cartridge for reloading.

Getting back to his feet and looking directly down the barrel of the shotgun, Abner examined the bear more closely and could plainly see that the animal's throat had been blown open. Ripped arteries pumped useless blood, having been destroyed by the 20 gauge blast the animal had practically swallowed. The eastern born turkey and black bear hunter was acutely aware that he was lucky to be alive.

As his nerves settled down, Abner paid more attention to Miguel who was still sitting with the Glock pistol in his visibly shaking hands. He thought of the incredible barrage of firing that had come from the strange man at his side.

"What the hell is that thing?" he asked.

"Heh?"

"That there pistol, or whatever it is."

Miguel turned his attention back to the pistol in his hands, then slowly handed it to Abner, who took in gingerly in his own, not knowing just what to expect.

"Ain't never seen no weapon like this—"

"It's a nine millimeter Glock, kinda new in the U.S. They're made in Austria."

About then Abner noticed the lump wedged under his shirt collar and dug it out, then held it in his hand, wondering what the dull, gray colored steel object was.

"Sorry about that," said Miguel. "You got in the way of my ejected empties. You don't want to stand too close to the right side of any automatic pistol." Then, moving around some to a less painful position, he added. "God, my leg hurts like hell. I think I may have busted it up worse."

"Yeah, sorry I let go of you, but that b'ar an all . . ."

Miguel then looked at the great bulk of the dead bear and just stared, feeling a surge of adrenaline and wishing the tingling sensation in his hands and leg would calm down. Even minutes after the shooting he could still feel his heartbeat pounding in his throat.

"How many times did you shoot—how'd you reload so fast," asked Abner.

"Didn't reload. It had sixteen rounds."

"Sixteen, not six, but *sixteen*?"

"Sure. Would have been more if I'd had the magazine full and the chamber loaded. Here, I'll show you what I mean," said Miguel as he took the gun back from Abner's hands and dropped out the used magazine and released the pistol's slide. He then got a fresh magazine from his knapsack and shoved it into the butt of the Glock. "There. It's all set to go again. Seventeen rounds now, since this magazine was full.

"That's it? *Seventeen* more shots? Damn!"

"Would have been eighteen if I had loaded the chamber before I put the magazine in, but I like to keep the chamber empty."

Abner, bewildered by what he had seen and heard, thought again about the sky. Could there really be people up there making those white streaks?"

As the two talked about the wonders of semi-automatic handguns, Miguel explained the ejected empty cartridge case Abner was holding, and even had the soldier fire a round into the bulk of the dead bear.

"Jesus, if we'd had these things back home we could of used 'em on them Rebs—"

"Give me a hand would ya? You better check my splint. Messed up my leg—hurts like hell."

Using adhesive tape from Miguel's pack, Abner carefully re-splinted Miguel's leg, then helped him to his feet so the two could resume their trek down Talavera Canyon.

"And hey fella," said Abner. "Next time you meet a b'ar, f'crist sake don't just start shootin' at the countryside he's standin' in like you done here. All you done was piss 'im off"

"Yeah, I won't. I've never shot at any animal before."

"Jesus, who in tarnation are you anyway?"

Miguel thought of his mother's maiden name, but didn't say anything.

Then the two men stepped to one side, passed the magnificent bear carcass, and headed down the canyon.

Minutes later Abner spoke again.

"Y' know, I've tacked a lot of b'ar hides on the barn door back home, but I ain't *never* seen a critter like that. I 'spect he's one o' them grizzel b'ars the boys talk of. That so?"

Miguel had reached the same conclusion after examining the great animal, and was trying desperately in his mind to deal with the fact that grizzly bears had been extinct in all the southwest for decades. "Yeah, that was a grizzly. The only one I've ever seen outside a zoo."

A little more comfortable after having the splint on his leg tightened, Miguel went back to thinking about the weird soldier that was obviously helping him, had probably saved his life. He decided to ask more questions.

"You mentioned that you have shot other bears back home, wherever that is. Do you always shove the muzzle of your rifle down the thing's mouth when you shoot one?"

"I would'a done a lot different if this here forager gun was a .45-70 like it oughta be. But it ain't." With that thought, Abner, who wasn't quite as calm as he appeared, realized that he still hadn't reloaded the Springfield. He promptly pulled the breechblock up and removed the fired cartridge case that was still in the chamber. As he started to toss it aside, he stopped and handed it to Miguel. Then he quickly took a fresh cartridge from his coat pocket, inserted it into the shotgun's chamber. He then pressed the breech bolt downward, closing the action.

Miguel held the shiny brass cartridge case in his hand, turned it over and read the head stamp on the back end. "Hey, this thing is a shotgun shell, a 20 gauge! But that gun is a Trap Door Springfield, ought to be a forty-five or fifty caliber rifle."

"Like I been tellin' ya this thing's one 'o them new forager guns. Same Springfield but it's got a shotgun barrel. Ain't for fightin' or anything. It's just for getting' a little game here and there for the camp cook pot. Sure ain't fer them damn grizzel b'ars you got out here in this mizzer'ble place!"

"Huh—Mind if I keep this thing?" muttered Miguel. Being an assistant professor of history with an interest in all things military, he found the antique forager gun fascinating.

"Suit yerself; ain't nothin' to me."

Miguel dropped the empty 20 gauge shotgun shell into the pocket of his hiking shorts and the two resumed their hobble down Talavera Canyon. The crippled hiker mulled over the fact that he had seen a historic firearm, a locally extinct bear, and a jet airliner, all within the last hour and all in the company of a Civil War soldier.

"Anyway, I don't think we are going to run into any wild Indians," muttered Miguel with a sarcastic tone of voice. "You look like you're expecting to be attacked any minute."

"Yeah, and I just was. I don't 'spect you thought we was gonna run into any o' them 'extincted grizzel b'ars you mentioned, either. Lets just us both keep my scattergun and that hand cannon of yourn handy case some o' them extincted 'pachies shows up!"

"OK," muttered Miguel, as he put his arm around Abner's neck to keep using the big man as a crutch as he had been doing all day. But in doing so he noticed that the back of Abner's shirt was bloody, and it wasn't just spattered blood from the bear. Abner had a wound that was still bleeding.

"Hey, man. You got cut up some back there."

"Yeah, I noticed. I think that critter managed to get a lick in at me durin' our little wrestlin' match. It ain't serious, but it hurts some."

"It's bleeding a little. Lets stop and take a look."

Reluctantly, Abner found a good place to set the crippled hiker down, and turn his own back so Miguel could check things out.

"Woo, man. You got a good gouge from two of those claws. Now it's my turn to play doctor. I've got plenty of stuff to fix that in my pack."

After cleaning the wound as best he could, Miguel smeared an antibiotic salve over the wound, then, using the last of his roll of wide adhesive tape and several adhesive bandages, he put a gauze compress on Abner's huge shoulder and stopped all the bleeding just fine. Then the two injured strangers continued their trek. For another hour they made slow but steady progress down Talavera Canyon.

"Hold up a mite, fella. I been watchin' yer leg and it appears yer splint's loosened up some. Best we fix it."

"Yeah, ok," muttered Miguel as he hopped toward a nearby boulder and dropped to a half-sitting, half-leaning position on the rock. He shucked off his pack and set it by his injured leg. But his sudden movement caused Abner to lose his balance for a moment, and the soldier fell on his rump, narrowly missing a large clump of prickly pear cactus and grass.

"Whoo-ee, glad I plunked my butt down here in this grass stead of on that damn cactus. Whole place is full o' stickers, one kind or another."

"Hey man. I warned you about staying clear of—"

Miguel stopped in mid sentence. What he saw in the cactus clump told him it was too late.

"Don't move! Man, I mean it. Don't move; there's a rattler right behind you." As he spoke Miguel tried to dig his Glock out of his pack.

"Haah?" Abner began scrambling to a standing position.

"Don't move, damn it!. Hold real still; he won't strike unless you scare 'im!" Miguel still hadn't been able to get his Glock out where he could use it yet.

"It's not a diamondback; it's a black tail rattler. They aren't very aggressive. Just hold real still 'till I find my gun!"

"Fuck that!" yelled Abner as he tried to scramble away from the snake. That was a big mistake. Frightened by the sudden motion, the rattler struck, hitting Abner high on his thigh.

"Oh shit, man. I told you to hold—"

"Oh lordy, it hit me, right in the butt! It bit me. Oh Jesus—this desert—I'm gonna die"

"Stand up, damn it, and stop hollering" yelled Miguel. "Drop your pants; let's see how bad you've been bitten."

Reluctantly the soldier did as he had been told.

"You sure he hit you? Where at? I can't see any sign of a bite."

"Right there! Right on my pocket. Oh Jesus, Oh Jesus, I'm dead. Fuckin desert, it's finally got me."

"Calm down, damn it. You said your pocket. You got anything in your pocket? Look and see."

Abner calmed just enough to pull his pants up enough to get his left hand into his pocket, and all he found was Miguel's silver coin. He pulled it out and handed it to Miguel. "Look. It's all slimy; got googley-goo on it," muttered the still panicky soldier.

Miguel took the coin and immediately saw that it had a liberal coating of rattlesnake venom smeared on one side.

With a grin on his face, Miguel broke into a hearty laugh as, for him, the tension was released.

"What's so damn funny, ass-hole. You ain't the one what's been butt-bit by that thing. Hey, where'd it go?" The snake had crawled away and disappeared in nearby brush and prickly pear cactus.

A few minutes later, after Abner had calmed down, the two sat talking about the events of the past few minutes. Miguel had handed the coin back to Abner who sat holding it in his hands after having rubbed all traces of venom off of it in the dirt at his feet. "Hoo-ee, this here token o' yourn, it's a lucky piece, sure enough."

"Yeah, well, I think you better keep it, man. If you keep up your habit of sitting down on rattlesnakes you're going to need it."

"Heh, I thank ya, fella," said Abner, laughing at Miguel's comment. "But I believe I'm gonna start breakin' that habit!"

"And about rattlers, man. Most of them are pretty timid; if you don't move too fast, they usually just stay put. If you had just sat still I could have shot the thing so you would not have been bitten in the first place."

"Oh yeah, fella. Back with that grizzel bar, I seen how you shoot. Hell, I'd of been more scared o' you and your scatter-pistol than that snake critter," said Abner with a grin.

"Yeah, maybe you're right, man."

For a few minutes more the two men sat together just enjoying each other's company. Abner then tightened Miguel's splint. Miguel suggested they each take on a little water and handed one of his plastic bottles to the soldier. Abner took a few sips, handed back the bottle with a grateful nod and a smile, then helped Miguel get his pack back together.

"Those eyes, so familiar," thought Miguel, and again he had a vague feeling that he ought to know this strange "Civil War" soldier from somewhere before.

The two then continued their trek down Talavara Canyon, with Miguel leaning heavily on the bigger man for support. Miguel was still trying to convince himself that the bear couldn't have been a grizzly. There just hadn't been any wild grizzlies in New Mexico since the 19th century. And Abner had uncomfortable thoughts of his own because of two more brilliant white streaks he had noticed against the deep blue of the fine, springtime sky. And in spite of wanting to trust this weird hiker fella, he just was not ready to believe those little black dots making the white tracks were stage coaches with hundreds of people in them.

The End of the Trek

Neither man said much as the day wore on, but they were making a little better time as they got more coordinated in thier walking. Abner had taken a few minutes to hunt up a short fir tree branch that Miguel could use in his right hand as a cane, which helped. By late afternoon they had reached the lower part of the canyon where the valley was wider and less steep. Miguel knew they weren't far from the point where Talavera Canyon joined the Gila River, but he hadn't mentioned that to Abner.

"Hey," said Abner, stopping and looking around. "I *been* here! I know where we are! I been here on maneuvers; the camp's just over that ridge jist a little ways. We made it!"

Abner was clearly relieved and no longer lost.

"Look, let's you wait here a spell so's I kin skedaddle over that hill t' the camp, get some boys with a litter. Make things easier on your bunged up pin, OK?"

"Hey, man. No, there isn't any military camp over that hill. There's just a meadow with a highway and my pickup—"

"Jist you wait here, fella. I'll be back in a jiffy with plenty o' help." Abner lowered Miguel to the ground in a sitting position and started up the low hill to the east, toward where Miguel knew his pickup was.

"No, wait, let me come with you." Miguel saw that his plea not to be abandoned so close to his truck was falling on deaf ears as Abner scurried up the low hill and disappeared over the top.

Miguel struggled to a stooped standing position and, using the scrub oak branch Abner had cut for him as a cane, began an agonizing climb up the hill in an attempt to follow.

Abner reached the top of the low hill and just as he expected, there was the military camp he had left many days earlier. With apprehension, he thought about the reception he knew he would receive, and then his thoughts went back to the strange young man he had been half carrying all day long. He glanced back at where he expected Miguel to be and the fella was nowhere to be seen. Probably crawled into some shade, thought Abner, feeling a little guilty that he'd left Miguel so abruptly. He should have helped the injured man get to a comfortable place to wait for help from the other soldiers. Then, holding his forager gun in one hand, he started trotting toward the encampment. He'd get help for Miguel and then face his own consequences. In any case it would be good to get plenty of water and some real chow instead of those cookie things the injured guy had.

An hour after Abner left, Miguel had managed to crawl and stumble to the crest of the hill and could see no sign of the strange soldier. Just an open, grass-covered meadow with a few scattered juniper trees. And there, just a little over a hundred yards away, was his Chevy pickup right where he had left it in a gravel parking area on the bank of the Gila River. And, much to the relief of the injured hiker, his truck was not alone. There was an elderly couple sitting in folding chairs in the shade of an awning sticking out from their fine, new recreational vehicle. With a sigh of relief, Miguel realized that his ordeal was about over.

Interrogation

The day of his return to camp, Abner was escorted from the camp's single stockade cell to the office of Captain Elias Miller, the commander of the little group of cavalrymen

"All right fella, I still got a few questions about your recent absence. You do realize what you have done?"

"Yes Sir, Cap'n Sir. I know I done wrong, getting' drunked up and all. Hadn't ough't'a been drinkin' with them civilians anyhow. I know better."

"Jesus, a sergeant with so many years of service! You damn well *ought* to know better."

"Cap'n Sir, I don't recollect much about it all, till I woke up in that minin' town."

"In Jail in Mogollon, soldier—eh, prisoner. Starting a brawl in a bar, getting arrested by a deputy U S Marshal, that messes things up good. You know I can't do much to fix anything that stupid. What happened anyway?"

"Sir, I really don't know. I ah, a bit too much to drink—"

"Steinmetz, how long have you been in this army?"

"Ah, countin' the war and all, then back there t' home, I'd say a little mor'n twenty years. Mostly back in Virginia and Maryland—even in the District O' Columbia for a spell."

"You have a great record for your wartime service; you were cited for bravery twice. Then you were cited again in the Capitol during those riots. Jesus, Steinmetz, you were doing great till you were transferred out here to the territory. How long have you been with us, Steinmetz?"

"Right at three, maybe four months, Sir"

"Yes, and during all that time it seems your best friend has been the bottle; what the hell happened? Staff Sergeant Anderson says you're scared of these hills—one pretty damn sorry excuse to say the least. You sure as hell weren't scared of anything during the mess back in Virginia."

"Cap'n Miller, Sir. Scared's got nothing to do with anythin' Sir. It's just this place. No water nowhere, just rocks, no farms. Everythin's got stickers on it, even the dam—ah, even the snakes is got stickers, Sir. It just ain't no place for a farm boy to be."

The captian just watched Abner for a moment, then, with a slight shake of his head, changed the subject.

"What about this civilian you claim you met. Tell me about him. Tell me who he was, where he went."

"A little fella he was, Sir. His duds—heh—like a school boy, but a growed up one. Said he belonged to some fancy school or som'thin'. Told me lots of stuff I don't want to think about. Streaks o' white in the sky, flyin' machines, talkin' machines, and about coaches what runs around by themselves without horses, Sir."

"Demented, he was demented."

"Sir?"

"Ah, means crazy, Steinmetz. The fella, if he existed at all, he was crazy."

"He saved my life, Sir. If he hadn't of give me that token the rattler hit I would'a been bad snake bit. And he shot the shi—ah, he shot up that b'ar some too."

"Yes, Steinmetz, and with a pistol that shoots all day long, from what you've been telling folks around here. If you really believe that then I have to think you're demented too!"

"Ah, Cap'n Miller, Sir, the patrol you sent out. They found the b'ar, I heerd talk that they did. And the fella who was hikin'—that's sort o' like marchin'—he saved my life, he did."

"*You* killed the bear, Steinmetz, killed the blazes out of it from what Sergeant Anderson found, and—"

"Cap'n Miller Sir, I got proof. Here, in my pocket." Abner took the single cartridge case from Miguel's Glock out of his trousers pocket where he had kept it since the incident with the bear. It was the one that had momentarily burned his neck while Miguel was blazing away at the animal. He set the little cartridge case down on the captain's desk.

The officer picked it up, examined it casually, then put into a desk drawer. At a glance he knew that it was a fired pistol round, but not like any one he had ever seen.

"Newfangled round," muttered the captain, knowing that there had been dozens of experimental rifles, pistols, and ammunition types in development since the war. But the odd gray color . . .

"Sir, I seen it shot Cap'n Sir. I even shot one of 'em my own self."

"Steinmetz, I hate to do this, but I have no other choice. Since that marshal has sent in a record of your arrest and because you went absent for a few days, I have to send you along to Santa Fe, let them figure out what to do with you."

Abner slumped some, and then reestablished his position of attention, and asked, "Cap'n Sir, what will the army do,—Sir?"

"Soldier, I can only make a guess, but because of your record I expect you will be sent back east to where you enlisted and then discharged."

"Well, Sir, at least I kin get away from these dried up hills what ain't nothin' but stickers and such."

"Steinmetz, you're going to be with us for a few more days. Out of respect for your record I'm not going to send you back to the stockade, that is if you can stay sober. That a deal?"

"Yes Sir, thank you Sir; I kin do that. Now that I'm goin' t' where there's water, and green stuff that feeds ya instead of cut's ya up."

The Captain's Report

Master Sergeant Charles Anderson walked into the office of the little cavalry camp on the Gila River, and came more or less to attention in front of the single desk. "You wanted to see me Cap'n?"

Captain Elias Miller looked up at the gray-haired Sergeant and told the man to take a seat. "Chuck, you and I have know each other for a lot of years; you know I've put some stock in your opinion more than once. I gotta write another report on that ruckus you had with those Apaches. Before I do I want you to tell me just what you think of that soldier, Steinmetz. You spent some time with the man and except for Private Dix you're the only man who didn't get shot up some."

"Cap'n, all I kin say is that it sure as hell warn't worth what we went through just to fetch a deserter."

"Right enough, Chuck, but you know the regulations say we gotta do that no matter what. Just tell me what you think. Is the fella a little crazy, or what?"

"Cap'n, I spent a few evenin's talkin' with Sergeant Steinmetz, and—"

"Just plain Abner Steinmetz. Deserters don't have rank, Chuck, at least not in my book."

"Cap'n, Sir, I'd respectfully like to say that Stienmetz ain't no deserter. He just got drunked up and went off for a bit. But he stayed army all the way—Sir."

"Sergeant, I count Steinmetz as a deserter for running off to Mogollon. And you know full well that when your detail went back to the attack site in Talavera Canyon, Steinmetz wasn't there, alive or dead. He had to have run off—"

"Cap'n, could be things was a little different. I ain't said much about it, but just before the ruckus they was somethin' I hadent oughta' done." Sergeant Anderson shifted his weight a little as he stood before the captain's desk. "I, ah, y'a see, Sir—"

"C'mon Chuck. Spit it out."

"Yes Sir, Cap'n. OK. Y'see, just before them 'paches hit us, I sent Steinmetz out huntin' turkeys."

"Heh? Turkeys? You sent your *prisoner* turkey hunting?"

"Yes Sir. That's what I done. Figured the bunch of us could use somethin' fresh in the cookin' pot. I give Steinmetz the forager gun and sent him out after birds I heard—thought I heard." The sergeant got a lump in his throat when he remembered Abner's remark that "Them don't sound like turkeys to me."

"Heh. So *that's* how he got that scattergun he went bear hunting with."

"Yes Sir, Cap'n. I figger he just wasn't handy to them 'paches t'kill, and couldn't do nothin' to help with that silly scattergun full 'o birdshot. He warn't no deserter, Sir. He just got his self lost in the ruckus."

Captain Miller thought for a moment. "Yeah, maybe, maybe not. What else do you think of the man?"

'Well, we talked quite a lot what with us both bein' from near t' the same county back home. And you know from them papers you got layin' on your desk, Steinmetz had a good record in the war. Fought in the Battle of the Wilderness, got a bayonet in his butt at Spotsylvania. Savin' three of his buddies near Richmond is what got him his stripes."

"You think maybe those Apaches scared him some, Sergeant?"

"Cap'n, after what he done more'n once in the war, I don't think he's scared of anythin' that moves, man or beast. I been solderin' for near thirty year, and was we back east I'd ride with Steinmetz anytime."

"Back east? What do you mean by 'anything that moves'?"

Sergeant Anderson resettled himself a little, started to reach for a chew of tobacco, then thought better of it. "Like I said, we spent a lot of time doin' campfire talk. And the fella's got one little problem. He's basically a farmer what got caught up in the war. He knows crops, forests, animals and such and is more'n usual attached to 'em."

"Sergeant, what the hell's that got to do with anything?"

"Cap'n, I know this sounds kinda strange, but I think he's just bothered by these hills around us."

"Heh? You mean the Apaches?"

"No Sir, not the savages. The cliffs & canyons, the bushes, the cactus, cat's claw, mesquite, and all them other damn kinds of brush what makes this place so different from the East."

"Chuck, you telling me that this hero of Richmond ran off to Mogollon because he's afraid of cactus?"

"No no, what I mean is I think he sorta got homesick, then drunked up, and then caught a ride with that mule train that supplies us. Still think we'd all be better off we hadn't of gone after 'im."

"I have to agree with that Sergeant. And we wouldn't have if he hadn't tried to bust up that saloon in that mining camp. But when a deputy marshal says he's caught a deserter, well, I've got no choice, you know that."

"Yeah. Is that all, Cap'n?"

"Yes, that's—no, wait. There's something else. I've been thinking about what you saw when you took a detail up Talavera Canyon looking for that weird civilian that Steinmetz claims he found. And that damn bear; at least some of his story was true."

"Hoo-ee, Cap'n. You should'a seen that critter. Big old grizzly sow, with her spine blowed apart at the neck. Steinmetz damn near took her head off; worst case of dead b'ar I ever seen!"

"Yes Chuck, I know about the bear. Ah, Sarge, did you see any sign at all of some civilian like Steinmetz keeps telling us about? Nobody else found any sign of some stranger, especially one in short pants, for God's sake. You think the fella might be a little off his rocker after that bear deal, maybe just imagined that civilian?"

"No sir, Cap'n. I think he's on the level. The medic showed me some bandages he took off of Steinmetz from where that b'ar got in a lick or two. They was right back of Steinmetz's shoulder; ain't no way he could'a put 'em there. And the bandages, they wasn't army kit neither. They was some sort of sticky things."

"But Christ Chuck. A pistol that fires *sixteen* rounds without reloading?"

"Ah, Cap'n, ah—they's somethin' else I found up that canyon by the dead b'ar. Didn't show 'em to you earlier 'cause they just don't make no sense, not one bit."

"Oh Jesus, Chuck. What else?"

Sergeant Anderson reached into the pocket of his light blue uniform pants with the yellow leg stripe and brought out a handful of small, metal objects and dumped them on the desk.

"These here c'atridge cases, they was about a dozen of 'em right where the b'ar was. But they ain't any kind I ever seen or heerd of. Funny color too."

The captain picked up one of the spent cartridges, looked it over, and read the identification head stamp on the base.

"WCC 9mm. Wonder what that means; never heard of any such! Where the hell did these come from?"

"Damn if I know, Cap'n. That's why I didn't show 'em to nobody."

"Oh Jesus. They'd make my report a whole lot harder to write. Anyhow thanks for your help Sergeant. I better get after the job at hand."

"Yes Sir. Ah, Cap'n, what are you gonna say about Sergeant—ah Mister Steinmetz?"

"Damned if I know." Captain Miller looked again at the hand full of spent nine millimeter cartridge cases and thought again about Steinmetz's comment that "The stove up civilian had a pistol that could shoot all afternoon on one load." Senseless ranting of a man

148

who had been through a bad fight with North America's biggest predator is what Captain Miller had thought. But those cartridge cases—

"Sergeant, did anybody see you pick up these empties?"

"Naw, most everybody in the detail was busy bein' impressed by that ole b'ar, Cap'n."

"OK, you're dismissed, Sergeant. I know you have your own work to do. And Chuck, next time you're sent to bring in a prisoner, don't give him any damn weapons!"

For half an hour Captain Elias Miller sat quietly at his desk thinking about what Steinmetz and Sergeant Anderson said about the civilian's strange pistol, the little bunch of fired cartridge cases there on his desk, and the report he had to write. "Gotta be aluminum," the puzzled officer muttered to himself. "Jesus, that stuff is almost as expensive as silver; nobody's going to make ammo out of it."

A few minutes later Captain Miller sat up straighter." Just a simple drunk and disorderly report, that's all that's needed. Who knows what the hell happened; best not seem like we're all crazy out here." Opening his desk drawer, he swept the handful of fired nine millimeter cartridge cases into it to join the single one Abner had given him. "The less said about these empties the better," he thought as he picked up a pencil and began to write.

Miguel's Office, New Mexico State University, March, 2007

One more time Professor Miguel Anaya read the photocopied document that he had received from U. S Army Archives at West Point. It was a copy of the service record for a soldier named Abner Abraham Steinmetz. Miguel read of two awards for valor during the War Between the States and another one years later for rescuing a senior officer who was nearly assassinated during some riots in Washington. But, at the end was an unusual notation. In 1884, Sergeant Steinmetz had become an incurable alcoholic during an assignment to New Mexico Territory. The report said that because of his previous record and the time he had already spent in the stockade, the man had been "retired by command decision with the right to keep his pension."

Drumming his fingers on the desk Miguel stared at the as yet unopened envelope just lying there, taunting him. It was from his great-aunt Wilma Martensen, a distant, elderly relative. Miguel almost wished he had never written to her, asking the question the letter was likely to answer.

Finally, knowing he had to face the inevitable, Miguel laid down the photocopied report, and picked up the envelope with the penciled address, noticing again that it was a little too heavy to contain just a letter. As he tore the envelope open, a small object, wrapped in a piece of red and white checkered, gingham cloth, fell out. Then he began to read.

"Yep son, yer family does have some folk in it name of Steinmetz, and one of 'em was in the Civil War. I heered talk of him a long ways back. Best I know is that he was mine and your mammy's grandpappy. Nobody talks on him much on account of he was a drunk what got shed of the army. Don't nobody know what happened to him 'cept he went t' army jail. Don't nobody know much what he done after he shucked the army 'cept he married up with my own personal granny and quit drinkin'. Some folk says he went t' farmin', found God, an run around talkin' nonsense about folks ridin' round the sky makin' streaks in the air. Don't rightly know and don't care. Fella couldn't hev amounted to much, what with army jail and all.

"They's one more thing though. My own personal ma used to talk about her pappy's lucky charm he seemed real fond of. Claimed it saved his life and give him luck. Ma said maybe it did 'cause if she done her cipherin' right he was near a hunderd years old when he kicked the bucket. She give the thing to me and it's been in my sewin' basket ever since. It ain't never been no luck to me so I'm sendin' it along cause you seem curious about the old feller. Thanks for writin'. When you're as old as me it's good t' hear from anybody about anythin'."

"Huh, old Abner, he sure as hell amounted to something as far as I'm concerned." muttered Miguel, now certain that his meeting with Abner Steinmetz was every bit as real as the brass shotgun shell he always carried in his pocket.

Miguel unwrapped the brightly colored cloth covering the object that had made his great-aunt's envelope seem a bit heavy. Instantly he recognized his great grandpappy's lucky token, and with a trembling hand picked up the big, silver, Mexican coin. Right away he noticed that it was very worn, not new-looking as it had been last time he had seen it. Then Miguel laid the coin on his desk beside the old brass shotgun shell and sat back in his chair, wondering how old great-grandpappy Abner had dealt with their meeting in Talavera Canyon.

Then, as Miguel leaned forward to examine their lucky token more closely, he noticed that the coin's date was no longer legible, having long ago been scratched away with some sharp pointed object. Miguel sat back, took a deep breath, let it out, and told himself that he better get used to the idea that his adventure had not been a hallucination.

The End

A TALE OF TWO FRIENDS

Lewiston, Montana, 1919

*W*ith the sheepskin collar of his coat turned up against the wet, winter wind, the young man stood listening with little interest to the frail, old minister's words. But his eyes never wavered from the scene in front of him, his almost-handsome face showing no emotion at all. Other people in the group that had gathered for the ceremony avoided looking at the man, uncomfortable about what might be in his heart. The occasional snorting from one of the nearby horses and the minor creaking of a carriage harness showed the animal's displeasure with standing in the rain with nothing to graze on.

One bystander sneaked a glance at the face framed by the heavy collar and, seeing something intense in the man's eyes, looked away. But no one noticed as the fellow reached inside his coat and put his hand on the cold, walnut and steel grip of the revolver stuffed in his belt.

As the minister finished reading, he closed the black, leather-bound Bible and nodded at a burly assistant in heavy overalls who was leaning on a nearby work wagon. Hunching his shoulders against the weather, the workman threw down his cigarette and, along with two fellow gravediggers, ambled over to the ceremony. Two of the men took up the slack in two ropes slung under the coffin as the third bent over, about to remove one of the wooden supports just above the open grave.

But all three stopped still as they sensed several mourners turn in apprehension toward the man in the sheepskin coat. He had stepped forward, with the authority of an outdoorsman used to behaving as he saw fit. He was holding the revolver in his two hands.

The minister, his face a bit more pale than even the winter season could justify, clutched his Bible closer to his dark vestments as he stepped back from the head of the grave. All whispering stopped as the mourners watched the not yet thirty-year-old man walk up to the coffin with the heavy revolver in his right hand. As he reached the simple pine box he pointed the Colt's muzzle at the sawn board top.

"Open it," he ordered to the world in general.

No one moved, that is until the squinted eyes framed in the sheepskin collar turned toward one of the workmen. Motioning with the revolver's barrel, the man made it plain that the workman should fetch a claw hammer from the nearby wagon and open the box.

After the lid had been pried open, the workman, whose trembling hand had let the hammer slide into the open grave, stepped back, hoping his involvement was over. The minister held his breath as the man in the sheepskin coat pointed the Colt .44 toward the partly opened, head end of the casket. Time ticked by in silence except for the patter of raindrops on nearby black umbrellas.

Three Years Earlier, Springtime, 1916

Jason Banner plodded along through the freshly turned soil watching just two things. One was the single bottom plow he was following as it cut its furrow through the rich, black earth. The other was the view across the gray's rump, back and head, right between the horse's ears. Jason was making sure that his plowed furrows were straight and parallel to the fence line at the edge of the field. Two more passes and this field would be done, ready for seeding.

Thirty minutes later Jason was in Mr. Manchester's barn, one of the finest in southern Montana. He was giving the tired horse a rubdown and inspection to make sure that the plough's harness hadn't caused any undue abrasions on the old mare's hide. He gave the animal a little grain and then turned her loose in the corral where she headed toward the water trough.

As he struggled to hang the heavy, leather horse collar and harness on its rack, Jason's glance outside caught sight of a rider a couple of hundred yards away heading toward the barn. He knew who it was, but he stopped his task to wonder why Johnny MacFee was in such a hurry. Whapping his hat against the little sorrel's rump and howling like a banshee, Johnny was riding like half the Sioux nation was chasing him.

As Johnny skidded the excited quarter horse to a stop in front of the barn, Jason saw what was chasing his friend. No wild Indians. Only Duncan Manchester whose father owned the ranch Johnny and Jason worked for. The elderly Mr. Manchester had long ago taken in the two orphaned boys and Margie, Johnny's little sister, in exchange for the work the boys could do around the farm.

Years earlier little Margie, just six years old, died in the street because of a carelessly driven freight wagon running much too fast. The wagon driver claimed it was an accident and most of the town decided to agree. But Johnny hadn't agreed. He had become a bitter and remorseful eight-year-old rebel. Because of his loss, Johnny and Jason grew close, and around the Manchester ranch the pair shared a near stepbrother relationship with Duncan.

"Hey, you cheated!" yelled Duncan, as he arrived just seconds behind Johnny. "You didn't say anything about riding bareback or cutting across that pasture—"

"Nobody said I couldn't; you could have dumped your saddle too if you had the balls for it. Now you owe me three bucks!"

"You could have busted up that filly or yourself jumping fences like that."

"Three bucks, three bucks," said Johnny, holding out his hand.

After both riders had dismounted, Duncan Manchester magnanimously counted out three silver dollars into the outstretched hand, along with his mount's reins and said, "Winner has to put the animals away." Then he turned and ran toward the farmhouse, feigning fear of retaliation from his friend.

Jason stepped forward to help his buddy with the two excited horses. "Jesus. You bet three dollars on a race using Mr. Manchester's sorrel? Three whole dollars? You don't even have *one*. What would you do if you lost?"

"Hey Jace. You know I don't gamble to lose! Besides, I knew that if I went bareback and got that sorrel fired up some she could beat anything Duncan had the courage to ride. That filly can run like a fox with its tail on fire when she needs to."

"Yeah, well, looked to me like you barely made it."

"Heh—Dunc rode better than I thought he would. That's why I took a short cut; he doesn't like jumping fences."

"Jesus, bareback I wouldn't either," muttered Jason as he joined his friend in walking the two horses around before rubbing them down.

"I talked to Mr. Manchester today, Jace. He said sure enough, we can use his .32-40 in the tournament tomorrow. We can load some cartridges tonight after dinner. You cast and size the bullets; I'll prime and charge the cases and do the crimping, OK?"

"Yeah, man, leave me working over the hot forge and greasing slugs while you do the easy part, as usual."

As they headed to the farmhouse for chow the two continued their good-natured banter about competitive shooting, something both boys enthusiastically participated in.

"I'm gonna shoot your socks off in that match tomorrow, old buddy," said Johnny. "I'm bound to win 'cause that Colt for first prize is just what I need to be the fastest *pistolero* in the west, right?"

The first prize in the tournament was a brand new Colt Single Action Army model revolver that had been on display for the last month in a local hardware store window.

"Not a chance. You've never beaten me yet" said Jason. "Long range rifle shooting is precision work, the stuff of steady-handed, sharp-eyed guys like me. Not for smart aleck, fast mouth types like someone else around here."

Much as he had used it to spur the sorrel to a win, Johnny whapped Jason with his hat and yelled, "Bet I beat ya to the house!" With that he sprinted toward the farmhouse with Jason at his heels. When they arrived, with Johnny ahead of Jason, they were met by Duncan, who reminded Johnny that he had to go back and fetch the saddle he had taken off the sorrel just before their race had started.

***

The next day, after having returned the borrowed rifle to Mr. Manchester, the two boys were walking amid good-natured scuffling as they left the Grant County fairgrounds heading home. The rifle tournament, which had been mostly slow fire shooting at ranges of 200 yards, was over.

"Well Jace, you are now the official county champ," said Johnny with a grin as he slapped his buddy on the back one more time. "And I have something for you." He then handed Jason a cloth-wrapped bundle.

"Ho, now we find out what the mystery is you've been carrying around all day and wouldn't let me touch!" Unwrapping the gift he found a brand new, steel mold designed for casting .44 caliber bullets from scrap lead.

Grinning at Jason's surprise at the gift, Johnny added, "It's not just for you, you know. I figure we're both going to shoot that nifty trophy you won and we can't afford to buy all the store-bought ammo we're gonna put through that thing." Pointing at the bullet mold, he added "And that's for hollow point slugs; lots better for medium and small game, right?"

"But you had to order this thing weeks ago! What if I hadn't won the tournament? You'd have been out—"

"Shoot man, we both know you're the best long-distance rifleman in these parts. I'd bet on you anytime."

"All right," said Jason, holding the new bullet mold in both hands and the trophy Colt revolver, chambered for the modern .44 Smith & Wesson Special cartridges, under his arm. "Tonight we'll load some cases then take it out tomorrow after work, OK?"

"Yeah man and I know where I can find a leather belt and old holster that ought to fit," said Johnny.

***

Several months later Johnny and Jason were hunting quail together. They had worked out a way of taking turns with their jointly owned .410 gauge shotgun. As they walked together down scrub oak-filled draws near wheat fields, they would occasionally come across a covey of Gamble's quail which would then flush in a near explosion of birds flying in several directions. The one with the shotgun would get a shot; if he missed, then it was the other guy's turn to carry the shotgun. As they scared up one covey of quail after another during the day, Johnny got most of the shooting, because he rarely ever missed.

The little Iver-Johnson was a single shot shotgun, which meant that the shooter usually got just one bird out of a flock. But Johnny had developed a technique of holding extra cartridges between the fingers of his left hand that was gripping the fore-end of the little .410 and he could fire, break open the action, reload, and get a second bird. Once he managed to flush a flock and get three quail before they were all out of range, with Jason staring open mouthed in admiration for his friend's speed and coordination.

On this day they came near an abandoned farmhouse and found the usual junk pile, mostly rusty cans and empty bottles.

"Hey Jace, I'll make you a bet," said Johnny, eyeing the glass bottles lying around.

"A-ha, another bet," said Jason, referring to his buddy's quick interest in any kind of gamble.

"Yep. Unstrap that .44 you've got around your worthless belly and hand it over." Johnny then bent over and picked up a light green bottle partially plugged with dirt.

"I'll bet you a day's chores that I can toss this in the air, draw your .44, and bust the thing with one shot."

Knowing that Johnny had been frequently borrowing the Colt .44 for practice shooting, and aware of how well his buddy could handle a shotgun on moving targets, Jason wasn't about to take that bet.

"Heh, I ain't that dumb fella. Get yourself another sucker."

"Ok, man with no guts, I'll give you a better chance." Johnny then picked up a brown beer bottle and said, "Both of 'em, OK?"

"Are you serious? "Jason had a skeptical expression.

"Still no courage eh? Some gambler you'd make," said Johnny as he picked up a small, white colored jug.

Jason, looking at the three bottles, unbuckled his new .44 Colt and handed it to his friend. "I'm gonna enjoy sitting in the shade watching you do my chores, man with big mouth!"

Having strapped the gun belt around his waist, Johnny held all three bottles by their necks in his left hand.

"OK, look out for flying glass!" Johnny then threw all three bottles as high as he could as he drew the Colt. Clouds of white smoke belched from the revolver's muzzle as it roared three times in what sounded almost like one explosion. As the noise died away, a rain of green, white and brown glass fragments peppered down on Jason's amazed gaze.

"Jesus. Now I know what kind of practice you've been doing when you borrowed that thing."

With Jason carrying the shotgun and Johnny their sack of birds, and with a lot of scuffling and shoulder punching, the two friends headed back to town. As they walked past the local post office they saw a prominently displayed sign in the large glass window. It was a poster proclaiming the country's need for young men to join the U.S. Army—now. The post office was doubling as an army recruiting office. And surrounding the big poster were fresh copies of the daily newspaper with red headlines reading:

"AMERICA JOINS BRITAIN IN FIGHT AGAINST THE KAISER!"

"Whoa, said Johnny. Looky there."

Both boys read the details confirming local suspicions that the United States would soon be involved in the war in Europe. Without discussing it, both had decided they would join up when the time came. Now, the time had come.

"I'm gonna join, right now."

"Me too, but we have to wait till tomorrow. This place isn't open on Sunday."

"Yeah, OK Jace. And while we're in that big army, I expect to see you shoot at Camp Perry and take a military rifleman's championship or two, right old buddy? And I'm gonna be right there with you, shooting a pistol faster than anyone has ever done yet. Then we're off to fight the Hun! You can bet on it."

"Yeah," muttered Jason, slightly annoyed at his friend's lighthearted reaction to such a serious subject.

The two walked on home in silence, each with thoughts about what the future had in store.

***

Ten days later Jason, having enlisted in the U.S. Army, knew he would be leaving soon for training as an infantryman. But he was bothered because Johnny had been behaving oddly for the last day or two and hadn't mentioned the war or the army. Jason decided to confront Johnny, hoping there wasn't some serious problem. That evening he did so as they walked to the bunkhouse after dinner.

"Well, we're joined up. When did they tell you you're gonna go?" asked Jason. "Same as me I suppose."

"I'm not gonna go."

"What? What'd you say?"

"I said I'm not gonna go, damn it!"

"Hey, c'mon. We signed up at the same time; they'll probably send us to the same training camp, right?"

"I *can't* go. I got me a job right here!"

"You got a job? A *job?* The army, we gotta go fight the Hun. You know that. Jesus, you're kidding, right?"

Johnny's shoulders slumped, and he gave in.

"Oh hell, Jace. I *can't* go; the damned army won't take me!"

"What—"

"Jace, the physical exam. They say I've got a murmurey heart or something. All I know's that I can't go."

"Jesus, Johnny. I—"

"Jace, it means that you gotta go fight the Hun alone. You, ah . . . you won't have me there to keep your butt out of trouble." Johnny was trying to take the conversation lightly, but not doing well.

The two walked along in silence for a while, then Jason spoke. "You said a job, man. What job?"

"I talked to Sheriff Swenson; he says I can hire on as a deputy." With his voice almost choking, Johnny said, "I'm gonna be a deputy sheriff, Jace. And you, you're gonna be a war hero."

***

Two days later Jason Banner was standing on the town's railroad platform waiting for a troop train that was due to pick up the town of Lewiston's contribution to the war effort. Like a flock of sheep, nine scruffy new recruits stood with parents, friends, and wives, all trying to be optimistic about the war. Jason and Johnny stood a little apart from the crowd, Jason with a package under his right arm. As the train arrived and folks filed on board, Jason handed the package to his only friend.

"Johnny, this is for you. It's all yours now; a sheriff's deputy can make better use of it than a lowly infantryman can."

From the shape of the package Johnny knew Jason was giving him the .44 Colt revolver he had won in the rifle tournament.

With his voice cracking a little with emotion, Johnny said, "Jace, your trophy Colt. Man, I know what that means. I promise to take good care of it till you get home. Then we'll both be back hunting quail, busting bottles and winning tournaments, right?"

With moist eyes Jason shook Johnny's hand and then embraced the friend who was practically his brother.

"Hey, you don't have to get blubbery, Jace," said Johnny, choked up himself. "When you get back, why with my shiny deputy star and your war hero medals we'll be the talk of the town amongst the ladies, right?"

Jason climbed on the train, which had already started moving. "Keep in practice, man."

"Yeah, Jace. You too, and you damn well better come back in one piece old buddy."

With that, Infantryman Jason Banner went off to war and Deputy Johnny MacFee went to work.

Winter, 1917, Somewhere in France

Corporal Jason Banner looked up and down the cold, muddy trench at his fellow infantrymen. In his little corner of France, he and fewer than ninety fellow soldiers, along with a handful of French civilians, huddled against the rain. The miserable weather and the fact that they had not slept for more than 24 hours and had eaten cold, canned stew for the last week had many of the men thinking about giving up.

But the sloppy, almost garbage dump conditions in their frozen trenches were the least of their problems. They knew that just a few hundred yards away in another set of trenches another group of soldiers was waiting. A larger force of Germans whose officers were even then making plans for a massive charge into the smaller American group.

Jason, huddled under his wet overcoat and trying to keep his Springfield rifle as dry as possible, was listening to an American captain talking to two older sergeants.

"Reinforcements—our reinforcements—won't be here till about dark. You boys are going to have to hang on till then," said the captain.

"They's four, five hours of daylight between now and dark," said Master Sergeant Mitchell, a gray-haired veteran whose time in service went back almost to the Indian wars. "Them Bosch is gonna boil over here on top of us long before that."

Ignoring the comment the captain continued. "We've got about two hundred men and two tanks coming tonight; that will give us our edge. You fellas just have to keep the men on their toes for a few more hours."

"Oh hell, tanks," muttered Mackinly Drake, a heavy set staff sergeant. "Just pieces of junk for us to dig out'a the mud!"

"Enough of that talk, Sergeant. You got a job to do, so do it," said the captain.

"Shit, we've been—"

"Staff Sergeant Drake! I don't give a damn what you've been doing; what your men are going to do is all I care about! None of that *can't* crap. You *can* and you *will* hold. Got it?"

For a time there was no further response from either of the sergeants, and Jason understood why. For two days the two sets of trenches had been trading shots and casualties with neither side gaining nor losing ground. Both sides had been waiting for the stalemate to be settled by the arrival of reinforcements, American or German, whichever came first. Unfortunately, the Germans had been reinforced just an hour earlier and no one had much doubt about the immediate future of the conflict.

Finally, Staff Sergeant Drake spoke up again, his voice almost like a whining child. "Cap'n, we're half starved and ain't got much ammo. Most guys got dysentery or pneumonia; we're already—"

Jason flinched in surprise as the captain, with the lightning speed of a prizefighter, delivered a flat hand slap to the side of the sergeant's head.

"You are not dead yet Sergeant. I've heard the talk about white flags and such, and there won't be any more of that! Like rats we're living in these stink holes, but it's a paradise compared to a German prison camp. You, either of you, hear any more talk about giving up, you fix it quick, same as how I just did with you."

Both sergeants stood up straighter, almost at attention as the captain glanced at Jason.

"What are you looking at Corporal? Get you eyes and your rifle pointed over there, at the Bosch, damn it."

Jason moved higher in the trench, pointed his Model 03 Springfield toward the muddy sky and stole a peek over a lower spot in the trench wall into the "no man's land" in front of him. He had been thinking about a big tree blown over on its side by an artillery hit, its big root structure looking like a many-armed monster silhouetted against the murky sky. And Jason kept listening to the conversation behind him.

"We got one advantage; they don't know much about our strength, and they'll want to know more before they decide when and where to charge," said the captain.

"It's about fifty yards to that tree" thought Jason, "and about two-fifty more to the German trenches." As he pondered the frozen mud of the battle-scarred desolation in front of him, he was still listening to the conversation behind him.

"Now lissen up both of you," continued the captain. "Those Krauts are going to poke at us some to learn what they can. They'll likely make a little run at us just to feel things out."

Looking at the rise and fall of the slightly hilly no man's land, Jason thought, "A fella'd have a pretty good view of the whole place from that tree. And there's that low swale between here and there, . . ."

Still listening Jason heard the lieutenant say, "Just keep this standoff going a few more hours men. Then Major Gershwin and his boys will show up and save our sorry butts, OK?"

"A few hours," Jason thought as he looked back at the three men and at the large wooden ammunition box near Sergeant Drake's foot. And he noticed the cased binocular the man had set on the box.

Then Jason made his decision. With his Springfield slung across his back Jason walked to the ammo box and picked up two cloth bandoleers of .30 Government cartridges in their five round stripper clips, grabbed the binocular, and scrambled up the side of the trench.

"Hey, what the fuck you doin' Corporal? Get your butt back here—now!" yelled the captain as Jason, scrunched down, started slogging toward the overturned tree. No one on the German side even noticed as Jason took advantage of the low swale.

"Shit," muttered Staff Sergeant Drake. "You think he went to do his own white flag?"

"With his rifle and extra ammo? Think again, Mac," said the gray-haired master sergeant. "And remember how Banner made corporal in the first place."

"Banner? That's Corporal Banner?" asked the captain.

"Yes sir, sure is. He's killed seven Bosch sneakin' around in no man's land with that Springfield of his. He can nail 'em from so far away the bastards don't even know where the shot come from," replied the old sergeant. With a grin Sergeant Mitchell added, "He's not the white flag type, Captain."

Remembering who Jason was and with his whiny tone in check, Staff Sergeant Drake added, "Yeah, a few weeks back on that sunny day we had we could see Kraut helmets as they was walking around in their holes. Sometimes you'd see one try to ease a peek over the top. They quit doin' that cause not just once but *twice* Banner shot the little pointy thing off the top of one of them helmets! I seen 'im do it."

Jason slid to a stop against the fallen tree glad that it had a trunk nearly three feet in diameter and noticed the cover the jumbled root mass would give him. With the higher ground behind him his hiding spot would be almost invisible to the observers on the German side. Jason had now become a sniper with a clear view of most of the German side of no man's land. "Just a few hours" he thought.

***

The next morning Staff Sergeant Mackinly Drake, summoned by Major Charles Gershwin, stood at attention in a newly-erected tent wondering what he had done wrong now.

"At ease, Sergeant, you're just here to tell me about Banner's actions yesterday, and Private Worth here is going to write it all down. I'm recommending Banner for decoration."

"Yes sir," said the relieved noncom. "I can tell you all of, well most of it anyhow."

"Y' see, just like Captain Sanders said they might, them Krauts tried to do a little testin' of us, feelin' us out. A couple o' their officers, one funny lookin' fat guy on horseback—"

"Refer to the man as a German officer, Sergeant."

"Uh, yes sir. Anyhow they was two of 'em—German Officers—on horses, with swords out sure enough, and they sent a bunch of guys up out o' their trench t' come over at us. Well, quick as they done that, the fat—ah, the first German officer, well he just fell out of his saddle, probably long before anybody heard a shot if they ever did."

"You saw this sergeant?"

"Yes sir, not as good as I might of, cause Banner, he stole my binoculars, more power to 'im. He used 'em better than I ever could of."

"All right Sergeant, then what?"

"Well, next thing the other officer he slides out o' his saddle just like the first. And the Kraut footsloggers, they seen it happen cause they most all stopped. While they was doin' that one of them dropped over, and the rest decided to regroup in their trench.

"All the rest o' the day, ever time any Kraut tried to come up out o' that trench he'd catch a bullet or at least get mud in his face. Bein' deep down in the trench got real popular.

"Then the Bosch tried throwing hand grenades; that was dumb; nobody could throw anywhere's near far enough and they didn't know where to throw anyway. They tried settin' up machine guns but nobody wanted to man 'em after the first gunner died. It got kinda funny watchin' them Krauts shootin' machine guns and rifles from just over the edge o' their bunkers where they couldn't see nothin', sprayin' no man's land with blind, eight millimeter lead."

Then Sergeant Drake's enthusiastic report got a little somber.

"Too bad the bastards got lucky," said the sergeant, thinking of the bullet that had hit Jason.

"Corporal Banner is doing just fine in the medic's tent; pass the word along, Sergeant. And thank you for your moving narration. You may go. Oh, and for your information, now that we are relieved, you boys are going to get a little rest."

"Yes sir, thank you sir." Staff Sergeant Drake saluted and left the command tent, thankful that he hadn't done anything wrong after all.

Lewiston, Montana, 1919

Jason Banner had only been in town for two hours, and already he was feeling uneasy. He had undergone a hero's welcome by the town with several politicians making speeches about how their local son had "helped save the world from the Hun" by using the exceptional marksmanship skill the townsfolk had always known he had. Having been offered far more drinks at a local bar than any man could handle and having turned down most of them, Jason felt self-conscious about the limelight.

The next morning found Jason thinking of leaving much sooner than he had planned, for two reasons. He had come to realize that there was nothing left in the town for him—no family or close friends. His old employer Mr. Manchester, had passed away during Jason's time in Europe.

But most of all Jason was bothered because Johnny hadn't met him at the train; in fact he wasn't even in town. When Jason asked about his old friend he got vague answers, people just saying that he was gone. Jason decided to go see the local sheriff, presumably Johnny's employer, and see if he knew where he was.

Sheriff Joe Swenson's office consisted of one room near the back of the courthouse, and two cells off to one side. The man himself was sitting at his old, walnut desk when Jason stepped through the open doorway and knocked lightly on the doorframe.

"Excuse me sir," said Jason as the elderly man looked up from his work. "If I'm not interrupting anything I'd like to ask about one of your deputies."

"Shoot no, son, y'er not interruptin' anything at all. Just some paper stuff I gotta' do," said the sheriff with a good-natured grin as he sat more upright in his chair. "But before I can help ya I gotta know which deputy, and how come you're interested in the man, right?"

"Well I'm —"

"C'mon over and have a sit young fella," interrupted the sheriff as he pointed toward a nearby chair. "Don't I know you from somewhere?"

"Yes sir, my name is Jason Banner. I've been out of town for a few years, but I grew up here."

"Shoot son, y'er Sergeant Banner, the fella that knocked off all them Krauts!" The sheriff stood up, walked around his desk and offered Jason his hand.

"I'm damned pleased to have you back in town, by golly. I'd of been down to the railroad station with the other folks yesterday, but I just got back home last night. We're all real proud of you son."

"Well thank you sir. I'm just glad it's all over."

Sheriff Swenson motioned again toward the chair and Jason sat down. Then the sherrif went back behind his desk. "Now, tell me all about it Sergeant. I heard you shot some of them Kraut fellas from half a mile away."

"No, nothing like that sir. I just got in a few lucky shots —"

"Well anyhow, you done your duty for God and Country as they say. And now, what can I do for ya? You maybe lookin' for a job?"

"Ah, no sir, I'm just trying to find out where Johnny MacFee went. I think he used to work for you and —"

"Oh jeez, Deputy MacFee. Yeah, he worked for me for about a year, then I had to let him go." The old lawman leaned forward with his elbows on his desk, and his face took on a trace of a frown.

"Let him go? Go where?"

"Oh cripes Sergeant. I'd kinda forgotten that you two boys was buddies awhile back. I hate to have to tell ya about Deputy MacFee."

"I know Johnny was doing OK just before I left for France and I wrote him a lot. Never got an answer. He's OK isn't he?"

"Yeah, I suppose he is but can't say for sure," said the sheriff, not enjoying the conversation.

"Y' see, MacFee was a good deputy for the first few months. Folks liked him, he done his work right, never hassled anybody that didn't need it, and I thought I had a good man on board. Then things started to change.

"He started hangin' out down to the White Star more than he needed to. You know the place, right?"

Jason did indeed know of the White Star. A local gambling joint and nightclub.

"Y' see, Johnny had to go there to break up brawls now and then. He got real well-acquainted with the management there, and they gave him a part time job as a bouncer. I'd of rather he hadn't done that, but it wouldn't have been too bad except that he got to playin' the tables hisself a little too much. Ran up a considerable gambling debt he couldn't pay," said the sheriff, shaking his grayed head to indicate his displeasure with events.

"I can't have a deputy like that. Got so' I couldn't tell just who MacFee was workin' for. I called him on it a couple times, told him to make a choice; was he goin' to be a lawman or a gamblin' bum. He didn't take that well, so I let him go."

The room was silent for a time while Jason soaked up the unbelievable words he had just heard.

"Then it looks like I better go down to the Star and see if anybody knows where he went," said Jason.

"Yeah, well before you go off down there, there's more I ought to tell ya. Y' see, MacFee was in debt, like I said. Now Brett Mathews, the Star's owner, had his own troubles. Seems that two fellas from who knows where had it in for Mathews, and showed up at the Star one night, late. Nobody knows for sure what happened, but there was some shootin' and them two fellas wound up dead. Mathews claimed he and MacFee done it, and it was self-defense. Probably was. In any case if them two fellas tried anything stupid with MacFee around they was bound to lose. One thing that boy was, was quick. He could draw and fire that .44 of his like a spring loaded bobcat."

"A Colt .44?"

"Oh yeah, that one you won at the shootin' match a few years back. MacFee always said that it was his best friend's gun—your gun. He was real proud of that.

"Y' see, after that shootin' MacFee's debt seemed to disappear, and he sported a lot more spendin' money than you might expect from a bouncer's pay. Some folks figgered it was Mathews gratitude for savin' his butt, but I had a different theory."

"What do you mean, Sheriff?"

"Oh hell, I don't know for sure. But there's been several piddlin' bank jobs done around the state, and some folks think one of the fellas involved looked a lot like my ex-deputy. Same kind of horse too. Thing is, somebody got hurt in the bank robbery up t' Kalispell, but I don't know the details."

Sheriff Swenson was getting worked up as he recalled events, and then realized he was talking about a friend of Jason's

"Jeez son, I'm sorry as hell to have to tell ya about all this. I'd rather be buyin' you a beer across the street. Hell of a homecomin' to hear news like that about an old friend."

"Yeah, well, I guess I'll go see if Mr. Mathews knows where his ex-bouncer is. Then maybe Johnny and I can clear up some of these rumors."

Jason stood up and stuck out his hand to the sheriff. "Thanks for your help sir. I guess I'll be on my way."

"Hey, like I mentioned son, if you're lookin' for work—"

"No, Sheriff, thanks anyway. I've signed up with the Pinkertons, so I already have a job."

"Hey, good enough. I guess that makes you a Pinkerton detective then. Though I hate to say it about your old buddy, it wouldn't surprise me if you run across a wanted poster on 'im one day, the way he seemed headed."

Tamarack Strike, Idaho

The following week Jason stepped off a train onto the station platform of a little town called Tamarack Strike in the Idaho Panhandle. One look up the unpaved main street of the small town showed Jason that it was little more than a mining camp with two bars, one hotel, a telegraph office and little else to offer. Jason headed for the Aces Up Bar and Gambling Emporium, the place Brett Mathews had said was Johnny's current employer.

Jason stopped at the entrance and looked inside some before entering. The large room with a bar down one side, a magnificent mirrored back bar and about twenty-five tables, was nearly empty on this Thursday afternoon.

Just as Jason stepped inside, he saw his old friend talking with the barkeep at the back of the room. When Jason saw Johnny he almost didn't recognize him. Well-fitted dark pants, white shirt and black silk vest were not at all what he was expecting from his old orphanage buddy. But glad to see his old friend, Jason walked toward the other man.

Johnny instantly recognized his buddy.

"Son of a bitch! Looky here folks," said MacFee to the bar's few patrons in general. "By the grace of God, Johnny's come marching home again, hurrah, hurrah!"

Grabbing Jason's right hand in his own and with his left slapping his friend on the back, Johnny said, "My God it's good to see you, Jace. I been keeping my fingers crossed for ya all through the war and hearing about your exploits all over."

Jason too bubbled over with excitement at seeing his only real friend and both engaged in a bit of horseplay that knocked a chair over.

"Sit down, Jace, sit down," said Johnny as he picked up the chair and set it upright. Motioning to the barkeep who was staring at the commotion, he said, "Mack, get me my own bottle and some glasses; bring 'em here. This is the best friend a man ever had!"

"No whisky for me," said Jason, "but I could sure use a cold beer."

"Beer it is, old buddy."

Mack promptly brought a foaming draft beer, a bottle of expensive Canadian malt whisky and one shot glass.

"Man you gotta tell me what you were doing over there in Europe. All about the Krauts, the war, and oh yes, about the nice French ladies, hey?"

"Oh man it wasn't much, just a big mess. Cold, muddy, hungry, and scared, that's all I remember."

"Yeah sure, from what I heard you shot half the German Army and got the medals to prove it!"

"No, it wasn't like that, just a few lucky shots is all."

"Yeah, sure, we both know that when Jace Banner uses a rifle luck has nothing to do with anything. Hey, that Springfield you used, you still got it? I'd sure like to fire it some."

"Nope, the Army kept it when I mustered out. I'm not so sure I'd want it around anyway. I marched, ate, and slept with that thing for almost two years. All it meant to me was bad times and dead people."

"I see the government let you keep that," said Johnny, nodding toward the Government Model .45 Automatic Jason carried in a cross-draw holster near his left hip. "I never could develop a liking for those modern automatics."

"The army didn't give this one to me. I had to buy it. It feels right in my hand since I got so familiar with one during the war."

"Well," said Johnny, undaunted by Jason's comment, "Later tonight this place will get cranked up and we'll find something better than an old rifle for you to eat and sleep with, hey old buddy?"

"Geez, I wish I could, but come eight o'clock I gotta be back on the train. Gotta be in Kalispel tomorrow." Jason's employer had telegraphed him about a bank robbery in the city and asked him to look into it.

"You can't even stay the night?"

"Next time I'll stay longer," said Jason, and then, to change the subject, added, "Hey, judging from the fancy duds, you must be doing pretty well working here, right?"

"Yep. I'm what you call an assistant manager and general handyman of sorts. I'm getting along pretty good," said Johnny with a grin. "And what are you going to do in Kalispel; you got a job there, or a girl, or what?"

"A job, just starting out. I'm a detective for the Pinkerton Agency. How about that." Jason couldn't help a little show of pride in his new line of work. "I guess I'm gonna try being a lawman too," he added, and then, remembering that Johnny got fired as a deputy, Jason wished he hadn't made his last remark.

"What's up in Kalispel?" asked Johnny, his tone just a little less casual.

"Somebody knocked off a bank up there, one that had some government money in it, and I'm just supposed to talk to the local law and get the details, then report to my boss."

"Banks!" said Johnny, with a definite note of derision in his voice. "People can't get work, miners are going broke, and yet the banks, with all their dough, won't loan to anybody. Can ya blame some fella for grabbing a little out of a bank when his kids are getting hungry? Besides, those robberies don't hurt the banks anyway. They're all insured."

"Hey man. I didn't know you were so sympathetic to bank robbers. What happened to all that enthusiasm for putting thieves and murderers in jail I used to hear you talk about before the war? Back when you signed on as a deputy sheriff?"

"Yeah, back when I was a lawman," said Johnny as he sat back and slumped a little in his chair. "Jace, I learned a lot when I was a deputy." Johnny's voice had almost a pleading quality to it as he looked his old friend directly in the eyes.

"Y' see Jace, there's more than one kind of thief in this world. Stealing from real folks, that's wrong, sure enough. The golden rule and all that. But there's another kind of stealing that banks and their insurance companies do all the time. Just hoarding people's hard-earned money and not giving something back when times get tough for folks. That's stealing too, Jace. An' I've seen plenty of it."

Surprised and a little discomforted by Johnny's attitude, Jason changed the subject.

"Hey man, you still got that old .44 I gave you?"

Back in a jubilant frame of mind again Johnny replied, "Sure Jace. I'm not gonna part with that, at least not till somebody takes it out of my cold, dead hand." In one smooth, almost startling motion Johnny pulled the Colt out of his holster and handed it to Jason.

"Of course I keep it in a better piece of leather these days, hey?"

Taking the Colt in his right hand, Jason noticed that it felt good, almost like meeting an old friend again. With his right thumb, he brought the hammer to the second notch, opened the loading gate, and with his left hand ejected one of the cartridges. He noticed that it was a hand-loaded cartridge, and the lead bullet was one of those from the special bullet mold the two friends had used years before.

Johnny sat back and smiled, pleased that Jason had noticed that he was still loading his own ammo just as before.

"How about that? You still don't use factory mades."

"Nope. Those wad cutter target bullets we used for so long, they work just fine close up too. I guess I've put several hundred pounds of lead down that barrel since you gave it to me. I still practice a lot."

"The barrel might be a little bent from breaking up bar fights," joked Johnny as Jason returned the cartridge to the cylinder and continued to examine their Colt revolver.

"Hey, what's this?" asked Jason as his thumb found two small notches carved in the left side of the Colt's walnut grip.

"Yeah, well, I never went to war, but I've had an exciting moment or two myself Jace."

"Yeah, I guess," said Jason as he handed back the weapon, butt first.

The next few hours passed fast for the two old friends with talk of the good times as they grew up together. Then they walked to the railroad station so Jason could catch his train.

Kalispel, Montana

Stepping off of the train the next day in Kalispel, Montana, Jason scrunched his shoulders some against the cold rain of a dismal spring day and was glad he had managed to keep his olive drab, canvas raincoat from his army days. Glancing for a moment at his muddy military boots he had the fleeting thought that he was out of uniform and sure not ready for inspection. Feeling out of place in the big city and fancy marble-floored building he had just entered, the new Pinkerton man searched a glass-cased directory on the wall for the office of Walter Forrester, the local assistant chief of police. A few minutes later he found himself sitting near the man's desk, holding a cup of coffee that had been provided by a secretary in the front office.

"Well, Detective Banner," said the assistant chief as he examined the business card Jason had just handed him, "What can we do to help a big city detective now?"

"Sir, I've come to learn what you can tell me about the recent bank robbery. The government is interested because they had the bank insured and they hired the Pinkerton Agency to look into things."

"Yeah, I thought that's what you wanted. I got a telegram from your boss saying you'd drop by. Just to make things easy I had Belinda—the lady that gave you that coffee—write down stuff from all the records we have. You can pick it up on your way out." The assistant chief then made busy motions on his desk and added, "If you need anything else, Belinda can get one of our boys to help. I got a meeting to catch."

"I presume there was a newspaper story too sir. Will that be in the stuff your secretary has for me?"

"Newspaper? Naw, we can't copy something like that. Pictures and all. Wasn't much there anyway but stuff about the funeral. Little Marlene was a city counselor's niece so the paper gave it a lot of space. You can get copies of all that at the newspaper office."

"A funeral? A girl was killed? How did she die?"

"Got shot, what'd ya think during a bank robbery!" The assistant chief stood up, anxious to get on with his next meeting. "If you need to know more about Little Marlene or the shooting, check the newspaper office or, better yet, go see Doc Martensen. His office is just across the street from the bank that got robbed."

Jason stood up too and offered his hand to Assistant Chief Forrester. "Well, thanks for your help, sir and—"

"Sorry I gotta go," said the harried assistant chief as he quickly shook Jason's hand. "Belinda, she'll help you with anything else you need."

Two hours later Jason had his folder of transcribed notes from Belinda, had been by the newspaper office, had talked to several employees at the bank itself and had made notes of all he had learned. Then, as he walked out of the bank, he thought of Doctor Martensen.

Jason slogged across the muddy street, glad at least that the sun was coming out, and found that the Doc's office was indeed just opposite the bank. Apparently it had been the best place to take the little girl during the emergency.

***

"Nope, she wasn't in the bank," said Doc Martensen. "She was way off up the street on the other side. There was a lot of shooting going on from robbers and cops too. It was just some stray bullet that got the little tyke."

The doctor stood up from his chair as he filled Jason in on the girl's injury. "Damn chunk of lead severed her spine and broke her hip," he said as he reached into a drawer behind his desk for a little cardboard box he then handed to Jason. "It's bent up some. Hitting bone does that."

Inside, wrapped in cotton, Jason saw a single lead bullet. Immediately he felt a knot in his stomach, as he was reminded of the dozens of chunks of lead and copper he himself had left among the German trenches in France.

Tamarack Strike, Idaho

For the second time Jason found himself on the station platform in the little mining camp of Tamarack Strike. Pleased that it was a nice, sunny day, he headed down the town's single, unpaved street. As he entered the front door of the Aces Up Bar and Gambling Emporium he was startled to hear three gunshots in rapid succession. He stopped, instinctively thinking of the .45 automatic at his waist, and listened, but heard nothing more. He knew that the shots had come from behind the bar. Since he could hear men's jovial, unalarmed voices coming from the bar itself, Jason walked in just as he had a few days earlier.

Again he saw his friend, the bar's "assistant manager and handyman," come in through the back door holding the Colt .44 in both hands, about to reload it. Spotting Jason, Johnny strode over to his friend.

"Hey Jace! Y'er Back again; gonna stay longer this time I hope!"

As before Jason felt good to see his friend, even in the unfamiliar clothes. This time the silk vest was red, and with the white shirt with red garters on the sleeves and black pants, Jason was reminded of a dime novel gunfighter. As Johnny casually dropped the .44 into its hand-fitted, black leather holster, the image seemed complete.

"Hey fella. What was that fuss out back I just heard?" asked Jason with a grin, having already guessed what the single, tight burst of three gunshots shots meant.

"Yep, three busted bottles. Even around here where folks ought'a know better there's always somebody who wants to bet I'm gonna miss sooner or later. I just collected four beers off these fellas." Johnny waved an arm at several men who good-naturedly made derisive remarks in response.

"C'm on Jace; let's have a drink. Chow too. Wan Lee, the cook, has just fixed up a tasty beef roast and some spuds. You gotta be hungry riding that train and all."

Johnny motioned toward a corner of the room. Mack, the barkeep, remembering who Jason was, had already set Johnny's favorite whiskey bottle and a foamy beer for Jason on a table with a fresh, white tablecloth.

For the next hour the two men talked again of old times, and then new times, and how things were in the life of a small, Idaho mining camp. Johnny had introduced Jason to several local friends, business men and miners, and all had made him feel welcome. Clearly, Johnny MacFee was a respected part of the rough, but typical, mining camp community.

But throughout the meal, Jason was tense, and his closest friend noticed it and brought it up.

"Hey, Jace. Is something bothering you? Maybe the detective business isn't suiting you or something?"

Jason swallowed the buttery potatoes he'd been chewing, then picked up his beer glass and held it in both hands, staring at the half inch of yellow fluid. Mack brought him another full glass, which Jason ignored.

"Johnny, you remember when I was here a while back we talked about bank robbing and such?"

"Sure Jace, just nonsense talk—"

"No, let me finish. I think maybe you've got a little sympathy for the business of armed robbery. I need to talk about it with—"

"Oh jeez Jace. I don't hold with robbery, you know that. You walk up to a man and put a pistol in his back and say 'gimme your polk,' that's robbery. But taking a little bit out of the pile of dough in some damn bank, that's different."

Jason sat back for a few moments then said, "Robbery is robbery, Johnny. There's no two ways about—"

"No, that ain't so Jace. Like—like killing somebody. Shooting Krauts by the barrelful like you did, that's killing people, but it ain't murder, not by a long shot."

174

Jason's stomach tightened up again in the knot he had come to know too frequently in recent days as he slumped back in his chair and laid his two hands palm down on the white tablecloth.

Seeing the discomfort in his friend's expression, Johnny tried to take some of the awkwardness out of the remark he had just made.

"Aw hell, Jace. Have some more of that beer. And Mack can fetch us a big slab of apple pie and—"

"Johnny," said Jason. "Did you know that little Marlene died during the robbery up in Kalispel? She got shot!"

"Marlene? Who the hell is she? And what's Kalispell got to do with anything?"

"Marlene was a little eight year old blue-eyed, blond girl with pigtails and a blue ribbon in her hair, that's who the hell she was," replied Jason. And I gotta know. I just gotta know; were you ever up there in Kalispell?"

Johnny rocked forward in his chair and put both elbows on the table and looked Jason straight in the eye.

"Jace, if you'd been say, upstairs last night with Emma Sue over there," said Johnny, waving a hand toward a scantily-clad cocktail waitress across the room, "I wouldn't ask you a damn thing about it. Asking questions that can get a little too awkward is not what one friend does to another, you know that. Jeez, Jace. Let it alone."

"A little girl got killed, Johnny."

"Oh hell Jace. A robbery like that in a big city. There's lots of shooting all over. Those guards shoot at anything, and the robbers shoot too just to discourage people from coming after them. But Jesus, Jace. Nobody is gonna shoot a little girl. It had to be an accident, just an accident."

"An accident," muttered Jason.

"Yeah, damn it. Lots of things are accidents. Things happen in this world Jace. Sometimes you can't control 'em. That's what life is all about. Everything's a matter of taking chances, taking the right ones, and coming out ahead if you're lucky."

Jason could see in Johnny's eyes that his friend hadn't known about the child's death, and the news bothered him. Jason thought of the tragic death of Johnny's own little sister Margie, many years earlier when they all three had been new arrivals on the Manchester ranch.

"Just like little Margie was an accident," said Jason, immediately wishing he hadn't made the remark that would bring all that pain back to his friend's mind.

Johnny's jaw dropped just a little, and his eyes bored into Jason. Both sat frozen in silence for several seconds. Jason had never before seen such hatred in his best friend's eyes.

"Hey," said Jason. "There's gotta be some way we can get this cleared up. If you'd just go with me to the court—"

"Go with you! to a courthouse? To jail? You came here to try and arrest me for what I did to that stupid bank? I can't believe you'd do that Jace! I didn't shoot anybody; you know that. You think I'd shoot a little girl?"

Jason felt a surge of fear as he saw how agitated Johnny was getting. He wished he had never heard of Kalispel Montana. Or Pinkertons. Or dead little girls.

Jason reached into his shirt pocket and took out the cardboard box Doctor Martensen had given him. As Johnny's eyes dropped to the box, Jason opened the lid and let the single chunk of lead clunk out onto the table.

"Here's the slug that killed her."

Johnny picked up the bullet and saw its familiar, hollow point, wad-cutter design. Not a common thing among bank robbers.

Jason watched his friend's face lose all color as he sat up straighter holding the chunk of lead clenched in his right hand.

"Oh God, no, Jace, no." Johnny's shoulders slumped and his speech faltered as he almost cried.

Jason relaxed some and with his left hand reached out to touch his friend's hand clenching the bullet. In doing so he let his right hand drop into his lap.

Misinterpreting Jason's movement as an attempt to draw his .45 automatic, Johnny became a blur of motion. He rose out of his chair, flipped the table over, and Jason found himself looking at the muzzle of the Colt .44 which had instantly become pointed at Jason's own middle.

"Jesus Jace. That was stupid. You draw on me? You're the long distance champ you bet, but we always knew who was faster than greased lightening, right?"

"Oh Jesus; I wasn't draw—you're going to shoot me? With my own gun? Our gun?" Jason could feel his heart pounding in his chest.

"I'm not going to let you arrest me Jace. I won't go to jail for just an accident. Nobody would believe me; the big banks would have me hanged for sure."

"No Johnny," pleaded Jason, desperate to fix the situation. "There's gotta be a way out of this."

"There is, old buddy. We can just forget about this crap and finish off a great evening and you can go on your way."

"Johnny, I can't—"

Then with his left hand Johnny took a pack of cards out of his vest pocket.

"OK then, we'll let fate decide. This is a new deck; we break the seal, you shuffle, and whoever draws the high card walks out the door. Then you stay away from me, and I'll stay away from banks."

Jason believed his old friend. He knew Johnny's bank-robbing career was over. But things just weren't right.

"No, man. I can't go that way. And you, you gamble through life as though it was all the fun in the world, but you can't gamble away the death of little Margie—Marlene." Jason was horrified by the slip of the tongue he had just made. He'd said the name of Johnny's little sister who died as a child.

After a prolonged silence where every customer in the bar held his breath, Johnny spoke.

"Stand up, Jace."

Slowly Jason rose to his feet, the .45 automatic feeling like a useless anvil tied to his waist.

"A gunfight? Johnny you know I—"

"I know you're damn good with any gun Jace. And you've had more experience than I have."

The two old friends looked at each other for a few more seconds, and Jason felt that maybe things might relax some. He saw Johnny spin the cylinder on the Colt .44 by rolling it against his left forearm twice, then holster the weapon.

"I'll give you a chance, Jace. A chance." Then the two stood facing each other just eight feet apart.

"All we had is gone Jace. There's no way out of this for us both, not even a draw of cards. But it's gotta be settled, right?"

Jason could feel and hear a sad, almost trembling tone in Johnny's voice as his friend said "I know you're no fool around guns Jace; I know you've practiced plenty with that damn government automatic hanging from your belly. You can grab it now man. That's the chance I'm giving you."

"No Johnny, no," cried Jason. But he saw in his friend's eyes and pained face that times were now past all reason, so in near panic Jason grabbed his automatic with the reflex draw he had indeed practiced for countless hours.

But Jason was no match for Johnny when time counted. In the slow motion that the mind gives a man when horror is happening, Jason saw the Colt .44 appear in the other man's hand. As Jason felt the grip of his government automatic in his own hand he saw the Colt's hammer cock back under Johnny's right thumb. And then the hammer fell, . . .

***

In the fading afternoon light a broken man sat slumped in a chair in the silent barroom holding a .44 caliber Colt Single Action revolver in one hand and a modern, U.S. Government .45 Automatic in the other. Amid the acrid smell of gun smoke and with his ears still ringing from the sound of one single shot, he sat with his eyes scrunched closed, both hands trembling, and with his best friend lying dead at his feet.

Lewiston, Montana, 1919

At the little cemetery, raindrops collecting on the sheepskin collar of his overcoat felt cold against the man's freshly shaven face. In the tense silence, and watched by the nervous mourners, he let his gaze drop from the somber sky overhead, down past the rain spattered layer of umbrellas, to the Colt Single Action .44 caliber revolver he held in his hands. Its blued finish was worn, but it had been well cared-for and was in excellent condition. Moving the hammer to the half-cock notch, he opened the Colt's loading gate with his right thumb. Then, listening again to the familiar, crisp click each time he rotated the cylinder, he inspected each chamber. Feeling as alone as he ever had in his life in spite of the mourners standing near him at the gravesite, he squatted down beside the partially-open, rain soaked coffin. In one smooth motion he shoved the Colt inside and bashed the box closed with his fist.

"Lower it," he said to the nervous workmen.

Relieved, two of the men held the ropes as the third removed the supporting timbers and the coffin was lowered to its final resting place. The man in the sheepskin coat kept his place beside the open grave, oblivious to the wind and rain that were making man and horse alike anxious to finish things up. After a few moments, the man picked up a wet clod of dirt, tossed it into the grave, and strode to a bay mare tethered nearby. He didn't even feel the cold, wet saddle as he took his seat and walked the animal away from the graveyard.

Only two of the six chambers were loaded in the Single Action .44 revolver that now rested in the dark of the coffin. Johnny, happy to see Jason arrive, had not yet reloaded after his exhibition shooting behind the bar.

"I'll give you a chance," Johnny had said as he spun the Colt's cylinder and holstered the revolver. With his horse's hooves making sucking noises in the muddy, cemetery road, Jason Banner rode away thinking about the bad odds in his best friend's last gamble.

The End

www.ingramcontent.com/pod-product-compliance
Lightning Source LLC
Chambersburg PA
CBHW030545180626
46816CB00010B/1018